continued . . .

"Echoes the . . . psychological suspense of Hitchcock's *Spellbound*. If this isn't movie-bound, Hollywood needs a brain transplant."
—*Kirkus Reviews*

"Takes the reader on a high-tech voyage to the brain centers of human memory . . . [a] vivid cyber-medical thriller . . . stunningly surreal."
—*Publishers Weekly*

"Fast-paced, fascinating . . . suspense, twisting and turning up through the emotional conclusion. Highly recommended."
—*Library Journal*

"A compelling psycho-medical suspense novel."
—*The Trenton Times*

"Takes the reader on a roller-coaster ride through the darkest corridors of memory and personality." —Rick Hautala

See How She Runs

"Thrilling, suspenseful, and a whole lot of nail-biting fun."
—Ed Gorman, *Mystery Scene*

"A good solid read, a well-characterized thriller which works from start to finish. One of those rare books . . . I cared what happened to the characters." —Mike Baker

Homecoming

"A fast-paced, hard-edged killer of a book . . . it keeps the reader in a thoroughly satisfying state of anxiety."

—Dean Koontz

"[A] taut page-turner . . . Costello can write with power and pathos, and he gives his story a tragic twist."

—*Publishers Weekly*

"This is the real thing . . . the suspense is almost unbearable. There were spots where I was forced to turn my head and read out of the corner of my eye." —F. Paul Wilson

"A ride that will rival the biggest, roughest roller coaster you've ever ridden." —*Cemetery Dance*

"A truly gripping novel, a grabber from the start. The novel weaves the four tight characterizations into a single tapestry of terror. Costello takes his place among our finest purveyors of suspense." —William D. Gagliani, *Booklovers*

"An incredible book. It takes you into dark and dangerous places. This is powerful stuff." —Rick Hautala

"A gasp-a-minute thriller that is also a powerful novel of character." —Ed Gorman, *Mystery Scene*

Unidentified

Matthew Costello

BERKLEY BOOKS, NEW YORK

UNIDENTIFIED

A Berkley Book / published by arrangement with
the author

Copyright © 2002 by Matthew Costello.
Cover art by Charlotte Schulz.
Interior text design by Julie Rogers.

ISBN: 0-7394-2640-0

BERKLEY
Berkley Books are published by The Berkley Publishing Group,
a division of Penguin Putnam Inc.,
375 Hudson Street, New York, New York 10014.
BERKLEY and the "B" design
are trademarks belonging to Penguin Putnam Inc.

PRINTED IN THE UNITED STATES OF AMERICA

To Frank Boyd and Neil Richards . . .
After all, how often do people give you a whole country?

acknowledgments

Unidentified is indebted to the incredible (and nightmarish) thesis of H. L. Stauf's *Quantum Biology: The New Physics of Life*. The book should come with a warning: Read it, and abandon everything you used to think about reality. Thanks to Neil MacDonald of BBC Scotland for hands-on information about climbing the Glen Coe.

prologue

one, two, three

One

"Dr. Bill, how you doing down there, buddy?"

And Dr. Bill—Dr. William Steiner, professor of paleobiology at USC—moved the tiny mouthpiece of the microphone closer to his mouth.

"Er, fine . . . everything is . . ." He hesitated, hearing how thin his voice sounded in the cramped twenty cubic feet of the submersible. ". . . A-OK."

After he said it, he felt ridiculous. *A-OK*. As if he were some kind of astronaut. Though he did feel like some kind of inner space astronaut. He looked at the depth gauge.

Eight thousand feet below sea level, and still going down.

Still going down, God, like an elevator to a watery hell.

Next stop, the human weenie roast.

And that analogy wasn't a bad one. Things were roasting down here—though hopefully not his weenie.

"Sounds good, Bill. Just watch your air, outside temp . . . you know the drill."

That he did. He had practiced "the drill" for weeks in

a dock not far from the college campus. And after all that practice, he still didn't feel at all comfortable in the spherical submersible. Smaller than Alvin, this diving minisub was much less sophisticated than Alvin. Modeled by the French on the Russian Mir subs, it shared the same thrown-together technology found on the infamous Russian space station. Nothing in the inside cabin screamed "Relax . . . what could go wrong?"

It kind of whispered . . . "You know, you're a mile down and a hell of a lot *could* go wrong."

He had to pee.

For the second time since the eight-hour dive began.

And damned embarrassing—since he knew everyone topside could hear the fumbling, the hiss of water. He grabbed one of the bottles and looked at his watch. Another forty-five minutes until he hit target depth.

He unzipped his fly.

Elaina Dali—no relation to Salvador, she was quick to point out—grabbed the stack of printouts and riffled through them.

Interesting stuff, she thought.

No—way more than interesting.

She looked up. Her window overlooked the Hudson River from the hillside office in Ossining. The morning was beautiful, the sun glinting on the distant city.

She looked at the stacks of paper, two sets of identical information. And she knew she wanted to get this information out of here. She looked around the office, at the rows of cubicles peopled by young computer techies, isolated from the main offices of the fashionable business types who ran the people side of GenTech.

Business was booming for GenTech.

Ever since the human genome had been cracked, a new world in copyright and patenting had opened—actually less a world than a legal minefield. But GenTech—currently valued at twice what it was last month, and still growing despite the market slump—believed that there was gold in them there genes. Designer genes promised a lot . . . the end to cancer, no more AIDS . . . blond hair and blue eyes for everyone though Elaina was happy with her matching dark brown eyes and hair.

She looked at the pages in her hands. For a moment she wondered if she should throw the data on a floppy and shred the hardcopy.

Might be safer doing that.

Safer.

Amazing that she even thought in such terms. *Safer.* As in . . . there's danger here. She felt chilled—and it wasn't the sleek building's carefully controlled AC raising goosebumps on her arms.

No. Best to get up, stuff the pages in her purse, and walk out as though she were going to get a cup of coffee.

Safer. She thought for a second . . . what's the danger I feel? The GenTech brass? The government? No. Then . . . who?

And that was it. She wasn't sure, she only knew that the pages in her hand, all filled with numbers and code, were bad.

There was no way she could just toss them in the trash and forget about it. Everything you do these days leaves a trail. It was too late to pretend it hadn't happened, that she hadn't found this file, looked at it, and printed out two copies.

She looked at the name on the top of the page . . . Einbank.

Einbank. What was it? A project? A code name? The name out of a fantasy story? And at the end of the file, two initials . . . MR. The coder for this bizarre genetic string?

Elaina got up—took a breath.

She grabbed her purse and started walking toward the

commissary and the bank of coffee machines, casually stuffing the papers into her bag.

She felt as if she could barely walk.

Sophie leaned against the smeary window of the commuter train.

The ride out of London on a good day was an hour, an hour of the gray city slowly melting into deep green suburbia and farmland. Usually Sophie hardly ever looked out the window, immediately jumping on her homework so she'd have some kind of life when she got back home.

Tonight she wanted to just daydream a bit.

Already it was dark, and the long walk from the station to her home would be chilly. She'd want to do nothing but grab some supper, and go to bed.

To start the whole thing again tomorrow.

It was worth it—at least that's what her dad said. She went to the best girls' school in London, the London Academy, with a full scholarship. She should be grateful.

Instead she was usually exhausted. No friends—nobody lived this far away from London, no social life, no way she could do anything after school.

There was another problem . . . falling asleep on the train. Despite an interior color scheme that screamed clowns gone mad, with seats of crimson and flaming orange, more than once Sophie had fallen asleep on the train, waking up in Piggotts-on-Bromley, or some other nowhere stop miles from home.

She looked up and saw an old woman hovering in the aisle beside her. "Now, dearie, is this seat free?"

Strange, thought Sophie. *The train is virtually empty and this woman has to sit next to me.* Sophie shrugged, nodded, and then scrunched over.

"There," the lady said, exhaling, a great sigh of relief. She clutched an umbrella and an oversized handbag.

"Been threatening rain all day, it has . . ."

God, thought Sophie, *she wants to talk.*

"Yes, I'm sure it will rain," the woman said. Then she reached out and patted Sophie's arm. "Just hope we can get home safe and sound before all the trouble starts, hm?"

Sophie smiled. She knew that people—like this lady—often thought she was younger than twelve. She wasn't going to be tall like her dad.

Thank God the next stop was hers because it didn't seem like the woman needed absolutely any feedback to go rambling on. Sophie turned to look out the window again—and just at that moment, a single spear of lightning shot to the ground.

Miles away, she thought.

I've got plenty of time.

And the woman went on talking about weather, and trains, and the unpredictability of England.

Nature's call answered, Dr. Bill put the HRE—the human range extender, essentially a soda bottle to collect pee—in a small compartment to his right. It joined a second bottle.

Maybe I can go for a new record, he thought.

"Everything okay down there, Bill?" Topside had been quiet for the past hour.

The privacy thing was getting to him.

"Yes, just fine. Couldn't be better."

"And your depth shows . . . ?"

Bill looked at the gauge . . . thirteen thousand feet, more than halfway toward the five-mile mark. Every few seconds he heard a little disturbing squeak as the metal adjusted to even more pressure. He remembered a joke they'd made topside.

Don't worry, you're diving in the best Russian technology available.

They all laughed.

He didn't.

"Thirteen point one and counting," he said. "Everything looking good."

"Lights working fine?"

He flipped the exterior light switch back and forth. Wasn't much to see outside save for the ever-present rain of organic snow dribbling down from the surface—bits of algae, fish scales, and debris that made the ocean outside look as though it were in the midst of a snow squall.

"Lights work fine and ready to party."

As soon as he said the line he regretted it. He never could pull off any macho poses. He might as well have said "Lock and load," "Make my day," or—

Thud.

He looked up, eyes wide, his heart immediately clicking into a higher rate. Something had smacked the small viewport of the submersible. It took a second to see that it was . . . a fish—hard to identify—and it seemed stuck to the port for a second and then it slipped away, trailing a filament-thin tail. It was a creature from another planet, all mouth and teeth and nearly sightless . . . a gulper, aka *Eurypharynx pelecanoides.* Giving it a Latin name didn't make it any weirder.

"You okay, Doc?"

"Fine," he said. Then he repeated himself to reassure them. "Just fine."

"You're dropping pretty fast, Doc. Start giving your down props a little blast."

Down props. For a second, the scientist froze. He had rehearsed this endlessly; they should be . . . right there. But he could see only flat black metal where the switch should be.

He muttered to himself: "Can't give them any thrust . . . if I can't find them. . . ."

"What's that, Bill? Missed that."

"Nothing."

Too loud. Revealing anxiety. Anxiety. He remembered one of the sessions with the shrinks. Watch out for anxiety, because anxiety can turn into panic.

And panic can kill you.

Where the hell is the switch?

He shot a look to his left. And there it was. Exactly where it always was. *Just anxious,* he told himself as he got close. *Never been five miles under the surface before. Could be a dream come true.*

I wanted this, he thought. *Wanted to do this dive real bad.*

And now I got it.

"Yo, Bill, everything okay down there?"

"Yup." He hit the switch, and squeezed the right throttle. For a second he thought that nothing was happening but then he saw the depth meter slow, growing sluggish as if the submersible had suddenly hit molasses.

"Slowing the dive. Looking okay down here."

He looked out the viewport and noticed that when the gulper hit the thick port, it left a smear . . . not a red smear exactly. More like the mottled color of a bird flying into a window.

No wipers to clear it off.

Not down here.

He took a breath and prepared for hitting bottom.

As Elaina walked she noticed how carefully she moved, as if revealing the slightest intent to *hurry* might somehow signal that she was doing something wrong.

Workers in their cubicles looked up, nodded, and smiled—and she smiled back. The papers stuffed in her purse felt as if they were burning, flame red.

Anyone can see I have something I shouldn't have.

God, she wondered. *Why am I doing this?*

She only knew one thing. She came from a fierce family of Catalans. She had grown up with her wonderful gentle father railing against Franco, explaining how the dictator had nearly destroyed Spain, the crown jewel of Western culture. She had grown up with the idea that when bad things happened, you acted. You did something.

She didn't quite understand everything in the papers she had. She didn't even know if they were really that dangerous. She just knew that the information had been well hidden, a secret meant never to escape—and she needed to talk to someone from the outside, maybe from the old genetics team. Someone like Peter.

Yes, he'd be good. Safe. Tucked away in his Manhattan apartment, working on his book, his research, far from the real world of genetic commerce.

But first she had to get out of the building without fainting dead away.

She reached the bank of elevators and stood there. As usual the elevators took forever when you most wanted them. She watched the indicator tick off the floors.

"Elaina?"

She turned and saw chubby Andy Pastore. Not her favorite person at GenTech.

"Bit early for lunch, girl? Or are they sending you on some god-awful road trip?"

She glanced up at the elevator indicator.

"No. Just need to—"

She didn't even have a story. She licked her lips.

She thought of something. Fast. Stupid.

"Female emergency, if you must know."

Andy made a big O with his mouth. A world he didn't comprehend.

Of all the lame excuses.

A high-pitched *ping* sounded.

She walked into the elevator and Andy followed.

"Are you going to the little goodbye for Walter on Friday?"

She turned and looked at him. Can he read anything on

my face, anything that would make him mention something to someone later . . . *Say, did you see Elaina? Looking all nervous, upset, almost as if she was hiding something.*

She forced a smile.

"Yes," she lied. "Wouldn't miss it."

And Andy, happy for the bone, smiled back. "Great." The elevator stopped, door slid open. "See you then."

A nod, another light smile, and she walked out, turning toward the stairs leading to the underground car park.

Was Andy watching her from behind, standing there, wondering . . . female emergency? What female emergency?

After an eternity, she got to the stairway door, opened it, and went down the stairs leading to the cavernous garage and her maroon Buick Century.

Sophie trudged past the small village center, right past the Lamb and Slaughter Pub—such a charming name, and already inside it was glowing warmly with the twilight and smoke. She passed the scattering of shops, a news agent, a Royal Mail post office the size of a big closet. . . . it wasn't much of a village.

And she started up the winding road that led to Portlach Hill. Her father could have picked her up, but he was always so busy, so preoccupied. With Mom gone, he had slipped even further into his work. Further, deeper, until almost nothing else existed.

She thought of the picture zipped in her backpack . . . the family at the beach, all together, so many years ago. Before Mom disappeared into the middle of the Atlantic Ocean after her plane just dropped out of the sky.

Now, Dad didn't have much time for anything else but his work.

Not, Sophie had to admit . . . *not even me.*

His work was everything.

More than that. Her father had left the big project in Einbank to move to this sleepy village, to a small house off by itself at the end of a tiny road that literally went nowhere.

He even seemed . . . what was the word . . . *paranoid.*

He asked Sophie sometimes, "Do you ever talk to anyone about what I'm doing? What we've talked about?"

With soup stains on his shirt and his glasses smeary, dotted with flakes of dandruff. A new wife was completely out of the question.

"No, Dad—you see most of my friends would rather talk movies and music than physics. Amazing, hm?" She laughed. But he didn't . . . though he would force a smile after a bit, as if getting it, nod, and go back to his notebooks, or back to his lab in the rear of the small house.

And each week he would hand her a small object in tinfoil the size of a matchbox.

"A thumb drive," he said. A tiny storage device. "Has all my work. Just in case," he said, smiling. "Just keep it in your backpack."

I'm a walking backup, Sophie knew. A backup—but also she knew . . . something more.

Looking at the cottage, no one would ever suspect that virtually half of it had been taken over by so much strange equipment that Sophie didn't have a clue about. Long ago she had learned not to ask about it. Though she was pretty sure that one of the machines was some kind of laser. Probably purchased from Dr. Evil's Supply House.

One laser, please.

She shifted her backpack to the other shoulder.

She worried about Dad. And—she worried about herself.

Now Sophie looked up the road. Her small house was just visible now, off the side of the road, at the end of the cul-de-sac. A few windows in the house glowed warmly but that meant nothing. Nothing, because the lights would have stayed on all the time, her father either falling asleep in his chair, or stumbling off to bed exhausted leaving lights on, dishes piled up.

She blew air out of her mouth.

So cold, that now a little puffy cloud formed. Be nicer to live close to London. Pointless to ask him, she knew. Never going to happen.

She looked up. The sky, nearly dark now, still showed the gunmetal gray of a cloudy day. At least it wasn't raining. Could easily have been raining.

She turned off the road onto the winding yellow-stoned gravel driveway that led to the house. She didn't question whether this was wrong or right. He was her father; this was how they lived. Though lately she had been inching closer to asking him more questions—*What exactly are you doing right now? And why here? And why do you need secrecy? And . . . and—*

He had told her some things. But always handed out the information in little pieces. The information and—like the thumb drive—special instructions.

She reached the door.

Which was ajar.

Strange.

Her dad might have gone out.

Sure he *could* have done that, got his daily gulp of fresh air then hurried back in. But he would have closed the door tight. He always complained of the cold, and the heating bill; money *was* tight.

The door was open.

She pushed it open more, and let her backpack slide to the floor.

"Dad! I'm home . . ."

She looked around. The clutter and mess was unchanged from the morning, exactly as she had left it. Crumpled bits of paper, opened mail, a tin of biscuits uncovered, now probably gone quite soggy, and—

Through the hallway, she saw a kitchen chair over-turned.

Lying on the floor.

And there was something about that chair that wasn't *right*. A quick thought: *If Dad had knocked it over he would have picked it up. And I didn't do it this morning, so, so—*

Another thought, remembering:

The door was ajar. Open.

As if someone had come in.

She knew how alone they were up here, so far from the tiny village, all alone. But she never felt scared.

But now—

"Dad," she called again. She took a few steps to the right, toward his lab. Sometimes she would just let him be, to continue working, and go up to her bedroom on the second floor, start her homework, and try and catch an episode of *Microsoap* on BBC.

But no—

She took a few more steps. "Dad, everything okay? How was your—"

A sound. Movement from the lab area. As if . . . as if . . . in response. She stopped for a moment, heart beating, thumping loudly.

And she happened to look down.

To the floor.

To the shut door of the lab.

As something seeped out from under the crack. Glistening, thick, red.

She took a step backward. Then another. And another.

And then she tumbled backward, falling over her backpack, crashing to the hardwood floor, her eyes locked on the door—as the handle rattled and the door slowly opened.

two

He pulled back on the rear propellers' throttle, and the small submersible moved forward.

There, Bill thought. *Not so hard. Kind of like flying a plane without the danger of crashing.*

He leaned forward to see if he could spot the bottom— but the viewport and the reach of the light were both too small to show anything other than the organic snow-filled water ahead.

No matter. The depth gauge gave him a smooth picture of the surface below. A smooth, sandy bottom. And it would stay that way for the next couple of hundred meters. He looked left, to the temp gauge. A chilly eighteen degrees Fahrenheit. A deep freeze at the bottom of the ocean.

But that would change.

"Kind of quiet down there, Dr. Bill? How's your ride?"

"Couldn't be better. Nice and smooth, all systems"— he looked around—"are fine."

And Bill did feel relaxed. For the first time since he

had begun the mammoth plunge nearly eight hours earlier, he felt good.

"Yup, everything's looking perfect."

Ping.

The sharp, high-pitched sound was an unwanted punctuation to his report.

A little warning bell, warning of—

He looked at the slide-sonar display of the bottom, and he "saw" the change in the bottom, dead ahead. The sonar showed a slow rise, then a jagged underwater outcrop of sea floor. According to the depth gauge he was still fine. He'd pass over the escarpment without a problem.

Everything was still okay.

And by then he should see it, the hydrothermal field, filled with such strange creatures, the bizarre wonderland of animals that should never exist.

This is exciting, he thought.

This is going to be cool.

He grabbed the throttle firmly in his right hand while his feet rested gently on the pedal operating the small wing-style flaps outside the sub. He leaned close to the viewport, his nose touching it, until he could see nothing, just the constant "snow"—and then—

He saw a shape. Rising like some behemoth in the distance, the blurry outline of something. An outcrop of volcanic rock. He looked down to the depth gauge. The rock looked mighty close, as if the sub might scrape it . . . but everything was okay according to the sonar.

Back to the port, the murky shape resolved itself, turning into something recognizable. A nasty bit of jagged rock.

Back to the gauge, still showing plenty of room . . . but . . . but—

I'm going to hit it, Bill thought.

Something's wrong here, the gauge isn't picking up one

of those stony fingers that could prick the shell of the sub like a balloon.

He pressed down on the wing flap, and the sub slowly tilted up.

Why was the gauge wrong? It was sending him right into the rock. *Or did I just panic, lose it, and—*

Christ, now he was shooting up at a ten-degree angle; he'd lose sight of the bottom completely, miss the thermal field and, damn. He was screwing up.

"Whoa, what's going on down there? You were fine, Bill, and then—up periscope?"

He hesitated. Maybe he should tell them that he thought something was wrong with the gauge. But then maybe they'd scrap the whole dive, or worse . . . think that he was losing it.

He took a breath.

"I wanted to come down on the thermal with a better visual, guys." He waited. "That okay?"

They hesitated.

"Guess so, Bill. Guess so. But next time tell us, Doc. Got a little worried here."

"Will do."

As he spoke he tilted the floor pedal to aim the sub down. He got a better visual of the field swooping down like this, a bird's-eye view of one of the strangest places on the planet.

He eased up on the throttle. The sub had enough thrust to glide downward, slowly.

Then, from out of the mist he saw . . . something. Scattered boulders, giant rocks sitting on the bottom, probably all volcanic. Then movement. A whitish blur darted across one rock, fell to the sandy bottom . . . scurried away. The giant albino crab kept moving like the rabbit from *Alice in Wonderland*, hurrying away frantically. Five miles down, and somehow a giant crustacean figured out a way to live.

Strange, but things would get even stranger.

He checked the digicam. Everything looked okay.

Bill eased back on the floor pedal, straightening out the sub, bringing into view—

The smokers! Dead ahead, the giant stone columns spewing superheated, deadly poisonous sulfides into the water, underwater chimneys heating the water to a cloudy three-hundred-plus degrees.

Incredible, like a vision from Brueghel, he thought. *Welcome to hell.*

And yet, it all seemed beautiful, the dozen stone chimneys, the black smoky gas bubbling into the water.

Ping.

Ping!

He snapped around to check gauges. Depth okay. Close to the bottom, but he was okay. Temperature was rising fast though. The outside temp seventy degrees and climbing fast. A hundred and fifty was his limit, and the sub could stand that for only a brief time. After that, no telling what the superheated water could do to the quirky Russian technology.

Closer to the smokers, and then, just behind the first row of chimneys, Bill saw what he was looking for.

A cluster of giant albino mussels, the size of dinner plates, ghostly white, mouths open, sucking in the nutrient-rich sea water.

Nutrient-rich because, just behind the mussels, there was—

He still couldn't see . . .

Still . . . couldn't—

And then there they were!

The giant tube worms.

Bill gulped, licked his lips.

He wasn't prepared for the feeling that looking at them this close gave him.

Like a patch of lawn sprouting giant weeds and tall grass, the tube worms clustered together around the smokers, the bacteria in the worms feeding off the poisonous sulfides, the worms feeding off the bacteria, a perfect symbiotic relationship . . . waving in the thermal currents of the water. Some twenty feet . . . maybe—God—thirty feet tall. Weaving, dancing in the hot currents.

Bill released the throttle button, drifting, floating dreamlike toward them.

"Dr. Bill, you there? How's everything look?"

He nodded. He drifted a bit closer, the treelike worms waving in the blurry swirl of hot water. Closer still—and—

"Fine. God, they're beautiful, strange, I—"

Ping.

Then again.

Ping.

And Bill Steiner—for just a second—removed his gaze from the viewport.

Elaina Dali dug her keys out of her purse and hit the unlock button.

But in her nervousness, she hit the panic button and her Century gave out a loud squealing noise that filled the underground garage.

"Shit," she said, and she quickly hit the unlock button, silencing the shriek.

She stopped and looked round.

So quiet down here. The cars sitting quietly, lurking. She took a breath. A few minutes and she'd be out.

She heard a door shut.

Then sharp sound of a door slamming.

Someone else . . . down here.

She opened her door, slid into the car, and quickly hit the lock button. She heard the muffled sound of a car engine.

Steady, she told herself. *Calm down. No one could know anything yet.*

She stuck the key in the ignition, started her car, and eased out of the parking space. There was no sign of the other car.

She pulled up to the gate and stuck her credit card–sized pass in the slot. After a second, the gate began to so slowly rise. And she didn't wait until it was fully up before pulling out.

Once out, the bright midday morning sun hit her face, feeling good, safe. She looped down the GenTech driveway, to Route 9, filled as always with heavy traffic going in both directions.

What was she doing? Did she have any idea?

She looked at the stream of cars going left and right. Staying here was no good, that's for sure.

Got to get away from all this, think, plan . . .

Elaina waited until the light turned green, then pulled out onto Route 9 and headed north. She went only a few miles down the road before she saw a small turnoff. She made the left onto the Bear Mountain Parkway, a sleepy winding road that cut around Peekskill to the mountains of Harriman State Park.

No matter. She was across, and climbing up to the hills, away from the traffic, toward the isolation and ancient hills and the trees already tinged with gold and orange.

I'll drive a bit, she thought. *Then I'll find someplace to pull off to the side of the road.* Then she could look at the pages again—take another look and figure out what the hell they really meant—and what she was going to do about them.

She looked in the rearview mirror.

No one was there when she looked.

But then her eyes immediately shot forward to follow the winding road leading to the Hudson River Valley.

• • •

The door opened. Not in a hurried way, not like someone was rushing out after hearing the noise.

No, Sophie saw, the door opened *slowly*.

For a second she thought of her dad, letting the terrible possibility hit her, that he was gone.

Before something even more urgent took its place.

She had to move. Had to get up. Fast.

She put her hands to her sides and pushed up, standing quickly, one hand dragging her school bag up with her.

All the time, her eyes locked on the opening door. Until she saw a hand, a leather glove, and a dark, shiny floor-length leather jacket. A black hat, the collar of the jacket turned up.

He might as well be invisible.

She was backing away, sensing where the front door was, just a few steps more, and then she could turn and run.

She thought of class today. Geometry and the circle. How it has three hundred sixty degrees. Every circle, everywhere.

Three hundred sixty directions.

Sophie was almost at the door, when the figure looked up, the brim of the hat rising—and now she saw something of his face. Eyes dark, glowing, widening. He hadn't known she was there—but now he did.

Sophie reached behind her, flailing with one hand for the doorknob, feeling nothing. Another step, and she backed into the wall. The door—was to her left.

She quickly slid over and opened it.

The man held something in his hands . . . some papers, and those blank CDs her father used. Blood dripped from them.

Horrible moment—she turned. Now her back was to the man while she made the all-important steps to the open door, wondering if maybe her legs would refuse to move, that they would freeze, and she would find herself turned into a statue.

She heard a voice.

"No," calm, almost soothing. A voice filled with calm . . . authority.

She bolted, running out the door, opening it and then out, to the crisp night air, pumping her arms as hard as she could.

She looked up—half expecting that someone would be there, blocking her way. But no—the road was clear.

Though she did see a black car parked to the side. She hadn't noticed it racing home. Now she kept running as fast as she could, looking over her shoulder only once.

To see . . . the man outside the house, standing there as though the house were his, as though he couldn't be less interested or concerned about her escape.

She needed to hide, to think . . .

To remember.

Everything her father had told her. Those long conversations where she had only half listened, thinking him a bit dotty, lost to his work. To his half-crazy speculations. She had to remember it all.

Because now—she knew, she *knew*—her dad was dead. His work was gone. Except for what she had.

And now she thought she knew just how important it all was.

"Dr. Bill, we're picking up some severe temp spikes. Maybe you better—"

"Yeah, yeah . . ." He kept his gaze on the gauge. The outside temperature was climbing way too high . . . as if a smoker were right below him, suddenly turned on full blast, pumping superheated water straight at him.

"I don't know what the problem is. I should be—"

Thwack!

He looked up.

Something covered the viewport. It looked like he had hit one of the tube worms. Where the hell was he? Had he drifted into the worm field? Then—shit—he saw that he was too close to the vents and had to—

Thwack! Thwack!

The sound again, now coming from both sides of the submersible.

Bill's eyes widened.

"Bill, maybe you better come up a bit. Take a look from above the field, see—"

Bill nodded. *Good idea. Get out of here, and try a new approach, and—*

Thwack, thwack, thwack!

What was happening? The DV cameras were capturing whatever was happening—but Bill was completely in the dark.

All he could see was the pinky-rose-colored flesh now glued to the viewport. Surely a tube worm. Looked like it. But then—why wasn't it simply sliding away?

Bill flipped a switch and gave the up props a little burst. He heard a *whirrr,* then a sluggish grinding sound, as if the prop had hit a giant clump of seaweed. Another burst now, keeping his finger on the button.

But he only heard the sick sound of the prop struggling. Doing nothing.

Bill felt a small droplet of sweat fall off his upper lip. And he felt how hard he was breathing too, the air being sucked in and out so fast.

"Bill, you out of there yet? Still showing you at depth. Come on, get up now, a few hundred feet at least!"

He wanted to tell them that he was trying to do exactly that, trying so hard—and going nowhere. But then he was sure they'd hear the sound of panic in his voice. *Can't let them think I've panicked,* he thought. *I can't fold under the stress. Just tangled a bit, and if I can use the other props . . .*

He threw a switch, shifting power to the rear props. A moment's hesitation, fearing the worst. Then he hit the button.

Please. God. Work.

He pressed the button.

The sickening whine made his stomach tighten.

The props . . . did nothing.

What did that leave? What the hell other options—

Thwack!

Another noise from behind. And now he placed the sound. Sort of like the sound of mud being tossed at a window, hitting hard and sticking there.

He looked ahead.

At what he thought was a tube worm.

The pink flesh—in the light of the sub cabin—had turned rosier, deepened. And now—he thought he saw movement on the surface. He leaned close to the port.

And on the surface of the fleshy meat covering the port, movement . . . small, oversized amoebalike creatures shuttled left and right, like crazed ants seeking the path. Their movement kicked up speed as the color of the flesh behind them deepened in color . . . as if excited.

Which is when he heard the groan.

The sound of the sub protesting.

The metal *moaning.*

He looked up and around, as if there were something to see.

"Bill, you got your butt the hell out of there yet?"

Now he would speak. Had to speak. He licked his lips, nodded.

"I—I . . . I'm trying, but there seems . . ."

Groannnnnnnnn.

"To be—"

The flesh was so bright red now, the movement of the surface creatures dizzying, frantic, and—no.

The movement seemed almost hungry.

Impossible.

Can't be a tube worm. Has to be something el—

"Bill, what's wrong?"

He gave the only answer he could say. A fragment. Incomplete. Useless.

"I . . . don't . . ."

He looked down at his thumb, constantly hitting the props under the sub. The whine turned sluggish, resigned. Not going anywhere.

Groan.

And then the submersible imploded on him in the tiniest fraction of a second.

The Bear Mountain Parkway was quiet; the endless parade of auto malls, diners, and fast-food joints that filled nearby Route 35 was a world away.

Where am I going? she thought. *What exactly do I think I'm doing?*

It was all unfocused in her mind, unclear.

She just knew she needed time and—

Damn, she could use one of her laptops. Do some quick searches, send out a few e-mails, alert people.

But that would mean going back to GenTech or to her home. And that was impossible, not until she knew what she had.

More than anything she needed time to plan.

If the papers in her purse were . . . what she thought they were, she'd have to decide quickly what to do. Maybe call a newspaper—and tell them what?

Just explaining it would be so hard.

I work for this company, you see, a genetic engineering and analysis company, a place that holds patents, for God's sake, on genetic adaptations. And I found something that is mind-blowing . . . not only that, it looks dangerous.

She looked at her purse, the wad of papers stuck there

like some kind of giant shopping list. Quickly back to the road, she saw a curve to the right coming too fast. Her tires screeched as she peeled around the bend.

Steady, she thought. *Calm down.*

Then—she pictured where she might go. A little motel on 9W just past Bear Mountain, Heidi's . . . something. She could call ahead if she remembered the name— Heidi's Alpine Inn? Though there certainly wasn't any inn there, just a row of sad little rooms.

A good place to hide and think.

She turned onto the 9W bridge, and saw that the span was deserted. Busy and bustling in summer, during the week, the region went sleepy and quiet when fall came. She drove across the bridge and past Fort Hood—passing a rusty brown World War II tank left outside . . . Lucy.

Not a very appealing ad for signing up. Lucy could use a coat of paint.

Her eyes flickered to the mirror.

To see another car.

Not that deserted, she thought.

Off the bridge, she took the traffic circle around to start curling up the mountain road that led to a small cliff, then down to the Bear Mountain Bridge. She passed the Old- stone Restaurant, overlooking the whole river valley, and then an abandoned fieldstone toll house, probably not used in fifty years but still standing by the side of the road like a fairy-tale cottage.

Back to the mirror—but the car wasn't on her tail.

Good thing, since the two-lane road was narrow and twisting—not something to take fast. In winter, it would often be closed due to ice—but even on a hot summer's day, it was treacherous.

She swerved left and right, climbing steadily. Another quick look in the mirror, and again she saw the car. It disappeared behind one curve, and then reappeared.

Nothing alarming about it, she thought. Just a car.

Another look. Not there.

But funny, the way it came out of nowhere.

Just appeared, on the empty road, right behind her.

She looked back to the road, cut the wheel and—almost imperceptibly—she started going a little faster, just a bit. Not so fast to make the road dangerous—but . . .

Up to the mirror again. The trailing car maintained its distance, the same length behind her. Speeding up too, just to hold its position.

"Shit," she said.

Just paranoia. That's all. I'm going to see people chasing me everywhere. Until I do something about these pages—and the name on the pages. Einbank. What the hell is . . . Einbank? And the initials MR?

Another sharp curve, and she rounded a bend in the road that gave her an incredible view of the valley, from the obnoxious Indian Point nuclear power plant up to the fjordlike valley north of the bridge and the hulking mountain, shaped like a sleeping bear.

Now began the even more tricky downhill to the bridge, and to Heidi's . . . whatever.

At a bit of straightaway, she looked up.

The car was closer, its BMW emblem clear now; the driver, though, was shadowed by tinted glass.

A sharp curve, and Elaina hit the brakes to slow.

And the car behind her *bumped* her.

She screamed, gripping the wheel tight.

I braked too much, she thought.

But as soon as she gave herself that excuse, the car bumped her again, harder.

Now she speeded up. She didn't know who was behind her. Had she really been followed all that time? Or was this just some random crazy person, bored and angry and homicidal on a fall afternoon?

The next curve and her wheels screeched, but she

caught another sudden ram from behind, and her rear end fishtailed and smacked into the rocky cliff. Loose rock fell on the roof, and she felt the car suddenly driving funny . . . as if the left rear wheel was hitting something as it spun around.

She looked ahead.

A big hairpin curve.

"No," she muttered. "Please."

She had to slow, go slow or she'd go careening off the cliff, smashing to the rocks below.

Her fingers holding the wheel were bone white.

She kept licking her lips.

Slowing. Braking. In the mirror, the car amazingly no longer right behind her, maybe—she hoped—backing away.

She hit the bend of the hairpin curve, wheels screeching again, the cliff edge so close, the Bear Mountain Bridge glistening, and—

The sickening sound of the crunch of metal—and the steering wheel popped out of her hand as she jerked forward, the shoulder belt keeping her only inches away from smashing her head into the dash.

Quickly she grabbed the wheel again, looked up to see the beautiful valley ahead, the car now pointed straight out, flying toward it.

"No," she said again. A whisper.

Now the grinding sound of stone as the small embankment hit the front bumper, and then the wheels careened over the stone barrier. And then she heard more terrible grinding as the stone wall clawed the underneath of the car.

Until Elaina held the now useless wheel, and the car plummeted down the cliff, suddenly, sickly airborne to what—she knew in that amazing infinity of time—had to be her death.

book one

last dance

three

"Dad, did you see that?"

Nick Fowles quickly turned back to the bowling lane where he saw the remains of his son's last turn, the scattering of ten pins already being scooped up by an electronic rake.

No, he hadn't seen it.

He had been idly looking at the guy spraying some kind of aerosol into the clown-colored bowling shoes. What a job.

"Er, I—" Nick smiled. He didn't want to lie. Been doing too much of that already. One of his new vows was to try to summon a little truth in his life.

His half-grin said it all.

"It was great," his son, Joe, said. "You should have seen it." But Joe's enthusiasm had vaporized, drained of life by good old Dad's lack of attention.

"Sorry."

"It's your turn," Joe said, sitting down.

Nick nodded, stood up, and rubbed a hand through his

son's straw-colored hair. Nick's own hair, he noticed, seemed increasingly flecked with gray. "I did see the aftermath, buddy. Looks like you killed those pins."

A small nod from Joe. A hint of smile.

"Want some eats? Fries? A BowlBurger?"

More of a smile.

"Sure," Joe said, brightening a bit. "After this game."

Nick smiled, and turned back to the lane. "That last shot is going to be a tough act to follow." He picked up his ball, and when he threw it down the alley, he took care to keep it slightly off the strike mark.

Another lie, he wondered. Or just trying to stem the damage. And he thought: *How did my life get so screwed up?*

He let the ball fly, barely watching its progress . . . barely caring.

In the car, on the way home, Nick tried to keep up a steady stream of chatter. How's school? Do you like fifth grade? How's your teacher? But Joe had already slipped into a land where only one-word answers were possible, as if he were a prisoner behind enemy lines.

As soon as they began this return trek to home—to what was once *their* home—things turned weird.

Nick looked over at Joe, now looking at the window.

"Hope Mom doesn't have dinner for you . . ." he said.

She certainly won't have dinner for me, Nick thought. Though the breakup—in the end—was civil, polite, with all recriminations shelved in the interest of Joe, he felt the cold wave of Andrea's hate for him every time he delivered his son back home. Was *hate* too strong a word? He didn't think so, though he never imagined that he'd end up being someone who was hated.

But he had destroyed a perfectly good marriage, and that's what had happened.

And destroyed it for what?

A little fling with some too-young TV reporter, some-one who looked oh-so-cute in her stylish suit, who showered him with so much attention, wanting to hear about his latest story, his last trip . . . so *interested*.

But no, it wasn't beauty that killed the beast.

It was *attention*.

"Dad . . ."

He looked over at his son.

"Yeah, Joe?"

"How long will you be away this time?"

This time. It was another swipe, another nasty brick in a nasty wall of guilt.

"Three weeks, tops. Then back for a few weeks. Just have to do some interviews, maybe head over to Ireland, and—"

He saw that Joe had already turned away. He just wanted a time report, not an itinerary. For all that Joe seemed to care or know, Nick could be a plumber and not a successful, award-winning international journalist.

Successful . . . respected . . . but not here.

He turned the corner to the quiet street that had once seemed so welcoming. Now it was alien territory.

He pulled up to the house and stopped the car.

"Well, Joe—here you are, and—"

"Dad . . . can you come in? For just a minute? I want to show you what I built for the LEGO contest."

Nick looked away. That wouldn't go down too well with Andrea. Not at all.

"Come on, Dad, just for a minute. It's really cool."

Nick smiled. "Okay, champ. Lets see what the Lego-meister has cooked up this time."

Joe popped open his door and Nick followed, wondering if his son thought that somehow, that maybe just by getting his dad into the house, it would all go away, all could go back to the way it was . . .

Such is a kid's faith in magic.

•   •   •

Joe bolted into the house while Nick waited at the entrance. After a few steps, Joe called back. "Come on, Dad!"

Then Andrea was there. She looked . . . beautiful. As though she might be going out later. Certainly a possibility. Guys always checked her out, and she wouldn't be one to curl up and disappear.

"Hi," he said.

"Hi," Andrea said back. Cold, nothing. Might as well have parachuted into the Arctic.

"Joe has this LEGO thing he built, wants to show me."

Andrea looked at Joe . . . her face softened a bit, then back to Nick, instantly hardening again.

"Okay. But I'm going out."

Nick shrugged. "Just a minute, to run up, see what he made."

Andrea nodded. "Go ahead." She turned and walked away.

Nick took the hint, and then followed Joe up the stairs, trying to walk steady, trying to move as though his whole body hadn't turned into something wobbly and insecure.

When he came down, after admiring the Lego structure and absorbing the feel of Joe's room through his pores, Andrea was nowhere in sight. He heard the TV in the kitchen. She was staying there, minimizing her contact with the enemy. He could go in and tell her when he'd be back for his next visit.

But she knew that already.

It was time to go, time to retreat.

He walked out to the quiet street thinking two things: he had four hours until his flight to London . . . and—

How he wished a meteor would come screaming through the atmosphere toward him and make everything disappear in one blinding flash.

• • •

Hours later, no meteor—but the overnight flight to London was delayed, and then he ended up sitting next to some fat-armed businessman desperate for a chat. But Nick had an effective way to deal with such things. He slipped on his bright purple Aiwa headphones and popped a CD in his player. Didn't matter whether he had music playing or not; the headphones were an effective barrier to any long-winded attempts to "bond" by the person next to him.

Maybe—he wondered—there were times he might like to talk to the person next to him. But it was a chance he dare not take. Besides, he liked to sleep on the way over and wake in London with at least a few hours of shut-eye under his belt.

The flight attendant came over with a tray of champagne and OJ. She mouthed something, and Nick smiled and scooped up the champagne. One or two of these, then a melatonin, and he'd sleep like a baby.

Finally he heard a pinging noise and the jumbo 747 began to ease away from the gate.

Finally . . .

It was so late . . . near midnight . . . In minutes, the engines began to roar, cabin lights dimmed, and the plane roared down the runway; in the jumbo jet it felt as though the attempt to become lighter than air were impossible, ludicrous, until finally, amazingly, Nick felt the traction of the wheels disappear, and the plane smoothly began its gradual climb five miles up.

He dozed.

When he woke he saw that the man next to him was gone, having finished off a tray full of food, a chunk of filet mignon, and a bit of shrimp cocktail, leaving only a half-full glass of red wine—probably not the first.

The attendant came over quickly—cute, short blond

hair. Dazzling smile. The type Nick would have flirted with in the old days. And he might again one day, he thought. The nameplate read "Carrie."

"Like some dinner?" she asked.

Nick shook his head. He really just wanted to go back to sleep—and then he felt a bump.

The plane acted as though it had hit something in the road . . . jiggling up a few feet before settling down once again into a nice flat groove. Then another. The attendant grabbed the tray next to Nick.

A bigger bump and the fat man's half-filled wineglass tipped over, sloshing red wine to the aisle. Carrie mouthed something that looked like an inaudible "shit."

Nick pushed his headphones off. He wanted to hear what she said next.

"Turbulence?" he said.

Carrie smiled. "You heard the announcement?"

"No."

"Big storm system. We're above it but it's causing some problems, little pressure pockets that—"

A giant bump, and now the attendant flew into the fat man's abandoned seat, one arm landing right next to Nick's head. She looked embarrassed.

"Maybe you better strap in?" Nick said.

He realized: *I'm* way *calmer than she is.* Carrie looked on the edge of losing it. She nodded—and instead of moving to her seat near the exit door, she buckled up.

The plane gave a sudden lurch to the left, a nasty lurch that triggered some yelps from the rear of the plane.

She looked at Nick.

And Nick thought of that old question . . . If you knew you were going to die, that it was all over, would you—very quickly—fuck the person next to you?—assuming of course that they were attractive. Stupid. He couldn't imagine being that close to Mr. Death and getting horny.

Death and horny didn't go together.

Nearly any other time, yes.

But not looking down the barrel of doom.

Another terrible lurch, bells pinging all over the plane, people wanting someone to come to their seat and tell them, please, we're not going to die.

The captain finally came on the speaker delivering the usual homily with a Midwest twang. "... a bit of that turbulence, folks, for the next few minutes. So, please keep those seat belts nice and tight and we'll fly you out of this just as soon as we can ..."

So wonderfully folksy ...

Must be a class where they taught that laid-back, we're-gonna-be-okay type of style.

Carrie's eyes were on Nick.

"You don't look scared—" Another bump, like hitting a roadkill at eighty miles an hour—

Nick smiled. She was cute, this sweet, long-legged attendant whose fun job did have its occasional downside.

"I'm not." Delivered in true Clint Eastwood style. Then, "I've been in worse. Just a bit of bumpy air ... *you* should know that."

"I do. Still—" She hesitated, her eyes now alive with a sudden interest. Nick had made the transition from passenger to person, not easy to do with the flight attendant robots. "Do you ever get scared?"

"Do I?"

She nodded.

"Once in a while. Once in a great while."

She waited, as if expecting details. But the plane had suddenly leveled off, and the man sitting next to Nick would soon be waddling back from the lavatory, probably looking like a human milk shake.

"Gotta go," Carrie said.

Nick nodded.

No promise implied. He watched her unbuckle and

swing back into mile-high waitress mode. He looked out the window.

Scared . . . *What scares me?* he wondered.

Easy one to answer. Of course the day he learned that Andrea had learned about his affair, which was well over. The icy feeling that had claimed him was one of the worst things he'd ever felt. Actual goosebumps sprouted on his arms as he walked up the path to the front door knowing that when he went in, his entire life would change, vanish . . .

That was fear.

And then there was the other kind of fear.

Something more primal, direct.

He thought of today, the stocky man spraying the bowling shoes. And why he looked at him, thinking for some strange reason about Sierra Leone.

His personal nightmare.

Nick closed his eyes. Thinking: *Gotta get more shut-eye.*

Instead, he replayed the movie.

That night.

The sights, the sound, the blood . . .

Sierra Leone.

For most Americans Sierra Leone was a quaint-sounding name for a place who-knows-where.

In actuality, it was one of the most unstable African countries with rival warlords fighting over the lucrative diamond mines while the people tried to subsist on next to nothing.

Nick was supposed to fly in for three days of quick on-the-spot interviews with the head of the UN peacekeeping force, a French general. At the same time, a small British force was kept in place and the embassy was open, but they were sending women and kids home in droves because everyone knew something bad was coming.

And the something bad . . . was a paramilitary group known as the Westside Boys. And these "boys"—armed to the teeth with submachine guns and grenade launchers, high on ganja and maybe a bit of coca—were out to take the capital and make it theirs.

The means: Kill whoever got in their way.

Turn the capital into a charnel house.

On the second day of his visit, with nightly gunshots making sleep impossible, Nick knew that he was over his head. But now getting out would be damned difficult. He had to wait at least twelve hours before he could get a chartered plane to hop over to Monrovia in Liberia.

But that night the gunshots were matched by something new.

An explosion rocked the street below, and it signaled that the Westside Boys were making a move. The hotel was being attacked, and foreigners would have two options: become hostages or become dog meat.

Nick remembered how he had bolted up from the bed and slipped his clothes on, and how eerily beautiful the violent firefight outside the window looked. Monte Carlo on New Year's. Only this was a New Year's where, as a door prize, they cut off your arms.

Merry Christmas.

He grabbed his bag, his Sony Vaio, his passport, and his wallet—and the door flew open, the hotel manager, gibbering, wild-eyed.

"Quick, monsieur, to the embassy . . ."

"Embassy?" Nick was thinking . . . the U.S. embassy? No, that was blocks away. He'd be dead or worse before he got there.

"U.K.! U.K.!" the man shrieked.

Right. The U.K. embassy was half a block away. If even that was possible.

He ran out to the hallway filled with other frantic guests, most of them attached to embassies, or government offices, all pros but now feeling that the ship was going down with them in it.

Nick wasted no time navigating through them to the staircase, then racing down.

When he got to the lobby, he saw an even larger confused crowd looking around for guidance, searching for some tour director from hell who could lead them to safety.

For a moment he was tempted to shout, "Hey, follow me. The Brits will be okay."

But a large moving throng would only make a bigger target.

Nick ran to the door, the sky alive with the telltale tracks of artillery.

A few yards into the street, and Nick ran into a sea of people, chaos theory in action, as they moved one way or the other in search of that now elusive space . . . safety.

A quick burst of automatic gunfire, and Nick knew that the militia were nearby. The embassy was close—but not close enough. He looked down the block—a Jeep filled with drunken Westside Boys plowing through the screaming crowd.

There was nowhere to go—but back inside.

Where things had changed . . .

four

A man stood atop the hotel lobby bar, talking loudly, calmly.

Somebody had taken charge.

"Follow the manager to the basement. Please. Stay together, and don't come up until I come and get you."

Nick looked at the man. He had seen him the night before doing some nice work sampling the bar's limited vodka selection. Now, short sleeves rolled up, a handgun in a holster, and holding a machine gun and grenades, he looked like a one-man fucking army.

His eyes fell on Nick.

"Okay, everyone—get moving."

The man hopped down to the floor and ran over to Nick. "Hey, I could use a bit of help here."

Nick grinned nervously. "I'm just a reporter."

"Right, mate." A big grin back. "Now about that help . . ." The man picked up another sleek, black machine gun sitting on a table. "Ever fire one of these?"

Nick shook his head. The conversation was punctuated

with bursts of gunfire and screams from the street. *It's hell out there,* Nick thought. *And soon, the demons will want in here.*

"Okay, you pull back on the release here and, with a full clip, you aim and you're good to go." The accent was thick, no polished London sound to his voice. "Got it?"

"Sure."

And without ever giving his assent, Nick found himself with a machine gun. "Oh, and remember you point at the things you want to stop." Now the man laughed. Nick guessed he was SAS. The guy acted as though this grim business were some kind of romp.

He stuck out his hand. "The name's Jess White."

Nick shook his hand. "Nick Fowles."

"Great, Nick—now let's push some of this crap up to the door."

The door, blockaded, looked like it might be a significant barrier to the armed militia outside. They liked things . . . easy.

The SAS guy patted Nick on the back. "Good work. Now all we have to do is blow away anyone who tries to get in."

Nick had nodded, as if that were a common experience . . . blowing people away. He was a journalist, someone who wrote about events and didn't participate in them.

He didn't need this new line of work.

Then the first Westside Boys broke through the barrier, smashing in a window and trying to climb in. Jess quickly sprayed the area with automatic gunfire, and the raid subsided.

Then he heard an explosion from the rear of the hotel. Jess looked at Nick.

"I'm going to have to check that out, okay? You sit tight, mate—and make sure that no one gets through. Remember, you have two more clips in your pocket." Jess patted the side of Nick's pants, pressing the metal clips close to him.

And then Jess was gone.

And Nick waited.

For a long time nothing happened. Then the front door started to bulge as someone tried to push it open. Nick aimed his gun at the door and pulled the trigger. The spray of bullets riddled the heavy wood door and—like a wounded animal—it stopped moving.

Then someone with a long rifle in one hand and a machete in the other tried the window again. Nick fired, taking care to shoot above the head of the invader, and he withdrew.

How many of them are there out there? he wondered. *And how long before they come up with a plan that gets them in here? Why the hell do they want to come in here anyway?*

And when will Jess come back?

The gun started to feel heavy in his hands. Heavy, useless . . . when he heard voices.

From just outside, the excited, ganja-crazed voices of a hyper crowd—and Nick knew that they wanted in.

Come on, he thought. *Come back, Jess. I can't handle this—*

And at that moment the door gave a giant lurch and two Westside Boys dashed in. Nick had no choice. He fired, and they fell to the ground, still alive.

Didn't kill anyone, he thought.

Not yet.

Then by the window, three faces and a tangle of arms appeared, eyes wide, crazy as they crawled in, pushing the blockade of cheap lobby furniture away. Like worms they slithered onto the floor.

Nick hesitated.

I should shoot them, he thought. *Shoot them before they stand up and shoot me.*

His finger caressed the trigger, still hesitating, hesitating, until one of them, using his machete to stand, got to one knee, grinning.

Still caressing the trigger.

Nick gulped, and started to pull on the trigger.

Only now, nothing happened. The trigger didn't move. Didn't move—even as he pulled back hard. He looked down at the useless weapon. Jammed, he thought. Somehow . . . jammed.

And now one of the Westside Boys stood right in front of him. He could have easily aimed his gun at Nick, but instead, he raised the machete. And Nick saw that the blade had a pinkish-orange smear.

The attacker raised the weapon and ran straight for Nick.

Nick raised his gun to block and it caught the first downward smash of the blade, a smash that sent Nick reeling back and then tripping over the corner of the lobby rug that had been rolled back, falling now, while all the time his eyes were locked on the wild-eyed attacker.

This person who didn't know him—yet was so eager to hack and slash at him.

Nick kept squeezing the useless trigger.

Useless—and now the attacker leaped on Nick as if he were about to ride him. The blade went up again. Nick smelled the man, the mix of cheap alcohol, pot smoke, sweat, blood—a dizzying smell, surreal. And this seemed to take forever.

Kill me, Nick thought, not able to stand the sensation anymore.

Which is when the man's head exploded. A hole bloomed in his forehead and the back of his skull erupted.

But he didn't get off Nick.

Just sat there.

"Push him off, mate . . . and what the hell's wrong with your gun?"

On cue, Nick pushed his dead attacker to the side, and then scurried to his feet. Jess took the automatic weapon, flicked a switch, and said, "There you go . . . shoots better with the safety off."

"Must have . . . must have hit it by accident."

Nick realized it took every effort to speak, to make sense.

He looked at the door and the window, littered with bodies that he never noticed getting blown away. A few still twitched with life.

"I can see it wasn't such a great idea leaving you on guard duty, eh?" Jess was grinning.

Nick nodded. *Not such a good idea. Couldn't protect myself, couldn't protect anyone else.*

And he knew that he would feel that man's body on him, so eager to kill him, and feeling unable to do anything to stop it, for a long time . . .

He'd feel it in nightmares and in those quiet moments when he'd feel a little ripple of fear . . . and compare it to the big fear.

But mostly—in nightmares.

"Sir, could you put your seat back to its upright position?"

Nick opened his eyes and looked at the attendant standing over him. He had forgotten how he had considered flirting with her. Carrie was looking a little worn and sleepy at the other end of the transatlantic tunnel.

The words didn't mean anything for a second, and then he said . . . "Right."

He pressed the metal button and his chair slowly came to what was called its upright position.

Carrie smiled.

Nick licked his lips, dry, cracked from the disturbed sleep on the plane. He slid up the shade, and saw that it was morning in England. They were still well outside of London, but this day was—for England—remarkably clear. A few high cirrus clouds tinted a gentle rose color, the lush green of the fields and hedgerows—all looking brilliant even from this altitude.

He heard a grinding noise.

Landing gear coming down.

Nick felt no excitement, no anticipation about the days to come, the work, the people, the events. Numb almost.

He did notice—as the plane dipped down—one lone wisp of cirrus cloud, curled into what looked like a question mark, complete with a little period at the base.

But as he watched that cloud it seemed to drift away, transforming into a frothy, roaring wave crashing against the solid blue shoreline of the sky.

five

As he did most mornings, Professor Henry White stepped out into the crisp air, stretched, and took in a great big gulp, holding it a moment before releasing it with a satisfying "Ahhhh."

He looked down and checked that his pants legs were tightly tucked into his socks—and then he made sure his vest was buttoned. He then walked over and got onto his ten-speed bike.

He suspected he made a rather amusing figure as he straddled the thin-framed bike, especially with his herringbone cap. People smiled and waved at him, but he also heard the jeers and snickers of the schoolchildren and laborers. But that didn't matter.

He loved biking to Ian MacDonald's house a few times a week, arriving in time for some early-morning coffee, maybe some toast, while they talked about everything but his subject—philosophy—and MacDonald's subject—quantum physics.

He especially loved it since he had figured out that

whatever Ian was doing was something rather remarkable. Though Ian tried to keep it secret, bits and pieces leaked out in conversation, through the odd statement or question.

Like last week, when MacDonald had said, "Henry, tell me what you really think of evil."

Such a *strange* question.

Especially from a physicist.

And though MacDonald knew that White also had a degree in theology, it was the first time that religion had reared its head in any of their discussions.

And formulating an answer wasn't easy.

"Evil . . . is evil," White said at first. "We all know what it is when we see it. Like love, eh? Hard to define exactly what it is."

But the answer seemed to annoy MacDonald. "No. Not good enough. If everyone, especially—" He looked at White.

"Especially people like me?"

MacDonald had laughed. "No offense, Henry. Just that good and evil, right and wrong, is so much part of your world. In mine—with quantum physics—all that goes right out the window."

"And off to the other side of the universe. So you've told me . . . on those rare occasions you actually talk about your field with me."

"I'd much rather talk yours—when I take a break. So, no better answer? The nature of evil is . . . ?"

And White remembered stopping then, and thinking. What did he really believe? More to the point, what did he really feel? It wasn't easy to put into words. But he tried.

"It's like your unknown, all powerful X-force, Ian. You know, this mysterious thing that, you tell me, can some-how link one particle with another a million light-years away? Evil . . . is like that. A force, like good. As real, as mysterious, as—"

"Powerful?"

White nodded.

"Sure. And something else," White added. "Dangerous. The most dangerous thing in the universe."

MacDonald sat quiet for a second. Then he smiled.

"We're not so far apart, you and I, in our work, or our interests. But more tea—and enough about evil for now. So tell me, what have you been reading lately?"

And the conversation moved on.

Snapping out of his reverie, White took a turn in the narrow lane and started up the hill toward MacDonald's house. Then, struggling with the effort, as he once again faced the reality that he wasn't getting any younger, he looked up.

To see . . . a bunch of police vehicles, a hospital van, all with lights flashing in the misty morning light.

Five . . . maybe six vehicles.

All clustered around MacDonald's house.

And he thought: *This isn't good.*

White also thought a simple prayer, knowing that the time for prayer was probably long gone.

Elaina Dali looked at her left leg.

A shallow gash ran from the bottom of her kneecap all the way down to her midcalf. The blood had turned into a dry, brownish, crusty smear. She looked at her other leg—amazingly it was okay—and when she felt her head for any signs of blood, and openings, there was nothing.

And only then did she look around. She saw a brilliant orange-yellow canopy of leaves overhead, and she sat up slowly, then turned, leaning into a massive outcrop of blackish-gray rock.

When she shifted—sitting like some kind of homeless person squatting on the side of the road—the crispy fallen leaves crunched. The only difference here was that she could only beg from the squirrels.

But even they seemed to be avoiding her.

She licked her lips—dry, cracked—and then she looked around the ground.

She saw her purse. One strap was broken, her nice Prada bag looking like some Goodwill castaway.

She opened it, pushing past a sheaf of papers, digging, scrambling, searching for—

Lipstick.

She took the lipstick out. She could use a mirror; there was one somewhere in the bowels of her bag. But she didn't want to hunt for it . . . so she opened the lipstick and used her fingers to guide her as she applied the deep maroon color.

Immediately her lips felt better.

But her throat was so dry and parched. *I need water*, she thought. *Has to be some water around here somewhere, somewhere near this—*

First time she thought of it.

Where am I?

So hard to let the pieces fall into place.

Where am I?

She remembered . . . her car.

Yes. She was in her car and it went off the cliff, tumbling end over end, so slowly, and now—

She felt it.

Could *feel* those sickening rolls, happening so slowly, her body sliding left and right, and the terrible thoughts having so much time to appear. *I should have my seat belt on. Then I wouldn't be rolling around like this.*

She looked right during one flip of her car and saw the right passenger windows implode, and then with the next roll, the front passenger door vanished.

She knew then that the next roll would send her flying

over there, to where there was no door, nothing to stop her.

And then, like a doll, she was thrown toward the open hole of the door, toward it, and then out the hole, past the car . . . flying into the leafy cover of the massive bushes that filled the hill.

Those bushes seemed to catch her, even cushion her fall.

And next? What happened next?

She remembered getting to her knees quickly. She remembered a voice that said . . . Don't stay here. You *can't* stay here. You have to move, get under cover of the bushes, the trees still heavy with their reddish leaves.

She had taken a few babylike crawls and somehow she saw her purse, the strap torn, but zipped, right there in front of her. For a moment she considered not taking it.

Just . . . *move*, the voice demanded.

But she took the purse and, throwing it over her shoulder like a rucksack, she'd crawled forward, away from the car, curling around the hill.

And she didn't stop until it grew dark, and she finally stopped, collapsed, and fell asleep.

Until—now.

Other thoughts, images occurred, sitting there in the shadow of the cool stone.

Another car. There was another car behind her. And the sound of metal hitting metal. Then she remembered something more important. Something—inside her bag. She looked at the bag. It was a good thing she still had the bag. So good.

She remembered what she had.

She needed a plan now.

She felt almost powerful.

Look what happened to me.

And yet—here I am.

It was good thought, a powerful thought.

Here I am. Alive!
I should get moving. Moving. Need to move.
But first, a plan.
And so she sat on the crunchy leaves, oh so thirsty, and waited for a plan to somehow appear.

Henry White stopped his bike, realizing what an odd sight he made standing there in his tweed and black socks pulled high over his trouser bottoms. Bright ribbons of yellow tape crossed and girded the tress around MacDonald's house.

Police walked in and out of the house, while paramedics stood beside their ambulance, talking. No rushing there. No rushing by the paramedics.

That wasn't good.

"Oh dear," White said.

He had inched the bike closer, until he was only meters away from the yellow tape, when a man in a long Burberry coat spotted him. The man stopped talking to the uniformed policeman by his side and walked over.

White watched the man duck under the yellow tape cautiously and approach him.

"Can I help you?" the man said.

It wasn't a real question. More like: *What are you doing here and don't you think you should move on?*

"Excuse me, but is something wrong?"

Such a stupid question.

No, nothing's wrong. We just circled this house with pretty yellow ribbon and turned on all the lights just for the hell of it.

The man in the coat took a step closer.

"I'm Inspector Thomas Murphy and you are—?"

White introduced himself. The police inspector, thin, balding, with eyes that had trouble landing squarely on White's face, nodded. "And how do you know"—he shrugged in the direction of the house—"Dr. MacDonald?"

White cleared his throat. The morning air still felt so chilly, as if the sun had failed to burn the haze off and a typical English fall clamminess claimed the day.

"We're friends. We meet a few mornings a week, talk over things . . ."

The inspector entered the information in a Palm Pilot. Funny. Almost a moment from a commercial. *Even detectives use it . . .*

"Was Mr. MacDonald expecting you?"

"Yes—er, can you tell me what's—"

The inspector looked up.

"A few more questions, then I will."

White nodded. Yes, definitely turning colder, and his herringbone jacket offered little protection. He waited, astride his bike.

"Dr. MacDonald had a daughter?"

White nodded. "Yes. Sophie. Her mum died, and Ian—"

"And she goes to school in London?"

"Yes, she's very bright, a real wonderful student."

"London Academy?" White nodded. "Tell me, when was the last time you saw her?"

Suddenly the image of the police, the idle paramedics, the tape became even more ominous.

"Two mornings ago. Passed her on her way to the station. Please, Inspector, could you tell me now what happened?"

Finally, Murphy nodded. "Yes. Last night"—he hesitated, a little unsure about the next word—"someone came into this house and killed MacDonald. Brutally. I won't give you any details—but trust me, the scene inside is like nothing *I've* ever seen."

White licked his lips.

"God, poor Ian. And Sophie?"

"There's no sign of the girl. We put the time of the murder at about the time she would get home."

For moment White wondered if somehow this cadaverous man had the crazy idea that Sophie had something to do with the death. But he quickly saw that wasn't the point at all. The inspector was concerned.

"We don't know where she is. A few of my people are in the village, asking questions. Nothing so far. Would you . . . know anything?"

"No. I came here for one of our regular chats. I don't have a clue where she might be."

The inspector closed his Palm Pilot.

"We'd like you to stay available. We'll keep you posted. Beyond finding who did this—God, and why— we want to find the girl."

"Y-yes, I won't be going anywhere."

Murphy smiled—eerie and uncomfortable. "Great. And we'll keep in touch."

The inspector waited, and White knew that he was waiting for him to bike away.

And so he did.

Elaina stood up and—amazingly—she felt almost okay.

I can tumble off a cliff, she thought, *and somehow be all right.* Though without a mirror she didn't know what her face looked like.

She looked down and saw that her pants suit was torn in a few places and a dark brownish crust revealed the telltale sign of bleeding.

She stood up and started moving. Her footing in the dry crunchy leaves was unsure, and after every step she'd slip down the slope a few inches. She walked, grabbing at branches for support, barely looking up, until she came to an opening, looked ahead—and saw the Bear Mountain Bridge.

The bridge caught the brilliant fall sunlight, shimmering as it spanned the Hudson.

A plan. That's why she was moving. She had a plan. And that plan involved her crossing the bridge. Were people looking for her? Had they searched the crash site and discovered that she was gone? How far was she from her car now? Had the car exploded? She seemed to remember seeing fire . . .

Or was that just the burning pain she felt as she moved?

She knew only one thing: She was alive.

She looked up at the deep blue sky, and wondered if her father could look down and see her. Did she still believe in that?

Then she continued hiking to the bridge.

The cab stopped dead in Piccadilly Circus.

The driver seemed totally unperturbed, as if he could sit idly in the intersection forever, quite happily letting the meter run on.

"No way around this mess?" Nick asked.

For a second the driver didn't respond and Nick wondered if he'd been heard. Then the driver turned around.

" 'Fraid not, sir. They're doing some work up on Charing Cross. Diverting a lot of traffic this way. Could be a while . . ."

Nick looked at his watch. Getting out of Heathrow had been a piece of cake, but now he had lost so much time fighting London traffic. He was blocks away from his meeting that was due to start *now*.

He dug into his pocket and handed the driver a ten-pound note.

"I'll just run!" Nick grabbed the door and bolted out into the sea of immobile cabs and cars. He looked around, trying to remember the most direct route to Soho . . . The streets of London curve around dizzyingly, and getting anyplace was never easy.

He couldn't blow this meeting. A one-on-one interview with Tish Barrett about her recent meetings with the Northern Ireland leaders.

Most Americans knew little about the fragile coalition trying to move the troubled region past the state of religious civil war. Parliament member Tish Barrett, with her short gray pageboy and ever-cheerful smile, was key to that process.

Nick jogged away from Piccadilly over to Leicester Square, and then he cut up, racing past the mayhem of Chinatown and into the heart of Soho. They were meeting at Forum, a private club for political figures, writers, and the occasional West End star.

At this time of day it would be deserted.

He jogged past Boardwalk, a late-night bar that had trapped him on more than one night. Might be a good place to unwind tonight, he thought.

Forum was just ahead, its beveled glass windows revealing only a blurry interior.

He pulled the door open and saw Tish Barrett sitting at a back table, a teacup in front of her. Nick smiled, checked his watch, and then made an apologetic grimace.

"Ms. Barrett—I'm so sorry . . . traffic was a mess."

Barrett smiled and dug into a small black purse, whipping out a cigarette.

"You don't mind?" she said in a husky voice.

"Not at all . . ."

Nick had grown used to the smoking in the United Kingdom. She lit up and inhaled deeply.

Nick pulled out a microcassette recorder and held it up. "And . . . is this okay?"

Barrett coughed. Have another drag, why not. "Of course—just make sure I see the transcript. I can be *so* stupid in these things."

Nick smiled. "You got it. So shall we start . . . Tell me,

just how much in jeopardy do you think the coalition is? How close are we to more violence?"

Like the caterpillar in *Alice,* the negotiator blew a stream of smoke that nearly seemed aimed at Nick. "Close? I would say we're more than . . . close. If we don't do something bloody fast, Belfast will be a war zone again."

A waiter hovered. Nick pointed to Barrett's cup, and he kept asking questions as the bluish smoke from her cigarette filled the room.

Henry White pedaled his bike along the road, his jacket struggling mightily to stay buttoned in the wind.

He felt chilled, and not just by the air. Something bad had happened to someone he knew. Something bad, something unknown. And in Henry White's universe, the unknown was always dangerous.

He had once read something about Alfred Hitchcock— that the director viewed any change, any variation of routine as potentially dangerous. It fueled his movies . . . people did something different, and terrible things happened.

White related to that.

But what to make of this? Whatever happened to Mac-Donald and his daughter?

White looked up ahead and saw the narrow path that cut right into the woods, then across some farmland, straight to his house. Normally he enjoyed taking the bumpy path.

But this morning, it felt oddly ominous.

Silly thought, that. In the light of day, what could happen?

He hit the dirt curb and then bumped his way onto the narrow rutted path. He had to pump harder now.

The air turned cooler here . . . with tall hedges on either side. Past this broad field, the path then cut into a small wooded area before ending at the tiny lane that led to his house.

A nice ride, usually. But why was he hurrying so much now?

The wall of hedges came to an abrupt end, one turning sharply left as the other continued to the edge of the woods.

Most of the trees had lost their foliage, but a few still had clusters of browning leaves, turning the morning light mottled.

The path grew even bumpier, and White jiggled on his narrow bicycle seat. He gripped the handlebars more tightly. He wanted nothing more than to get home, make a nice cup of tea, and maybe try to do a little work on his book on epistemology.

The path veered right past a close stand of three huge oaks, easily a few hundred years old, and then climbed a small incline. White pulled on the handlebars to get extra force for biking up—

When someone jumped in front of the path.

He reached around and grabbed both hand brakes, with just enough time to stop.

Right in front of Sophie MacDonald.

six

The bike stopped only inches from her feet.

"Sophie?"

She stepped aside. "I—I knew that you'd come this way. So I waited. I thought maybe I missed you, or had the wrong day."

"God, no, I just came from your house." White got off his bike. "Your house, Sophie . . . your father . . . I'm so, so sorry." He took a breath. "Sophie . . . what happened?"

She looked around. It had been such a long night, so cold, hiding here, not knowing what to do. Who to trust.

Until she knew there was only one person she could trust.

"What happened?" White said.

Sophie chewed her lower lip, a habit her dad was always telling her to stop.

Sophie, stop, you're going to chew it right off.

She knew . . . and her dad knew . . . that she had only started doing it when Mom died.

"Can we go someplace warm?" she asked.

Someplace warm, someplace with food, and especially a place to sleep, she thought.

White stepped off his bike. "Yes, walk with me; it's not too far to my house." He smiled at her. "Fix you up with a bit of tea, some breakfast, hm? And then we'll talk . . ."

Elaina fell, scrambling down the slope to the highway below and the narrow sidewalk.

She quickly sprung to her feet as if embarrassed by the fall, as if someone might see and wonder, *Whatever is wrong with that strange woman?* There was a path across the bridge—but she wondered, how odd would it look to walk across the bridge? How bad did she look? Did she look like a homeless person, some crazy nut escaped from Wingdale?

And another thing . . . it was late October and already the sun was close to dipping below the mountain. She had a few hours of light left—if that.

She started across the bridge. Too early for rush hour, only a few cars were crossing either way. No one seemed to take any notice of her, though she still felt her paranoia.

Elaina reached a hand up to her hair, seeing how horribly disheveled it might be. Then she touched her face. It didn't feel as though there was any blood on her face, no cuts.

Good, she thought, *then I don't look like a zombie. That will be important.*

Was she in shock? she thought. Could any of her thoughts, actions be taken as reasonable?

Halfway across the bridge, and she stopped and looked down. The river shimmered under the sun, still free from the mammoth shade of Bear Mountain, the water still, dark, looking cold, deep.

Funny about bridges. They always seem to whisper . . .

Jump. Go on. You could do it, just climb onto the railing and leap.

She pulled back, away from the railing, away from that voice. Then back to hurry across the bridge. The toll booths were ahead, and she'd have to walk past them.

Just have to smile and look okay, she thought. *Force myself to . . . look okay.*

"You sure you wouldn't want anything to eat?" Tish Barrett asked. "They have delicious pastries . . ."

Nick imagined that she was feeling, as they say, a bit peckish.

"Not for me, but—" He looked around and waved at a waiter who was chatting up a young waitress.

The lanky waiter ambled over, taking his time.

Nick smiled. "What would you like?"

"Oh, I don't know. Maybe some biscuits . . . a scone?"

"Great," Nick said. "And another pot of tea."

The waiter nodded and, without a word, left. One of the main things on the menu must be attitude.

Nick turned back to Barrett and gave her his toughest question.

"What about the guns?"

The abruptness of the question obviously shocked Barrett. One thing Nick had learned working international stories was that Americans were way too fast, way too uncivil for most of the civilized world.

But as an interview technique, it could be useful.

Barrett used a thoughtful sip of tea—though she had to be down to a mere sugary deposit—to hesitate.

"The guns—the guns . . . the IRA guns are a tough issue, Mr. Fowles. It's something most British don't understand, so I wouldn't expect an American to 'get it.' "

Was that a dig? Nick wondered. A subtle put-down for shooting such a question at her in a straightforward manner? Now Barrett leaned close and lowered her voice, though they were the only two patrons in the place.

"And here is what no one really gets. For decades, those guns have symbolized the dreams and goals of those who wanted an independent Northern Ireland. Just like the Palestinians, as long as they were armed, they had their dreams."

Her eyes glowed, and Nick felt chilled by the power that this roly-poly woman generated. He could well imagine her going head-to-head in meetings with loyalists and Sinn Fein.

"So you're saying—"

"I'm saying that if we take their guns we"—and here her fist curled into a ball, and for a moment Nick thought that she was about to slam it down on the starched white linen tablecloth—"damn well better leave their dreams and their hopes intact. Does that explain anything?"

Nick paused. He wasn't about to risk another blunt question, though her answer was . . . incredible. Eloquent, to the point. Insightful. Everything he had hoped to get from an interview with her.

"Yes. I do. Now, can I ask a hypothetical question?"

The woman laughed, the tension dismissed as though it were merely a theatrical tool for her, part of her repertoire. There was a bit of Churchill in this formidable woman. "Of course you can. I have no agenda for this little chat."

On cue, the waiter materialized with a plate of "biscuits"—sugary cookies—that were guarded by two fluffy-looking scones dotted with raisins.

"Yummy," she said. She winked at Nick. "I had no lunch and these look lovely." Amazing thing about the Brits . . . everything was *lovely*, from a cup of tea to having the right change for the tube. It was all so . . . cute.

"So, my question is—"

Nick felt a blast of cool air. He turned around to see the door open . . . and watched someone walk in.

A woman. Short auburn hair, incredible blue eyes, a rust-brown poncho over a stylish skirt-and-boot combination. Some celebrity? Lots of TV companies were based in this area, publishing too—

But she looked at Tish Barrett, then Nick. Then she walked straight over to Barrett, ignoring Nick, and stuck out her hand.

"Hello, Ms. Barrett—I'm Maddy Hodge."

For a second Barrett paused, scone half gone, staring at the woman.

Then a big light bulb went off. Barrett knew the name, Nick saw.

Only now did the woman look at Nick, a quick glance, quick and targeted, as if she were checking out his reaction time.

"Maddy Hodge! Yes, I've enjoyed your work. Your photos from . . . Iceland . . . incredible stuff really."

And the young woman smiled and quickly gestured at a nearby chair. "Do you mind?"

Nick was still studying her as if observing a phenomenon, a whirlwind that had spun into the room. Because that's what it felt like—the door opened . . . and *this creature blew in.*

He thought . . . *Who is she? And what is she doing here, and—more important—what should I do?*

"I found out that you were meeting here," Rogers said. "And I had to come and see if I could take a few quick pictures . . ."

The woman absolutely sparked with energy. She fired another quick glance at Nick, another test.

Barrett's face turned a bit somber. "I've been trying to breeze in and out . . . not kick up too much new dust. Just this one feature for America—what magazine did you say?"

It was all coming together for Nick.

"*Vanity Fair* magazine."

Maddy's eyes went wide—an expression of being impressed. Could have been complete baloney, since Nick was sure that this woman knew how to perform.

"Long lead time, I imagine—it won't appear for months," Barrett said.

Nick . . . got it. This woman was a photographer. And with Barrett trying to stay out of sight, she was suddenly very hard to photograph while the negotiations continued—or crumbled, depending on your point of view.

Somehow . . . Maddy Hodge had learned about this secret interview and was now crashing it.

In seconds, Rogers had her camera out.

"Just a few shots and then I'm off . . ."

Barrett didn't seem to know what to say. But Nick did, as he leaned across the table and blocked her shot of Barrett.

"Excuse me," he said. And for the first time Maddy Hodge turned and gave Nick a dead-on look.

Henry White held the door open for Sophie and she walked into his small house.

For a moment Sophie stood at the threshold, looking at the small entryway, the cozy living room, the stacks of books everywhere as though they had fallen from the sky.

She sniffed.

The smell of last night's dinner . . .

"Would you like some tea . . . maybe a bit of juice?" White looked away. "At least, I *think* I have some juice."

Sophie shook her head.

"No. A glass of water would be fine."

In truth she was horribly hungry and thirsty and terribly tired. But all that would wait till later.

"Be right back . . ." And White dashed away into the kitchen. "You sure you don't want something to eat?"

No, Sophie thought. Then she said the word quietly . . .
"No."

White hurried back with a glass of water.

He gestured at an overstuffed couch. "Sit. Go on. You must be exhausted."

Sophie took a seat, and folded her hands. She kept looking at the room, so different from her father's. Prints filled every available space on the walls. Statues and over-sized books occupied all the open flat spaces.

No high-tech equipment here. Just ideas and words.

And despite everything, she immediately liked it.

She allowed herself—for a moment—to feel safe.

"Sorry for the clutter. The life of a bachelor academic." White grimaced. "Sophie, I just came . . . from your house."

Sophie looked away. For a while she had been so good at not thinking about it . . . almost as if by morning's light it could have been a dream, a fantasy. That, like all the other bad dreams, it would melt away.

But now this man, this kind, almost silly man, made it real.

She felt a familiar pressure behind her eyes. The tears. She thought she might have none left. The tears, married with the fear.

Sophie fixed her gaze on the windows, the light muted by yellowish, sheer curtains. She recognized another smell, a pipe.

"There were police there, Sophie, and they asked me about you . . . ."

Sophie turned sharply toward White.

Her voice was low, flat.

"What did you tell them?"

"Why, I said I didn't have a clue where you were . . . which was true. I'm so glad you're fine, that everything's all right for you—"

"Everything's not fine. Not all right."

"I know, I mean, I understand that something terrible happened, some kind of accident, some mishap with your father's—"

Sophie stood up. Maybe this place wasn't safe. Maybe she had been foolish to come here. She scanned the room again as if what was once cozy and warming could suddenly turn—dangerous.

She looked at Professor White, sitting so uncomfortably.

She needed someone to trust.

Someone she could talk to.

There was no one except her mom's parents, on the Isle of Wight, so old. She hadn't heard from them, not since she lost her mother. Perhaps they were hurt too much. So there was no one, except some school friends—but what could they do?

Now there was just this man, this tweedy professor who enjoyed talking to her father.

A man who hadn't seen the blood seeping out from under the lab door.

How could he understand?

"Can I trust you?"

"Why, certainly, you can, Sophie, I wouldn't—"

She took a step closer to him.

"Can . . . I . . . trust you completely?"

He understood the question now. He took a moment to answer.

Then Henry White said, "Yes."

seven

Elaina pushed open the door to the small motel office, and a little bell jingled.

For a moment this place—Heidi's Motel—reminded her of nothing more than the Bates Motel. Of course, it wasn't out in the deserted Midwest . . . and being so close to Bear Mountain, it was probably busy with hikers, foliage hunters, skiers . . .

She stood at the desk. A small wooden cradle held postcards displaying three different views of the motel, all under a brilliant blue sky, just like today. She heard shuffling feet . . . slippers . . .

And a little gray-haired woman walked out of the back room, wearing giant bifocals that seemed to indicate she didn't miss a thing. She stopped for a second and looked at Elaina, instantly unsure.

"Yes?" she said, her voice loaded with suspicion.

Elaina wondered whether this was "Heidi." Or was the hotel named for the fictional little girl who went to live with her kindly, bearded grandfather?

"Can I help you?" the woman repeated.

Elaina smiled. She had passed the toll booths expecting to be stopped. One of the uniformed attendants looked at her as she blithely passed the booths and turned toward 9W, as if people always strolled this way.

She didn't look back. But she felt their eyes boring into her.

"Yes, I'd like a room. I saw the vacancy sign."

The woman didn't move; her bulbous eyes under so much split glass locked on Elaina, looking at the condition of her clothes.

"No reservation?"

Elaina's smile faded. Reservation? Was she kidding? A reservation? Here?

"No. I didn't know—" she stumbled.

Now the woman took a step closer to her desk.

"I have a room. Are you okay? You look like . . . something happened to you?"

Elaina looked out the back door. Cars streamed left and right.

She looked back at the woman. Elaina was so tired; she had to rest, think, *plan.*

I nearly died back there, she thought.

I could still die.

No. Not die. Be killed.

Because she knew—admitted—that's what it was.

They knew she had taken these papers—and oh so swiftly, they had moved to eliminate her.

Elaina licked her dry, cracked lips. Thirsty, and hungry too. Could she trust this woman? Could Heidi be trusted? She saw a religious picture on the wall, Christ holding two fingers up in a closed peace sign.

Trust. No reason she should trust her. But Elaina had no choice.

"I had an accident. I nearly died . . ."

"Oh, dear, should I call—"

"No." She realized she nearly yelled the response. Then, more calmly, "No. I'll tell you why. I wonder—" Elaina looked around, and she saw a single red plastic-covered straight-backed chair sitting against the front window, an artifact from some lost Formica kitchen of the fifties.

The woman immediately picked up on Elaina's longing glance.

"Yes, go on . . . sit."

Elaina backed up and sat on the chair, immediately feeling how her body ached.

The woman slowly came out from behind the counter, her slippers shuffling on the floor.

"What happened to you?"

"A car . . . pushed me off the side of the cliff."

"Oh God, how horrible—and the police never came?"

Elaina looked out the window. She had to trust someone, and like it or not, Heidi was the last stop. She couldn't go on any further on her own.

"I—I'm sure they did. I didn't stay."

"Whyever not?"

Elaina looked up at the woman's eyes.

"Because—they *wanted* me to go flying off the cliff. They wanted me dead. And"—a big breath—"they probably still do . . ."

Nick stared at the photographer's face. She had an elfin beauty that was remarkable. But, elf or no, right now she was screwing up his feature interview.

"Er, if you don't mind, I was having an interview with Ms. Barrett."

Maddy Hodge laughed. "Don't let me stop you, I just want to get a few pictures." She leaned over to Tish Barrett and patted the woman's arm. "You don't mind, do you?"

Tish Barrett looked around the dark tea room. "Well, I

was trying to keep a low profile this trip—things are so tense. But I go back to Belfast tonight, so go on . . . snap away. Though I would have dressed better . . ."

Whoever this Hodge was, she obviously had a reputation. Barrett was clearly charmed.

She took out a massive Leica, and started to shoot.

Nick shook his head and turned back. "You were saying, about the importance of an exchange, the guns—"

Maddy interrupted. "A little this way . . . oh lovely . . ."

Nick rolled his eyes. Was he going to have to fight to get every question out while she snapped pictures?

"The exchange of guns . . . ?" he asked.

Finally Barrett answered, and then she answered his other questions while Maddy Hodge snapped photos, interrupting both.

Finally she stood up.

"There, all done." She quickly stuck her camera in her equipment bag.

"Oh, that's too bad," Nick said.

Maddy fired him a glance. Sarcasm didn't go over so well in the oh-so-polite United Kingdom. Then she turned to Barrett and shook her head. "Thank you, I'll make sure you see the contact sheet—you will love them."

"Yes, that would be nice."

"And thank you!" she said to Barrett. Completely ignoring Nick.

And then Maddy Hodge bolted from the café with a wave of her hand.

"Well, that was pretty nervy."

Barrett turned to him, a querulous expression on her face.

"What?"

"I mean, the way she just barged in."

Barrett looked at the door, and pointed.

"But you know she is an *amazing* photographer. Perhaps one of the U.K.'s best."

Nick got the sense that he should rein in his criticism of Maddy Hodge. Quickly.

"And not only that, she's a pioneer in something called—I think—extreme photography . . . deep underwater, mountains . . . she's a real national treasure, amazing girl . . . absolutely amazing, fearless."

And now Nick looked at the door, and Greek Street right outside. And he had the thought that maybe he had been too hasty.

Barrett looked at her watch.

"Oh, got to go! Get to Heathrow. Do you think you have enough from me?"

Nick smiled. Despite the interruption, he had plenty. "You were great."

Barrett smiled. "Good." And she gathered her stuff while Nick looked wistfully at the door.

"My dad didn't talk much about his work. I mean, he'd get lost in his lab, sometimes just disappearing for days."

White nodded. He had put out a plate of crumbly cookies that Sophie nibbled at. Sophie thought that she could easily finish the plate—she was that hungry.

"He didn't have much time to ask you about school, friends . . . your world?"

"He tried. He always tried. But he'd get that distant look, all sort of—"

"Absentminded?"

Sophie nodded. She thought of that silly movie. *The Absent-Minded Professor.* Her dad was a bit like that.

Then another image. The door, the blood. She shivered. She wondered what she would have seen if she had opened the door and walked in, walked in to see her father.

In his lab—

She looked away.

A big grandfather clock ticked noisily in a corner of the sitting room, marking the passing of every second as though every moment was important, as though time itself were slipping away.

She took a breath. "He tried. I appreciated that."

White nodded. "Did he talk about his work?"

"He didn't use to. But I was having . . . these dreams. And—one night—he had a few drinks, he didn't drink much, but that night . . . anyway, he started telling me things. He told me about kicking . . . a football."

White laughed. "A football?"

Sophie pressed on. "Yes, he said to me, laughing, 'Soph, do you know what happens when you kick a football?' I said of course. My foot . . . kicks the ball. And then he stood up, red-faced, almost angry—"

"That's unlike your father."

"Right. He was never angry. He was gentle, sweet. And he said to me, no. Then again, 'No—that's not what happens.' And he came close to me, as if it were so important for me to understand. He said . . . that when my foot gets close to the football, the electrons that surround my foot . . . approach the electrons that surround the ball . . . and the closer they get, the more those electrons push each other away."

"Interesting. Never quite thought about kicking a football that way."

"He said, 'You never ever really hit the ball. You never even touch it. And yet—everyone in the world thinks that they do . . . that *that's* the reality, that's the way the world works. That we actually touch, feel things.' "

"Your father should know—he is"—White he stumbled a moment, using the present tense—"a brilliant man, a great scientist."

"He told me that the world doesn't have a clue about what's real. He wanted me to know about that. Before he told me the other stuff . . . ."

"The other stuff?"

Sophie looked at the clock. More lazy ticks, the pendulum swinging.

"Yes, he talked about this place in Scotland where he used to work, about the people, about the experiments, about how dangerous it all was. He wanted me to know, just a little at first. Even though he knew it might scare me . . ."

"And it did?"

"Yes. All the time."

Professor White reached down and picked up his cup of tea.

"Tell me, then. Tell me what your father told you."

Sophie looked right at the man. "And you won't tell anyone I'm here?"

"No. You can stay here. Until you're ready to leave. What . . . did he tell you, Sophie?"

Sophie took a breath. There was so much that she didn't understand, fragments, bits, a jumble—all of it a scary jumble.

The only thing she knew for sure was that now her dad was dead.

And it all had something to do with what he told her.

Elaina stood in the doorway.

The small motel room was surreally cute, the bed covered by a white bedspread with blue trim, and a Hudson River landscape picture on the wall. A small dressing table with an oval mirror sat in the corner. She looked around for a phone—and saw one. She might need that.

"Is the room okay?"

And Heidi—it was her real name—looked at Elaina.

"Yes. Fine." She smiled. "I love it."

Heidi smiled. "Good, let's go back to the office and we'll get you all checked in."

Checked in. Elaina's mind raced. She needed to rest,

hide a bit. Figure out what to do. But . . . getting checked in?

Elaina followed the woman to her small office. Heidi went behind the desk and tapped the keyboard of an ancient computer.

"And how will you be paying for the room?"

Elaina reached into her purse, pushing past the sheaf of papers she carried. She removed her wallet, opening it to display a parade of credit cards. She started to select one.

And stopped.

If she gave the woman a credit card, she'd get a preapproval. And the system will know where she is. *The system.* And anyone who could access the system could find out where she was.

The woman noticed that she was hesitating.

"Is there a problem?"

Elaina looked away. She needed rest, she couldn't stay on her feet much longer.

"I . . . I . . ."

The woman seemed confused, even a bit worried. Elaina looked into the woman's eyes trying to see the unseeable. *Can I ask for her help? Is she a good woman?*

She didn't have a choice.

Elaina cleared her throat. For a moment she wondered if the woman might be considering a quick call to 911. *Got a nutcase here, someone escaped from a mental home.*

"If you run my card through . . . now . . . they'll find me. I know it."

The woman looked down at Elaina's open wallet.

"What I can do—" Elaina dug out a few of the credit cards, a rainbow of American Express, Visa, and MasterCard. "See these? They're all good. Keep them. I won't stay here long, and when I go, charge me. Charge extra. Just don't—run it through . . . now." And with that, Elaina handed the woman the cards.

"Your fingers," Heidi said, "they're so cold."

Was it cold? Elaina wondered. Or was it shock?

The woman released her hand.

"Okay. I'll keep—one of these. When you leave, I'll wait a few days. Then I'll run it through. Are you sure you don't want to get the police to help?"

Elaina shook her head.

"No. Not till I know who's doing it. And why . . ."

The woman smiled. "Okay. Here's the key. Go rest. Rest, sleep, and we'll talk more later."

Elaina took the key. "Thank you."

"You know—I think I have some of my daughter's things that might fit. Nothing fancy. Maybe some jeans . . ."

"That would be great."

And Elaina turned and walked the few steps back to the room where she fell into the bed, and into the deepest sleep of her life . . .

eight

Nick stayed at Hazlitt's in Soho, a favorite writers' haunt dating back two hundred years, filled with antiques and broad wood floors that creaked with every move. The clubs and bars and great restaurants of the West End of London, as well as the bookstores of Charing Cross, were only minutes away from the small hotel.

The phone rang. Not his cell phone—which could have meant his kids or his editor—but the room phone.

"Hello?"

"Hi . . . am I catching you at a bad time?"

Who was this? The female voice sounded as though she knew him. "Excuse me," Nick said, "but I think you have the wrong room."

"Is this Nick Fowles?"

Then he flashed on the voice. It was Maddy Hodge, the photographer. How did she track him down? And why?

"Oh—it's you. The photographer."

She laughed, an infectious sound.

"Very good. Sorry, didn't mean to startle you with a strange call from a woman."

Nick laughed. "I usually don't get such calls."

"Oh good, glad I could inject a bit of excitement into your life."

"Not that I'm looking for excitement."

"Oh, we can always use more of that, eh? Listen, I want to properly apologize for crashing your interview. I had to get those pics or I'd lose her for weeks, maybe months. But it was a bit wrong."

"A bit? Yes, it was. No harm done though. I have my story."

"Good. Then let me make it up to you. Drinks and dinner at Atlantic?"

Nick hadn't been to Atlantic yet. A trendy, subterranean place near Piccadilly. He had planned on just grabbing a pizza. But then he thought about Maddy, her sparkling eyes, dimples—and he was curious about her photo work.

At least—that's what he told himself.

"What do you say?"

"Okay. Give me thirty minutes."

"Oh, don't rush. I'll need at least an hour. I *must* shower. Hey, if you get there early, order drinks—a Sapphire gin and tonic will do nicely."

He laughed again. "Okay, see you . . . when you get there."

"By-ee," she said in that singsong way favored by the Brits.

Nick put down the phone.

And then he looked in his suitcase for what would be suitable to wear to a trendy restaurant.

"How's the soup?" White asked.

Sophie took a long slow slurp of the vegetable soup,

savoring the warmth, the crunchy vegetables. It was . . . delicious.

"Great."

"There's plenty more where that came from. Not much else in the house, I'm afraid. Tend to let the larder go bare quite a lot."

Sophie looked at this quiet gentle man whom she had to trust. She always wondered what Professor White and her dad talked about. Religion? Science? Art? Life?

They were so . . . different.

Then she put her spoon down in the bowl and placed the half-finished soup bowl on the table.

"You were telling me what your father used to tell you . . ."

"Yes. After a while . . . I knew one thing. He was scared."

"Scared?"

"Yes. Scared. He only let me really see it a few times. Once, late at night, I was up, doing schoolwork. Math . . . always hard for me. He came into the room."

Sophie looked at the professor, who was nodding, listening so thoughtfully. Was she going to be able to make any sense?

"He seemed upset. I asked him—had something gone wrong with an experiment? And he shook his head. No, nothing there. The experiments were going just fine. It was something else. He sat down on my bed, and then looked at me. And then he said something that really frightened me."

"Doesn't sound like Ian . . . had he been—"

"Drinking again?" Sophie asked. "No. I mean, Dad loved his single malts. But never while he was working. But that night he looked at me and said . . . If anything should happen to him, that there were some things I had to do, things I had to know."

"Happen to him? What did he mean?"

"He didn't say. But I could tell from the tone of his voice what he meant. Happen . . . as in something bad. I knew that there was a reason we lived way out here, why he cut himself off from nearly everybody. Reasons besides Mom's death. I knew there was a reason—I just didn't know what it was. And that night—he was going to tell me."

"Your soup," White said. "Getting cold . . . Want me to reheat it?"

Sophie shook her head. All of a sudden she didn't want any food, didn't want to eat and feel the satisfying crunch of the carrots between her teeth.

"I told Dad he was scaring me. He smiled, and told me that he didn't mean to do that. But he had to tell me these things. Something might happen, he said. He might disappear—or something else might happen. I didn't ask him what that would be. Somehow—I knew."

She took a deep breath in the quiet sunlit room.

"He said that if anything did happen—I had to get away. As fast as possible. 'Get away,' he said. 'And trust Henry to help you.' "

White nodded. "He's absolutely right, of course. I'll do anything I can to help you."

"He told me to ask you to help me travel to Glasgow. That I should go alone. It would be too suspicious if you left."

"Glasgow? Why Glasgow?"

"I had to find a man there. Someone who worked with my dad once. I have it all written down. I was to tell the man . . . that it had started. That my dad said it was beginning now. And then I was to give him this . . ."

And Sophie opened up her hand to reveal a small chunk of tinfoil. She unwrapped the foil, to show the little rectangular box.

"What is that?"

"It's a thumb drive. It's . . . like a CD-ROM disk, but smaller—and it holds so much more. My dad has me travel with it all the time. I even had dreams about it . . . about what's on it. Something he had been experimenting with? Some secret he learned?"

"Can I see?"

Sophie handed it to White, who turned it over and examined it.

He looked back to Sophie. "I haven't a clue. Never saw one of these before."

Sophie looked out the window. The sun had gone behind the trees, and the room had turned dark. The small house still felt cozy, safe, but she knew that it was an illusion. Today safety had gone away. And who knew when it would come back.

White handed the small box back.

"Will you help me?"

He nodded. "Of course, but Sophie"—he leaned forward—"don't you think you should get the authorities to help, I mean you are just a young person, and—"

She stood up. "No. My dad knew what he was asking me to do. If you won't—"

White reached a hand out and gently took her wrist. "Steady. I'll help. We can start . . . tomorrow morning. But now—you should get some rest, sleep, yes?"

Sophie relaxed.

Sleep. A big comfy guest bed with giant pillows.

"I—I'd like that."

"Good. Let me get you settled."

White stood up.

And Sophie followed him knowing that—though sleep sounded wonderful—the nightmares would surely be waiting for her the moment she drifted off . . .

Nick stood beside the elegant bar of the Atlantic, looking around at the tall gilded ceiling, the ocean-liner scope of the place. Trendy or not, the sound was deafening—a mix of noisy chatter, laughs, glasses clinking, waiters hurrying from the bar to the sprawling restaurant.

There was no sign of Maddy.

He felt oddly . . . expectant.

I should be amazingly pissed at her, he thought. *She crashed my interview.*

But he didn't feel like that at all. He remembered her smile, the craterlike dimples and such bright eyes. Killer eyes.

She had his attention.

And while still scanning the crowd at the packed bar, he felt a bump from behind.

"What, you didn't order me a drink yet?" He turned and looked at her.

She had changed and now she wore a brown suede skirt, brown leather boots, and under her jacket a shimmering green top.

For a moment he didn't say a word.

"Aren't you going to say 'hi'?"

"Er, hi. You look great—I don't travel with much of a wardrobe myself."

She made a comical expression, a big O. "I just threw on some party gear. Can't look too businessy in this joint—they'll toss you right out."

Nick looked around. "Some 'joint.' "

"You can see anyone and everyone in here. Once saw Bowie chatting with Cherie Blair." Now Maddy looked around—giving Nick a chance again to study her. "Though there doesn't seem anyone of interest here tonight—" Back to Nick. "Except for us."

"The night's young. Drink?"

"Absolutely. A G and T please, if you wouldn't mind. Twist."

Nick turned to the bar and ordered. And when the drinks arrived, they stayed standing at the bar—she obviously was as comfortable as he was holding up a bar. She started asking a lot of questions about his work—and especially his time in Sierra Leone.

But he wasn't interested in talking about himself, and—as the maître d' showed up to escort them to a table—he turned the questioning around to her.

"What's this I hear about your work? Extreme photography? What's that?"

Maddy smiled and leaned close. "Love to tell you but then I'd have to kill you. No, seriously though, I'd love another of these"—she suspended her glass in the air—"and then I will tell all."

With the ESP of a good server, the waiter appeared and whisked her glass away. Moments later he was back. Nick saw him watch as Maddy took a sip.

"Okay?" he asked.

"Lovely."

The waiter smiled. *He's flirting with her,* he thought. *Well, I can factor that into the . . . reduced tip.*

Funny. A twinge of jealousy there. For someone he hardly knew.

But then Maddy swung her attention back on him.

"Well, I do a lot of politicians, events, some celebs—" She took a sip. "But that's not how I made my mark. I trained at University of London in the tech end. Did everything—microphotography, special cameras for night work, digital image processing for high-speed events. Found myself a little niche in extreme conditions."

She took another large sip of her drink. Nick loved the way her lips looked against the clear class and clear liquid.

"Like to climb?" she asked.

"Climb? You mean—"

"Mountain climb. I do a lot of it. I've worked for everyone from National Geographic to the IMAX people . . . shooting video and film under totally crap conditions . . . miles high, and subzero temps. That's a piece of cake, though, compared to the underwater stuff. Salt water and pressure are the worst. Do you dive?"

Nick smiled. "Er, no."

Maddy laughed.

"Then what the hell do you do?"

And then Nick laughed.

"No, don't answer that." Another sip of her drink. "At least"—a dimpled smile—"not yet."

And all of a sudden, Nick just absolutely loved this place.

Henry White tiptoed closer to the shut door and stopped there.

Funny, he had lived alone for so many years it was so odd to have someone here, especially such a young person, full of life and energy and—now—fear.

He stood there, listening, just to make sure that she was asleep. No sounds from within. Very quiet. Maybe she felt safe here—or maybe she was just so exhausted.

For a moment, standing there by the door reminded him of the Poe story "The Tell-Tale Heart," with a would-be killer forever frozen at the door, creaking it open millimeter by millimeter.

White felt a chill then.

He didn't like scary things at all. That was one of the main drawbacks of living alone: He was always alone when the wind rattled the window sashes or the floorboards creaked for some unknown reason. There were nights where he would lie in bed, covers drawn up tight to his chin—and he would just listen. Unable to get up and look. Frozen, afraid.

But he felt safe tonight, with young Sophie in the house, probably because he was her protector. When you protect someone, it takes your fear away. That was his theory at least . . .

He turned away from the bedroom door and walked out

to his small living room. He went over to the window and pulled the heavy drapes aside. Totally dark outside save for a distant light down the lane.

His was the lone house on this quiet lane.

He let the drapes fall back into place and picked up the phone from the coffee table. Then he walked over to a small corkboard by the kitchen entrance, filled with bills that needed paying, reminders of dinner engagements, church functions; it all made his life seem so busy.

He saw the number for the local police. He'd never had call to use it.

Nervously, he entered the number and waited while it rang once, twice . . . then he heard a sleepy hello.

It was pretty late.

"Er, yes, hello. I'm . . . Professor Henry White, on Duck's Lane, and—" He thought he sounded silly, pompous. He was always aware of sounding pompous. The silly, pompous professor. Something to be avoided.

"Well, I have Sophie MacDonald here, yes, the girl, and no, no . . . she's asleep. I am—was—friends with her father. But the poor girl is so scared. Terrified. I think you should come tomorrow, talk to her . . . No, I don't think you should come now. She's sleeping."

White felt so protective of his charge. He knew she didn't want to see the police, that she seemed almost scared of them.

But he knew better . . .

"Very well then. I'll see you first thing. Good night." He pushed a button and the red light on the phone went off. He walked over to his easy chair and picked up a book by a colleague from Cambridge, *Aesthetics and Ethics*.

And he read until he fell asleep . . .

Nick picked up a wooden skewer filled with Thai shrimp.

"Food's good too. Surprising."

Maddy smiled. "Don't tell me you're one of those Americans who's constantly amazed that English cuisine has actually advanced past greasy fish and chips."

Nick bit on the shrimp and slid it off its wooden stake. "Oh, no—I fully realize that a *few* of the world's best restaurants are right here in London. It's just that all the rest are in New York City."

"Oh, please, along with a zillion souvlaki carts."

Nick laughed. Then, "Tell me something."

"Yes?"

"You called me. Why?"

Now it was Maddy's turn to take a slow sip of gin and tonic number two. "Well, I had been rude, barging in and all—"

"But that wasn't it."

"No. You're right, it wasn't. To be honest?"

Nick nodded. "I'm a selective consumer of honesty."

"After I took my pictures, I checked on who you were. Read about your work. You just came back from Sierra Leone."

"I'm trying to forget about that."

"And . . . you sounded like someone I'd like to know better."

Such bluntness. Nick wondered if Maddy also knew that he had been married, that he had blown his marriage, and he probably wasn't a guy a woman should want to know better.

"I'm flattered. How about another—"

Maddy's eyes widened.

"Drink? Love to. But—" She stood up. "I have an early trip to Kent tomorrow. And gear to pack. But tell you what—we will do this again . . ."

Amazing, Nick thought. What a tease. One minute all over me . . . then the next, vanishing like a Cheshire cat. And he recognized that on one level he was already a little hooked.

He stood up. "I'll hold you to that."

Maddy leaned forward and kissed him on the lips, and then pulled away so he got the full effect of her mischievous dimples and dark eyes.

"No, I'll hold *you* to it."

And she grabbed her bag and ran from the bustling crazy carnival of a bar.

nine

White stirred awake.

A filmy light filled the room. He sniffed the air, cool and damp. A cloudy, rainy English dawn. He looked around the room and had that momentary thought— *Where am I, what am I doing here, and—*

Another thought. A small one. A question, actually. *What awakened me?*

And as if in answer he heard the sound of a car slowly moving up Duck's Lane, tires banging into ruts, gravel spinning around—a familiar sound, an alarm.

Funny, an *alarm,* he thought.

No way anyone could pull up to his house without making some noise. White moved to the window and pushed aside the drapes. He expected to see a police car with a few local officers.

Instead—he saw a black car.

Strange, he thought. But then he nodded. No, not so strange. A murder case would certainly bring in detectives. And though White didn't watch TV—what was there worth watching?—he knew that detectives, the real sleuths, didn't travel in police cars. No, they used cars much like this one.

He let the drapes fall back.

He thought of Sophie. Perhaps he should wake her. *No, she'd be so mad. She'd feel betrayed. Best I talk to them first and maybe see if Sophie could stay here.* And that was a pleasant thought. She'd need a place to stay and he was always alone, with just his books, his work.

He heard the sound of car doors slamming.

Yes, he'd let Sophie sleep on.

I'll talk to the detectives. Then wake her up . . .

Sophie heard the noise.

Eyes shut, her head buried in the plump down pillow, she heard the sound. An angry noise, car wheels grinding on dirt and rock. Only then did she open her eyes.

Opened them to see the strange room, the little guest room of Henry White. A small bureau, a tiny table with a lamp. The room was filled with a dull light—as though some fog from outside had sneaked in during the night and hid here.

She raised her head a bit to better hear the sounds. Car doors slamming shut, now sounding so close. Someone coming here. And in that moment she remembered with incredible vividness the vision from the previous evening, her house, the blood, the door opening.

She had trusted sweet Professor White.

And she now knew she shouldn't trust anyone.

People were coming here. No, they were *here.* Sophie silently slipped out of her bed, letting her feet touch the chilly wooden floor. She grabbed her school shirt and blazer from the nearby straight-backed chair. She pulled on her socks, so cold on her legs. She slipped her skirt on.

Now, voices. Talking.

Talking about me, she knew.

They're talking about me. Is she in there? Still asleep? Good.

For a moment, Sophie wondered if this wasn't maybe better . . . if she should try to get help from the people here. After all, she didn't know what she was running from, what she was afraid of.

She only knew what her father had said.

If anything happens to me, Sophie, leave. Take this, and leave. He gave her the name of a man in Glasgow, someone named Cosgrove.

But Glasgow was so far away . . . she had been a little girl when they lived there.

The voices were louder now.

She slipped on her shoes and grabbed her backpack, still filled with her Discman and books . . . and in a small zipped pocket, the thumb drive her father had given her and a picture, all she had left of her father. And somewhere in her bag a red apple left over from lunch was turning soft, pulpy.

She crept to the door.

Bent down to the keyhole.

To see—

An eye looking into the keyhole.

She reeled back, her heart racing, her lungs unable to breathe. But when nothing happened, she thought: *It isn't an eye. I'm just scared, crazy.*

She leaned close again.

And this time when she looked through the keyhole, she definitely saw in the small circle of light another eye staring right back at her. The eye pulled away, and then she could see Henry White, his back to the door. They were speaking louder now, angry.

A glance over her shoulder.

She saw the closet, and one small window near the table with the animal-shade lamp.

She turned back to the door, frozen, unable to move.

• • •

The phone rang, from all the way across the white sea of bedclothes, on the other side of the bed.

Nick had been having a dream—he didn't remember much about it except a strange party, and loud techno music, and a beautiful girl wearing a mask. She took the mask off and the girl was Maddy.

He swam across the sea to snare the phone.

"Hello?" he said, sounding like the grizzled drunken mate of some down-on-its-heels pirate vessel. Mornings weren't his time to shine.

"My, don't you sound irresistible in the a.m."

Maddy. Funny, despite the dream, he thought she had sailed on. No stops on the loser express for her. Too smart, too strong.

"Okay, I have this caffeine thing. Without it, just can't function."

"I'll have to remember that," she said. Even at this early hour, the double entendre wasn't lost. And suddenly, he felt wide awake.

"Breakfast?" he said.

"No. That's not what I called for. In fact—I'm in my car about ten minutes from your hotel."

"And?"

"Get some clothes on and come down. I'm off to Kent to shoot these ruins just found near Seven Oaks. A day in the countryside."

Nick looked out the window. Didn't look like an idyllic fall day.

And he didn't even consider hesitating.

"I'm there."

"Hasta pronto," Maddy said. And the line went dead.

And Nick began racing to get dressed.

Sophie was at the keyhole.

Henry White was on his knees. And she saw a man in

a short leather jacket standing beside him. She heard no words now, she only saw Professor White shaking his head back and forth, as if moaning, complaining.

No sounds whatever.

Nobody made any sound.

Because, Sophie realized, something wasn't letting any noises out. Whatever was happening—would happen in silence.

And then—

There was a noise. A little squirting sound, as White brought his hand up to the right side of his face to stop—the stream of blood that shot out. But that did no good, as another stream erupted.

Sophie didn't know when was the last time that she breathed.

She backed up.

So ... silently, so carefully. Every step a potential creak, an alarm.

She took a breath, the air searing her lungs. Looked to the window.

Thinking: *What if it doesn't open? What if it's painted shut, nailed shut?* Then: she knew that she was taking way too long. Already the people from the car would be walking to her door, opening it.

Her eyes were riveted on the doorknob.

Looking for the telltale turn as they tried to creep in—and do to her what they did to her father, to Professor White, to—to—

She turned around and ran to the window. She pushed up.

Nothing happened. No, she begged, *pleaded*. If there was a God watching, he had to help her. She pushed up harder, her hands tight, wedged against the top of the window frame.

And then the window shot up.

The cold morning air raced in.

Steps outside. Voices, loud, not caring now.

She pushed aside the flimsy curtain and looked out, completely expecting someone to be there, ready to grab her by her hair and yank her out. But all she saw was the small backyard trailing off into a field.

Sophie bolted. She thought she could hear the door behind her, a voice yelling, but by then she had already landed on the dirt smoothly, and—legs pumping—she raced toward the tall grass of the field, racing, running, thinking: *Trust no one. Not anymore. Not again.*

For now, I'm all alone . . .

While overhead, two massive ravens circled the field, calling others to watch as Sophie cut a chaotic trail through the brush.

ten

Glen Coe Mountains, Northern Scotland

Paul Hodge threw his right hand at a triangular piece of rock—and missed. His fingertips grazed the rocks but then quickly slid away.

And he laughed.

Even though he was hanging from a ledge with a hundred-foot drop—and the ledge was less than an inch wide—he laughed.

"What's so funny?" The voice came from Simon Anders, Paul's best friend. Though Simon was a good climber, Paul knew that he depended way too much on Paul, needing him to show the way they could tackle this near-sheer chunk of rock.

Right now, Paul wasn't too sure they could tackle it.

But he had a lot of confidence. And there was nothing better than leaving the pressure cooker of London and scraping his skin against some good Scottish granite. Just touching the cold stone made him feel better, as if he had instantly tapped into something deep and ancient, something that mocked the world of cell phones and PDAs and wireless anything.

He wasn't sure Simon shared his attitude. Simon came from Canada, where he had done some big mountains near Banff.

Though this rock wasn't big, Paul was pretty sure that Simon had never faced a sheer climb like this before.

And the reason Paul knew that was because he himself had never tackled anything quite like this.

They had ignored the No Trespassing signs hours ago.

It had been a tough call for Simon to accept, this illegal climb.

"I don't know, Paul. They must have their reason they don't—"

"Sure they have *reasons*. But we're not going to steal the damn rock and rob them of any of their bloody military secrets. All we're going to do is climb the damn thing."

Paul grinned and slapped Simon on the back. He had used the force of his personality and charm to get his friend to do things worse than ignoring the warning signs. He just wanted to climb the rock.

He didn't tell him that there were other surprises in store . . . once they got to the top. Finally Simon had grinned and agreed, and—their hands white with rosin— they had started the tricky free climb.

Now Paul looked at his lone hand holding on.

Crazy, really. If his hand slipped from the ledge or if the rock turned crumbly all of a sudden—then it was a fall that might kill him, or at the very least leave his body so battered and bruised he'd be in the hospital for months.

So—what was so funny?

Looking at death, maybe. Looking, laughing, saying, *Go ahead. You don't scare me. Do your worst, but you won't see anything like fear from me.*

And what was it that Paul really felt? Did doing this make the fear go away?

Perhaps. He knew that he and his sister, Maddy, were similar. Both risk takers, total adrenaline junkies. She got her kicks from photographing impossible things in impossible situations. Paul enjoyed riding the world's financial markets and then channeling all that pent-up energy . . . into this.

"You see," he shouted down to Simon, his voice still lighthearted, "this rock suddenly reminds me . . . of a woman I met last week."

Simon's voice came back, more sober, questioning.

"Woman? What woman?"

"At that party. In the Great Northern Hotel. She dared me to make a move. And—usually, Simon, I'm not one . . . to press the question. But she did challenge me."

"And—she walked out, didn't she? You blew it."

Paul laughed.

"Yes. I know. I mean, I know that's what you *think* you saw. But when I left you—there she was out on the street. Waiting. For friends, supposedly."

And he waited now for that bit of late revealed information to sink in.

"You son of a bitch. How did you pull that off—"

"Sometimes—you simply have to be—patient."

And with that Paul looked back at the triangular chunk of rock he had tried for and swung his arm up and watched his fingers latch on, catching just above the first knuckle. Not a great handhold—but enough.

"Patience. And you can get what—"

He grunted—and using his new handhold, he pulled himself up and over the triangular rock, kicking his feet, and attaining the top of the cliff.

"—you want."

In seconds it was over; he was standing there.

"Your turn, Simon. The honor of Canada awaits."

And Paul looked down as his friend slowly, torturously made his way up the sheer rock face.

Elaina kept dabbing at her face with the tissue.

The bleeding had stopped, and the thin cuts on her face—from the bushes, the bits of glass—had healed into thin slices. Still nasty-looking but not so much that it would draw the stares of a convenience store worker.

Funny that she thought of that as the benchmark. Would some sleepy-eyed clerk at a 7-Eleven look at her and wonder . . . *Hey, is there something wrong here, should I call the police? Is this bad?*

Her face looked bad.

But not that bad.

She had slept horribly with weird nightmares and strange sweats—though the room was damp and cold. But Elaina awoke with a plan. At least, she told herself it was a plan. She now knew . . . that she had information she could be killed for. That meant—the information was dangerous, important. She also knew that for now she was safe. Maybe they thought she died in the crash.

But they hadn't found her, hadn't tracked her to this tiny, hidden motel. So far, at Heidi's, she was safe.

And she also knew one last thing: that she wouldn't be safe for long.

So she had to act fast. It was now a game of who do you trust. And Elaina had seen enough movies to know that—right now—she should trust no one.

She walked over to her bed and grabbed her purse, the damning printouts buried inside, stuffed down at the bottom. She hadn't let herself speculate too much on what they meant.

And why is that, she wondered . . . when she opened her eyes that morning, feeling so horribly disoriented?

Why do I stop myself from thinking about them?

Maybe—because when she let herself think about them she got a terrible, icy feeling all over.

Fear. As if she had stumbled onto the creation of some monstrous virus, some mad experiment in genocide. It was a fear powerful enough to make her shiver. She had entered a nightmare, only it was no dream—it was real.

So she wouldn't let herself think.

For now, she had to follow the plan. And maybe later, she could think . . .

Simon was almost there, only a meter below the ledge.

Paul looked down. He could easily reach with a hand and help hoist his friend up.

But that wasn't how it was done. And it wasn't some kind of macho code, more a matter of simple human pride. You didn't climb the rock . . . unless you *climbed* the rock. It was like using someone else's pitons or ropes on a tech climb. They did the hammering, they laid the line . . . use their stuff, and you were merely a passenger on their trip.

There was only one place that was excusable—accepted.

Everest. Oh, yeah, and K2. *Everyone* was a passenger on those rides, traveling on the backs of every Sherpa and climber who made it up and down—and even more, those who didn't.

But on a free climb like this, mastering a chunk of stone . . . that was a different sort of contest.

So he looked at Simon, his face set, grim and hard as the stone, his right hand holding on to the same narrow ledge that Paul had grabbed. Paul could see Simon's fingernails dug into a small, slightly angled slope of rock.

About as precarious a perch as there was.

And now Simon had to do the same move, shoot that left arm up and nail that triangular piece of rock.

For the first time, Paul was worried.

Simon was an experienced climber. But his next move was an all-or-nothing shot. Either he made it, or he'd slip off the rock.

Paul tried to keep the concern off his face.

Everything was crucial in climbing—including the vibe you sent out to your partner.

"Ready, Simon. Give her a shot." Paul flashed a confident grin. Simon forced a grimace out. There were only two steps in the process—freeing his left hand and then shooting it upward to the triangular outcrop.

"Here goes," Simon said quietly.

He removed his left hand. And at the same moment there was the smallest sound of crumbling stone—coming from his right hand.

Shit, Paul thought. But he didn't say anything. It was too late to say—or do—anything once this move was in progress. Simon's body coiled, ready to strike, and Paul was in the strange position of not being able to do anything—

—but watch it happen.

Elaina opened the office door and saw Heidi sitting in front of a small color TV.

"Oh, good morning, dear. How are you?"

Elaina thought . . . *Trust. I shouldn't trust anyone but have already trusted this plump little motelkeeper.*

"Good. I slept well. And I'm not"—she smiled—"too achy."

"That's good. You know, there's a sweet diner down the road. You could get a nice breakfast, and—"

"Yes, I'd like that. But I need something else . . ."

Elaina wondered if the woman was growing a bit suspicious. After all, she had let her check in, held off processing her credit card. And now—

"I'd like to use your computer."

The woman nodded. Not saying yes, or no. Just nodded, unsure. "My computer?"

Elaina smiled. She wondered how much she could tell her, what words would make her want to help.

"Yes. I need to find some things out, and then maybe contact people without anyone knowing where I am."

Another nod, and Elaina knew that the story had to sound odd.

"I don't know. I mean, it's really just for motel business. I'm not sure."

Elaina took a step closer to the woman. "I know all this seems"—Elaina smiled—"strange. It's strange for me. And scary. But someone tried . . . I mean, someone wanted to hurt me. I have to get some help."

She didn't say "kill." Just a guess, but she thought that the word *kill* would be a bad word to say in front of Heidi. It might make the woman nod one last time, reach for the phone, and call the trusty state police.

And who knew whether *they* could be trusted.

Elaina cleared her throat. "And I'm pretty sure that, given the chance, they will try to find me—and finish what they started. So, I need help. Your computer, just for a while."

The woman's face still revealed nothing of her potential answer.

Elaina added something to the plea. "I'll be gone by tomorrow. But your computer could make all the difference."

The woman stood up behind the desk. "This old thing? So slow. Herb—he's my, well, boyfriend—he says I need to upgrade." She laughed. "I said I need to upgrade my bod."

Elaina laughed.

Then the woman looked Elaina straight in the eye, fixed her with a steely stare that came from someone who's been around, someone who wasn't always the little lady behind the desk at Heidi's.

"You're in trouble. And it could be that your trouble could even come here, could—"

"No. I mean, I don't think—"

The woman put up a hand. "I don't have a lot of rules in my life. Never liked rules. But there's one rule I always had. If someone needed help—I helped. I figure—who knows when it will be my turn. So, go on. The machine's yours." Another step and she was beside Elaina. "Just one thing, hon. I think it will be best—for you *and* me—if you're gone by tomorrow."

Elaina took a breath. She had a machine. She could see the phone wire snaking into the back of the computer. "Don't worry . . . I will be out of here."

And Heidi pointed to the small office chair on wheels. "She's all yours."

Simon's left hand flew out.

And Paul watched it catch the edge of the triangular piece of rock . . . then slip away.

Now Simon dangled from one hand. Paul studied his friend's face, the muscles tight, the eyes wide. And Paul immediately knew that Simon wasn't as strong as he was, that he couldn't hang there forever, dangling while planning for another assault on the last perch before the ledge.

Paul debated options. He could dive down and shoot a hand out for Simon to grab. Or he could coach his friend to make the move quickly. Every second was another bit of strength sapping away from his arm. And once the slide down that slippery slope began, it quickly accelerated, fueled by fatigue and panic.

Panic was always bad—but never worse than when you were on a climb.

Grab, coach, watch—his eyes locked on Simon's trying

to get an indication of what he wanted—or what he needed.

And in that moment Paul fell to his knees and, taking care not to extend too far over the ledge, he shot out his right arm so it was only inches away from Simon, an easy target.

Simon looked at the hand.

Was he frozen, immobilized?

"Go on, Simon. Take the damn hand."

Simon did nothing and though Paul didn't want to, he looked at Simon's other hand, the crab claw of fingers dug into the rock.

Then, slowly, gently, he whispered again.

"Go for the *hand*, Simon . . ."

And he waited.

eleven

Simon blinked.

Perhaps a bit of salty sweat had crept into his eye. He didn't move. Paul could just reach out and grab his friend's free hand . . . But that could throw Simon's balance off—or worse. It could throw Simon into a panic reaction that could jerk the two of them off the rock.

Paul licked his lips. Then he smiled. As if this were no big deal. Thinking: *Come on. It's right there. Go for it.*

And as if reading his mind, Simon flung out his hand and—clumsily—they locked fingers. It wasn't the best grab, but it was good enough, and Paul began to pull up smoothly, and in seconds it was all over.

"Hey, nasty bit at the end, eh?"

Paul's voice was purposefully light, as if he had merely extended a helping hand to a friend who really had no need of it. But Simon looked rattled. They both knew . . . how close they had come. But Paul had a rule about climbing. You move on, whether moving up a mountain, or down, or simply getting past a bad moment . . . *you move on*.

Paul looked around. The valley below stretched to the sea, and from here they could see the small villages and the heath, already turned a dingy brown with the onset of fall. But the late-afternoon sun covered it with a rusty, golden color.

"Look at that. Quite the view, eh?"

For a second Simon didn't say anything. But then he dug into his down vest and pulled out a pack of cigarettes. He tapped one out, put it in his mouth, and lit up.

"Those things will kill you, Si."

Simon smiled. They both got the joke. Then he looked out over the valley, to the sea. "Gorgeous. Could go for a Glenmorangie right about now."

"Not sure you want to do that. We still have to get down."

Simon took a big drag. "Yeah, I almost took the express back, hm."

"What? Oh, you were fine. I just wanted to—end the suspense."

Simon made a small laugh. Some things were better left unsaid.

Then Paul turned and looked at the other view.

"Whoa. Look at that. Shit. Now that's something."

Simon turned and looked in the same direction. The ledge they were on looked as though it were manmade, maybe by some strip mining. The flat ledge stretched east for a few hundred yards before ending in a barbed-wire fence.

And just behind the fence, there was a small rocky outcrop, no more than two, three hundred meters high. And what lay behind that was anybody's guess.

But Paul was pretty sure that the rock they were looking at had to be the highest point within miles.

"Come on," he said to Simon. "Let's take a look."

Paul saw Simon take another drag and look at the sun, maybe only an hour away from slipping into the sea.

"Let's take a look at that," Paul again said. Simon tossed his butt over the side, and together they walked to the high fence.

Elaina sat before a dinosaur.

That's what the machine was, a 486 dinosaur PC. The only Internet access it had came via an antiquated version of America Online . . . bound to be slow and sleepy. Still Elaina could use it to access her AOL account—always good for traveling—and she could log on as a guest.

She waited for the sluggish computer to give her the guest screen and then she entered her screen name and password. More interminable waiting . . .

"Would you like a cup of tea, honey?"

Elaina turned back to Heidi and smiled. "No thanks. Maybe when I'm done."

Finally she was logged on, and she heard the cheery words . . . *You've got mail.*

She clicked on the mailbox. There were two dozen e-mails. She checked the return addresses. If she opened the wrong mail, they'd know she was out somewhere checking mail. A few came from GenTech, all with "No Subject" as headers. One mail came from a guy she had met at the Quantum Evolution conference a month ago in Boston. Her mother had sent one . . . with the heading "Where Are You???"

But even that shouldn't be answered.

Okay, now she had to act fast.

She made sure that her name was screened—nobody could see her online. Then she went to Hotmail and created another e-mail account.

Then she wrote her e-mails, using the new Hotmail account. Three e-mails. She would not know which if any of the people she was sending e-mail to could be trusted. One in New York, one at the University of Glasgow, another out in Sausalito. All colleagues, people she regularly spoke to, people she liked.

But now everything had changed.

The mail would be . . . a test.

One part of the game.

Who Can I Trust?

Or just how alone am I?

"Honey—"

The woman's voice made her jump. Elaina turned around to see Heidi holding a cup of tea.

Heidi smiled. "I made you one anyway."

And Elaina nodded, smiled, and tried to make herself relax, as she finished writing her e-mails and clicking the Send button.

Nick sat beside Maddy as she gunned her Land Rover through a winding, narrow road.

He tried to relax, knowing that driving these English country lanes at high speed was normal here. But all he could do was imagine another car taking a curve, hidden by a hedge, and smashing into them.

And he had this other thought: *She's going way too fast,* maybe even enjoying the white-knuckle effect she created in Nick.

Maddy looked over, taking her eyes off the road—which only made Nick lock *his* eyes on the next curvy bit ahead. "You okay?" she asked.

"Sure. Fine. Er, you want to look—" He gestured at the road ahead.

Then Maddy laughed—obviously not buying his protestations of being cool.

"I could . . . slow down."

"No. That's—" And at that moment, a small compact car took the curve, coming right at them. Maddy hit the brakes, stopping the Rover instantly, and the compact also stopped. She threw the car into reverse, and backed up to an indentation in the hedge where she could let the other car squeeze through.

Strange, Nick thought. This was like playing chicken. And they all take it in their stride. The smaller car passed, with the driver giving a friendly wave. No awareness there that they all had nearly died.

Got to relax, Nick thought.

Then Maddy wheeled out of the pull-off, and was again racing through the lanes.

"So tell me," she said. "You were married?"

"Yes."

Not a subject Nick expected to be raised.

"And?"

"And what?"

"What went wrong? Did you . . ." Maddy exaggerated the next words as though she didn't believe in the concept. ". . . grow apart?"

"No." Nick looked out the window. At least he wasn't thinking about the mad ride through the Kent farmlands anymore. "No. At least, not in any way that made a difference. I had an affair. She found out. And that was it."

She looked at him, and her dark eyes seemed to scan him even as she wore an impish smile.

"Was the affair worth it?"

"Is this a subject we need to go into in such . . . detail?"

She shrugged. "Just passing the time. And I always like to know who I'm traveling with. What if we became stranded out here in the wheat fields?"

"I don't know. I guess I felt . . . what, bored. Needing something. Some excitement."

"Excitement? Or illicit sex?"

Now Nick laughed. "Aren't they synonymous?"

Another look from Maddy. "Guess they can be."

So, Nick thought. *She hasn't written me off as damaged*

goods. Either that, or she's as crazy as I am.

"Hold on," Maddy said, slowing the four-wheel-drive vehicle. "Things get a bit bumpy from here. We have to take a dirt road up to that hill there." She pointed to the left, to a small hill filled with thick trees.

"The ruins are up there?"

Maddy nodded. "They're not Stonehenge. But . . . I think you'll be interested."

And the Rover began a slow bumpy crawl to the top of the hill.

Sophie walked up Oxford Street, the endless shopping boulevard of London.

Everyone moved so quickly around her, people hurrying to the shops, or to work—fashionable women racing on the sidewalk despite wearing trendy shoes with heels, men in leather jackets with cigarettes dangling from the corner of their mouths.

She had slipped onto a train to London just as the doors were about to close—and then watched everyone who got on at every stop, seeing if they seemed to take any special interest in her.

The ride took forever.

Sophie realized that she must look as though she just got off a spaceship. She moved slowly, deliberately, thinking.

What . . . now.

She knew this: Whoever had killed her dad, and probably killed Henry White, would want to find her, and would already be searching for her.

There was this one thought that kept all the other feelings away: *I don't want to die.*

And something else: She wanted to hurt whatever had taken her father away from her.

On the train, she had dug the photograph out of her backpack.

She had looked at the picture of her father, the way he smiled, always distracted, but filled with love for her, but so paranoid about his work. Her mom . . . standing on the other side . . . seemed like such a distant memory.

He couldn't be dead, she thought. She flashed on the image of the house, the door, the blood.

No. He was dead.

She took a breath. A young man all in black barreled into her, stopping only inches away, making a disgusted "what's wrong with you" face, before moving around her.

What . . . to . . . do.

She knew this: She couldn't be on her own for long. They would find her. And if they found her, she'd be dead. Not that she knew why . . . though again her imagination could conjure up all sorts of weird ideas—if she let it.

She had to get to Glasgow, to the man Cosgrove.

What if he couldn't be trusted?

She was so alone. She passed by a Pret A Manger, with its gleaming shelves of sandwiches. She was so hungry—but she knew she should keep any money she had.

Then again—she didn't have enough money for a ticket to Glasgow. So—why not eat?

And she walked in, her eye on a plump tuna fish sandwich on lovely whole-wheat bread.

"Hm, now this looks serious," Paul said. He stood before the massive fence, lined with razor ribbon at the top.

Simon was sorting his gear, crouching a few meters back. "What's the sign say?"

"Pretty blunt, Simon: 'Warning! This is a military testing area. Anyone breaching this fence is in extreme danger and will also be subject to severe penalties, including 10 years' imprisonment.' "

"I always thought that imprisonment sat at the very top

of the severe penalty list." Simon got up and walked to the fence. "What do you think it means?"

"Secret tests? Unexploded artillery shells? Don't know. Too bad. That rock"—he pointed to the skull-shaped rock dead ahead—"looks like a nice climb. It's definitely the highest point. We could have probably gotten up and down before dark, and gotten the best view of the valley. A magnificent view, I bet. Oh well—"

He turned away and saw that Simon still had his eyes fixed on the rock.

"Steady, Paul. Let's not dash away, I mean, we already broke the law in climbing up here."

Paul rattled the fence. "Yes, but I'm afraid this fence has other ideas."

"Look, we can get over that fence, shield ourselves from the barbed wire at the top, hop over, climb the rock. Come on, let's do it."

Paul looked at his friend. Simon was suddenly gung-ho, eager—and Paul guessed it might be in reaction to his near-fall. "I don't know, Simon. God knows what they're doing . . . on the other side. Maybe we call it a day, get back and check out the local pubs—"

Simon shook his head.

And he tossed his pack clean over the fence.

"Oops. Now look at what I did. Guess . . . I have to go over now."

Simon was grinning, but Paul looked at the sign. The fence was no small fence. And it wasn't the fear of getting caught that made Paul hold back. As a climber, he always liked to know exactly what was ahead—the mountain, the weather—it was best to remove all the imponderables, or as many as possible.

Here was this big warning sign. *Danger.* Something dangerous was on the other side of the fence.

Simon dug his hands into the chain mesh of the fence.

"You with me, huh, Paul?"

Paul looked at the domelike outcrop ahead. Not a bad climb . . . they could be up and down . . . fast.

"Okay. Since you're there. Sure. Let's do it."

And Paul locked his fingers into the fence.

twelve

Nick took a step, and the incredibly green grass seemed to slip away in great wedges under his foot like a toupee sliding off a bald man's head. One arm flew out to break his fall, rewarding him with a muddy hand, fully buried in the muck.

Maddy laughed. "Don't do much hiking, eh?"

Nick shot Maddy a less than amused look—but the truth was he *was* amused. The air was crisp, the weather clear, and it felt good to be here . . . though he didn't know what they were going to see.

Maddy came over and reached out a hand to help Nick up from his awkward stance.

"Thanks," he said.

Maddy looked down at his feet. "I should have told you to wear something else . . . sneakers maybe?" She looked up. "We're almost there—though you may have some fun getting down."

"I'll just walk down sideways . . . slowly. As long as you wait for me."

"I might."

Maddy turned and continued up the gentle slope with Nick following, cautious now, not wanting a full spill onto the sodden grassy earth. That would make for an unpleasant trip home, not to mention eliminating any other possibilities for the day.

And what were those . . . possibilities?

Maybe dinner with Maddy, some drinks—and he realized that he was already thinking about spending more time with her when . . . he was already with her.

Bad sign. Silly really. He thought those days of being infatuated were behind him.

Or so he thought.

Maddy reached the hill. Nick could see her taking her camera out of her bag, screwing on a lens. In a moment, Nick came beside her. He looked around . . . for the ruins.

"Er, and the ruins are where?"

Maddy was snapping pictures, using the hill as a vantage point to get shots of the rolling countryside, the farms, the hedges, the narrow strips of concrete winding their way through the Kent farmland.

"The ruins?" Maddy said, not removing the camera from her face. "You're"—*click*—"standing"—*click*—"on them."

Nick looked down, All he could see was a hill, a few scrawny trees, the grass, and dirt.

"Ruins?"

"Yes. The clue is the trees. No big trees up here . . . because there's not enough dirt for a big root system."

"So what is it?"

Finally Maddy took the camera down. "That's the funny thing. The experts, a consortium of scholars who are experts on ancient Britain, aren't at all bloody sure. They have, so far, kept it very quiet. Only a small circle knows of this discovery. They'll do some x-ray surveys of the mound, and they'll have a better idea of what's under here. But all they know now"—she took a step closer—"is that it's damned old."

"Can't they identify it based on similar mounds?"

"Could do. If there were any. Which there aren't. The closest thing, in the U.K. at least, are some small mounds that dot the outskirts of what was then called 'Londinium.' Places where loot was stored to keep it from invaders. But they were a fraction of the size of this thing. This is no loot bank."

Nick looked around, savoring the view of the rolling countryside that the hill gave him. It was a scene that couldn't be replicated anywhere else in the world—the brilliant, electric green of the English countryside. The civilized crisscrossing of the hedgerows. The gentle slope of the land said that it was an amazingly long time ago that any volcanoes or earthquakes ravaged and twisted *this* land.

And yet . . . there was this strange ruin.

"How did they find it?"

"An Oxford archaeologist on vacation near here; he had a country house in Seven Oaks. Walked over this way and suddenly, for the first time, realized that there was something really odd about this hill."

"You know the archaeologist?"

Maddy raised her giant Nikon and started snapping again. "Of course. That's why I'm here. He knew my work and got the little group of artifact commissars to approve my taking photos. They'll be used when they go public with what they found . . . part of their bid to get some government money."

Stupidly Nick looked down, as if he could understand something about the mound and its secrets by looking at it.

"And what will they do with the money?"

Maddy pulled the camera away. "Move a bit to the left . . ."

"Taking a picture of me?"

"Why not. Gives the mound a nice sense of scale."

She snapped a few pictures. And continued talking as she did. "They'll use the money to carry out a variety of tests before they uncover the thing. The fear is that any major excavation work could damage what's inside. Could even collapse. So they'll be doing lots of readings, taking samples, x-ray, and spectrographic work . . . then prepare for a major excavation . . . maybe next year. But I will have been here first."

Maddy unslung her bag and handed it to Nick.

"Could you hold this?" Nick took the bag and Maddy took more pictures.

"Don't you want to get some of the mound from a distance?"

"Oh, I will. The light will be great on the way down. Do you know why the archaeologist thought something was odd about this hill?"

"No. I mean it looks like a regular hill to me."

"He had been on vacation. To Belize. And besides seeing all the exposed Mayan ruins, like Xunantunich, he saw that there were hundreds of suspicious mounds in the jungle—and the government knew full well that more ruins were buried under the centuries of jungle. But they had no money—at least for now. But the shape—he told me— once you saw it, was immediately recognizable. And when he saw this hill, he *knew* something was here."

She put down the camera and walked up to Nick. "And he was right. Cool, huh."

"Very."

And she kept looking at Nick. "Hey," she said, "thanks for coming with me. Could be kinda lonely here. You're a sweetie."

She leaned forward and gave Nick a kiss—on the cheek this time.

It happened so fast, so unexpected for Nick.

But as soon as it happened, he knew that couldn't simply be it.

He reached out, took her shoulder. "No, thank *you*. This has been . . . great." He leaned forward and kissed her on the lips, hard, sweet, the warmth electric on this chilly windswept hill.

Simon used his pack to protect himself from the barbed wire. Then he took care to swing one leg at a time over the side, searching for a foothold in the mesh.

"See, it's a piece of cake."

Paul nodded. It wasn't climbing the fence that concerned him. No, he wondered why there was a big fence way up here, at the top of a difficult, forbidden climb. And the dramatic warning sign . . .

What the hell was on the other side?

Simon quickly scurried down, grinning. "Okay, your turn."

Too late now to turn back, so Paul started up the fence and, like Simon, protected himself with his pack. In minutes, he was down the other side.

"What now?" Paul said. He realized that he was also uncomfortable with Simon urging them on . . . uncomfortable, because he thought it might be a reaction to his near-fall.

Reactions were bad.

Simon brushed his sandy blond hair off his forehead. "A quick scurry up that neat chunk of rock, some great pictures, and then down in time for a lovely pub meal."

Paul nodded. Though the rock face ahead cut off the view to the east, it didn't look like a terribly severe climb. The pub supper—and a pint of Guinness—might indeed be closer than he thought.

"Let's do it," Paul said.

• • •

Sophie walked into Kings Cross Station—and it was as if she had fallen into a sea of people.

Like crazed ants, they scurried in all directions, all with grim, purposeful expressions. And Sophie realized that standing there, not moving, looking around, she must have seemed like a cork bobbing on the water.

She saw a policeman look over at her.

What is he thinking? she wondered. *Am I lost? Or maybe he wants to know why I'm not at school.*

She had never felt more alone.

She tried to focus on what she should be doing. She needed to get to Glasgow. There was help there, someone her dad said she had to trust. Glasgow. Big train trip, hours and hours, and she had almost no money.

So she formulated plans, trying each one out in her mind to see if maybe it might work.

She could get to the train . . . and then pretend she lost her ticket. And when the conductor asked her about it, she could say . . . she was on her way to visit . . . an uncle. And her parents would be so mad if they found out she lost her ticket.

That was one plan.

Except what if the conductor decided to check her story. What if he called from the train and tried to speak to her parents.

Then Sophie would be trapped.

No, she needed no questions, no phone calls.

Then there was the crazy idea that she could simply dodge the conductor, walk to the café car while he was checking tickets, or hide in the toilet, or—

Sophie had seen that done in a movie once. It looked as though it *could* be done.

But that was the movies, where fantasy ruled. In reality, the conductors probably had a way to catch that. She'd get caught, then she'd have to make up a story, the phone calls, and . . .

No. She needed to do something else.

She still didn't move. She looked right, and the policeman was still looking her way. So she started toward the tracks as if, yes, now she knew where to go. She moved past the line of tracks, dodging hurrying people, heading to the area where long escalators led down to the tube.

The crowds thinned, and when she looked behind her, she didn't see anybody.

She looked to the side and saw a homeless person holding a coffee cup, his long dreadlocks twisting past his shoulders, his trouser cuffs pushed up exposing legs with sores. She kept moving, all the time thinking.

Which is when she felt that she was being watched.

And at that moment she looked ahead.

The long escalator leading down to the tube stations seemed to turn blurry. The sound *shifted*.

One minute there was the noisy bustle of people moving. And then—there was something else—a faint, barely audible high-pitched sound.

She stopped. Something told her . . . *don't go ahead*. As soon as she stopped, she saw a thin plume of bluish-white smoke. No thicker than a broomstick, the plume seemed to grow out of the escalator. And at that moment the faint sound grew, swelling, turning into—

Screams. More stick-thin plumes of smoke erupted from the escalator until they resembled smoky columns, and then a *wall* of smoke.

Sophie backed up, and she covered her ears. The screams were horrible. People trapped on the escalator, engulfed in what now was a tunnel of smoke. She closed her eyes.

When she felt someone touch her elbow.

The screams stopped. She opened her eyes and turned to see the homeless person. His face was . . . a mess, little sores, and strange bumps, and eyes recessed deep into his face. But his voice was gentle, soothing.

"You okay?"

Sophie looked around. The smoke, the screams, all gone.

"I saw . . . smoke . . . smelled smoke." The man's eyes became suddenly alert. He looked at the escalator. Took a deep sniff.

"No smoke, I don't smell a thing. But—"

He hesitated. This was the type of man she should be afraid of—but his . . . *touching* her had ended the terrible scene.

"But what—you were about to say something?"

The man looked around and rubbed his long, scraggly beard. "It was . . ." He pointed at the escalator. "You said you smelled smoke, heard screams?"

Sophie nodded.

The man licked his lips. "A few years ago there was a fire here, and all the people—down there—got trapped. Trapped, choking, burned. Years ago."

Sophie looked at the stream of people coming out of the hole in the ground. Nothing wrong.

"I never knew that. It seemed so real."

Something had made her feel what had happened. She looked around, trying to see if anyone was watching.

Suddenly Sophie felt a cool breeze at her back, and gooseflesh sprouting other hairs. Was anyone watching them?

"What are you doing here?" the man said, snapping her attention back.

"I have to get to Glasgow. I think . . . I think I'm in danger. I'm trying not to be scared, to be, to be—"

The man put a hand—black in spots, the nails filthy—on Sophie's shoulder, and she welcomed it.

"No one to help you?"

She shook her head. "Not here. I have to get on the train . . . somehow."

"No money?"

Another nod.

The man laughed. "Face that problem, myself. A lot. Tell you what—" He handed Sophie the coffee cup. She looked into it and saw a few coins, even a five-pound note.

"I shouldn't—"

"Take it."

She smiled sweetly trying to be polite. "But I don't think it's enough."

Another laugh from the man. "Of course it isn't. But you just stand here with that cup out—and guess what?"

"What?"

"In one hour, you'll have enough for a trip to Glasgow—and back."

"Really?" The thought excited her. Panhandling? She never did *that* before, that's for sure.

The man nodded. "And I'll be sitting over there, my eyes on you to make sure no one bothers you. Okay?"

And for a moment Sophie had to wonder where this man came from, with his deep pained eyes, but so . . . gentle, so helpful.

"Thank you," she said.

The homeless man tilted his head to a new crowd of people streaming off the escalator.

"Get ready. Here they come."

The climb was a lot trickier than Paul had estimated. What looked like a gentle, easily manageable slope, quickly revealed itself to be a slippery, treacherous surface that screamed for pitons and technical gear.

Paul looked back to see Simon doing just fine, though, confidence restored. But Paul felt that his own muscles had been prepared for a quick run down the mountain, and they were none too happy with the added strain of this mammoth rock.

And he couldn't shake the nagging fear that the warning sign . . . should not have been ignored.

"Almost there, Paul?"

"Yes . . . a few meters." Though when Paul looked up he could see that those last meters were anything but easy. Be nice to have some kind of handhold that wasn't a mere sliver of rock protruding.

He licked his lips, studied the surface some more, and then reached up. The little lip he grabbed came flying away in his fingers, shattering into tiny flaky pieces like paper-thin mica.

Great, he thought.

He searched for another handhold, and saw one that looked a bit out of reach. But if he stretched and made a good grab, he could get it.

He took a breath.

He stretched up and—for a moment abandoning his right foothold—he caught the rock. Amazingly it held. Good rock, he thought. Nice steady rock.

He pulled himself up, and the slope lessened, and gravity became less an enemy, holding him a bit to the surface. It felt . . . almost sweet. The way his body suddenly had some weight against the cold rock.

And it was cold; the afternoon sun had vanished into a cloud, and though sunset was a few hours away, everything turned dark and gray.

Let's get up, Paul thought—*and down fast . . .*

"Nice catch," Simon shouted up to him. "Go on to the top . . . I'm right behind you . . ."

Probably going to be an amazing view, Paul thought. Something his sister, Maddy, would love to photograph. Nothing stopped her from getting the shot she wanted. Nothing stopped her from anything. He had to wonder: What made them both risk takers, thrill seekers? And was it a good thing?

Right now, it didn't seem so.

He brought his foot up to another bumpy chunk of rock, and pushed up, the surface flattening more, very near the top now.

Just one meter.

Another little scramble.

And then—

Then—he was there.

And for a moment he didn't move. He just . . . stood there, looking down at the bowllike depression girded by a ring of lower mountains, all of them well behind the military's fence that—Paul guessed—circled the entire area.

He stood there.

And though he knew it was cold, the wind whipping the top of this mountain—he felt the cold that had nothing to do with temperature.

Below him, he saw another fence, taller, a good twenty feet, something that looked as though it could keep King Kong at bay. And then, beyond that fence, he saw something, whatever it circled.

A house.

No, it couldn't be a house. This place looked like something that Frank Gehry might have built, all curves and shiny metal. It was someone's twisted version of a house.

Surrounded by one hell of a fence.

And on the far side of the fence . . . across the circular valley . . .

Paul didn't know what to make of it.

Tanks. Artillery, soldiers moving around with automatic weapons. A hell of a lot of firepower, all pointed directly at the "house," at this strange building caged as though it were the most dangerous beast ever.

A caged house with the massive firepower of an army pointed directly at it.

He heard Simon crawl up behind him.

"Whoa, nasty bit those last few feet, I thought—"

Simon stopped. Then Paul heard him say the obvious.

"Holy . . . shit."

book two
welcome home

thirteen

Paul didn't move for a second.

But he watched Simon take a step closer to the scene.

"Wow. What in the world . . . is that?"

Paul shook his head. "I don't know. I can't even guess." And then Paul looked up at the sky. He felt even colder, the sudden gulp of the sun being eaten by a dark cloud. Now the sky turned dark and a sneaky wind whipped around the small mountain.

When he looked back Simon was crouched low to the ground, digging in his bag.

"What are you doing?" Paul asked.

In answer, Simon turned around to reveal his camera.

"I'm taking a picture. I don't know what that is down there, but I'm sure people will be very . . . interested." He popped off the lens cap.

Paul stepped right next to him. "Are you crazy? Put that thing away. We have to get off this mountain now, and fast."

Again, he looked at the strange scene below them. The

metal house surrounded by a giant fence. Paul saw that electrical wires led from massive poles to two points in the fence.

An electrical fence . . .

Exactly the type of thing you'd use to keep King Kong in, as if the house were some kind of Skull Island. Whatever it was, Paul knew that they had to move fast. Simon went on getting the camera ready to take the picture.

"Simon—put that the hell away. We have to get off this damned rock. Now."

Another breeze. Colder now, cutting right to his skin . . .

"Hey man, relax. If you want to go down, go. I'm taking the damned picture."

Paul turned back to the path they had chosen.

And the path—was gone.

Not exactly gone . . . but now somehow the path ended in a sheer bit of rock. Unless Paul had the wrong place. Was the light tricking him, throwing him off?

"Simon. Where'd we come from . . . ?"

Simon gestured with his hand. "Thataway. Right"— Paul's climbing partner looked up—"there . . ."

Simon saw it too. The path—if it had ever been there— was gone.

"Must be somewhere else, we must have walked away and—" Paul scrambled, looking for an explanation, trying to find some rational thread. And both of them found nothing.

Paul walked over to where the path had been. He extended a hand to touch the rock but he hesitated—mere inches from the rock. There was something about the rock that bothered him. The color was too gray, marbled with dark streaks of black. And he saw bits of a deep rose quartz.

This was not a type of rock he had ever seen in the Glen Coe.

He turned back to Simon. But Simon was gone.

The camera lay on the ground. Just sitting there next to the backpack.

Must have gone for a pee, Paul thought.

Must have—but where?

He took a step closer to the pack. Overhead the clouds deepened, and now it was like the last glimmer of a rapidly fading twilight, as if night were racing here early.

Paul licked his lips. He recognized the feeling from countless close calls on the mountain. He was scared. And worse than that, he was more scared than he could remember ever being before.

"Simon," he said. Then louder. "Simon. Where the bloody hell are—"

A grinding sound, and Paul turned quickly around. And the rock wall that he had walked away from was right there, behind him, only inches away.

"Simon," he whispered.

And what happened next . . . transcended fear.

The rock seemed to slowly turn molten, into a bubbling liquid. Suddenly, the surface slowly moved, alive, swirling. The red veins of quartz that ran through the rock moved, now alive—like real veins.

Until the whole rock *pulsed*.

And Paul could feel his heart thumping. The insanity of this . . . too much. But not so overwhelming that he couldn't take a step backward.

Bumping into something solid.

He didn't turn around this time. No, that would require turning in place and stopping, watching the thing in front of him that was swirling faster, pulsing, throbbing. Instead, he reached both his hands behind himself and *felt* the rock.

As it turned . . . sticky.

He pulled his hands away.

But they didn't move.

All this—took place in seconds.

Only to Paul's perception, it happened so slowly.

The living stone in front of him now nearly touched his skin. He struggled against the imprisonment of his hands. But, like quicksand, each little jerk only seemed to make them slide in deeper behind him until he was up to his wrists.

He couldn't feel anything from his fingers, his hands.

Nothing at all.

Probably a good thing, he thought. *That's . . . a good thing*.

And with that last thought, the rock behind him closed the distance to his body, touching, enveloping, and enclosing it all until—in one last second—all thought became a thing of the past.

Elaina walked out of the motel. She had sent out three e-mails, and got only one response from—of course—Peter Friedman.

Did that mean anything? she thought. Did that mean she couldn't trust the other two people, or that something had happened to them, or, or—

She knew this. She couldn't stay at this little motel any longer; it was only a matter of time till she was found. And—God—she couldn't stay alone. She needed help and advice about what to do about the papers she had.

She walked along the road past the motel, heading back to the giant rotary that led up to the giant Bear Mountain Inn. With the summer season long over, the midday traffic was sparse, just a random car or two passing every now and then. The drivers barely glanced over at her as they roared by.

What do I do? she wondered. She needed information, but asking for help could get her killed. She believed that completely. The fall air was cool enough to make goose-flesh sprout as she thought about it.

No, she had no choice. She had to get someone to con-
firm what she thought the printouts showed. Then get
them to people who could help.

Who that was, she didn't know yet.

She kept walking along the highway as it sloped up to
the great Bear Mountain Inn itself. Been so long since she
had been there. She remembered being a little girl and
driving up from the Bronx with her father, so proud of
his new car that he wanted to make this great trip, out of
the summer's heat to the mountains.

Everything had seemed oversized to her then . . . the giant timbers that made up the lodge, the twin metal bears
that stood guard outside the inn, the fireplace as big as a
room. It was . . . a wonderful memory, rich with colors,
and light and smells.

But now—

It was as if that memory had been twisted into something dangerous, something ugly.

And—something deadly.

She entered the inn. A young couple stood to the right
at the registration desk, looking at a brochure. Maybe they
were planning their wedding—it could be such a nice
place to get married, the mountain in the background. A
memory—if you were lucky—to anchor a life together.

The young woman looked over at Elaina.

As if reading Elaina's mind, she smiled.

Yes. About to be married.

Elaina smiled back and continued down the hallway,
then up the great staircase.

And all the time she scanned the room, looking for a
phone. A secluded phone, a safe phone where she could
make a call that might lead people here. Though she knew
she had to get moving. Already she had stayed here too
long.

At the top of the stairs, she saw the great room with
windows on all sides that overlooked the grounds, and the

mountain and the ice-skating rink—all looking as if they were awaiting the first snow.

Then—in a corner behind the bar—she saw a bank of telephones. The white-jacketed bartender was polishing glasses. He might hear but she had no choice. She'd talk quietly.

It would have to do.

She walked over to the pay phone farthest from the bartender. The bartender looked up, smiled. Elaina flashed another smile, and then kept moving. The phone hung on the wall, open and exposed. Whatever happened to phone booths, to privacy? Now everything was public.

She picked up the phone.

She dialed the number, then her phone card number. She knew that her location could be tracked. It was a risk she'd have to take.

A sleepy voice answered the phone.

"Peter . . . it's Elaina."

For a second, there was nothing but silence. Then: "Elaina."

She had laid out to Peter in the e-mail what had happened, and how much she was in danger.

And how he could be in danger. But his e-mail said . . . "Okay, call, kiddo."

"Hold on," he said.

"Sure."

"Okay, I'm back. Just so you know, I'm taping this. Then sending it to some friends." He paused, letting the obvious message of his precaution sink in. "Just in case."

"Gotcha."

"How are you?"

"I'm okay. But scared. Alone. Too alone . . ."

She looked up. The bartender glanced at her, then looked away. She lowered her voice.

"Did you look at those numbers I sent you?"

"Yup. Look, I have to ask—how did you get them?"

"A mistake. Dumb luck. I was sorting some of the commercial files for GenTech, housekeeping the genetic projects they support around the world, all the cloning projects—when somehow I saw this file. And my password got me in. I shouldn't have been allowed to crack it, but I did."

"I see. Then you don't think that this stuff . . . is a joke of some kind?"

She took a breath.

"No. Not after they drove me off the side of the mountain."

"I know. Shit. Okay, I'm going to show these to a few people—"

"I don't think—"

"A few. This is way beyond me, Elaina, way beyond you. But if you have . . . what I think you have, we've got to get it to people who will do something about it."

"I know. That's why I took it."

"Good work. I mean it. You could have just . . . closed the file."

Peter had been a colleague at GenTech. He had tried a few awkward passes at Elaina but then he settled for a friendship. And when he left because GenTech thought he asked too many ethical questions—she became his link to what the company was doing.

Neither of them expected anything like this.

"Tell me first—what do you think this is?" Elaina said.

"Okay. I mean, it's just the hint of an idea, but I can tell you better after I see it all."

"Go on. Tell me."

"First, a meeting place."

"Where?"

"My family's summer place. You know, at the Jersey shore. Need the address?"

"No. I remember it."

"I'll meet you in the morning as soon I can get there.

And I'll be able to tell you more then. Okay?" Peter said.

"Okay. But what do you think this is . . . ?"

A pause. She could imagine Peter squinting his eyes, wondering if he should even say anything at all on the phone.

"Elaina, you know it's genetic code; maybe not a complete sequence but I bet that what you have is pretty damn close to a complete sequence. But it's a code with a difference. The structure is all wrong—there are extra pairs all over the place. They seem to run in sixes instead of fours. It's crazy. It's as if it was based on our genetic model of the helix with the four genetic bases, but with a big difference."

He took a breath.

"What else, Peter?"

"The sequence matches nothing that we know, that's for sure. This code—if it's real—is . . . off the chart, Elaina. Totally unknown."

"Could it have been something cooked up in a lab?"

Peter laughed. "Yeah, maybe after a few hundred years of experimentation by dozens of the world's best genetic scientists. No, what you sent looks like a code for a nearly complete organism. No way this was cooked up by GenTech."

"Then how— You mean—"

"Hey, no more now. I don't know what the hell I mean. Let me get some advice. Don't worry—I'll cover my tracks. And stay off the phone, okay?"

She nodded. The bartender had come closer, idly eavesdropping on her conversation.

"Okay."

"Check your e-mail. I'll dig up some places we can meet."

"Great."

"Then see you tomorrow."

Elaina said goodbye and reluctantly hung up the handset. She stood there for a moment. She almost had hoped that Peter would say it was nothing, a joke. Instead, he'd confirmed her worst fears.

"You okay, miss?"

The bartender stood close now. Probably got his share of tearful calls, lovers breaking up, and spouses fighting.

"I'm fine," she said. She smiled. "Really."

And she turned and walked out of the great room and down the staircase.

fourteen

Nick threaded his way past the packed pub patrons, one eye on the two pints in his hands, the other on the sea of moving bodies.

The crowd seemed affable enough so that a mistaken slosh of lager wouldn't precipitate a fight. But best to take no chances.

The pub—The Lamb and Flag—was tucked away on a tiny twisty street off Warren Street. And though it was only Thursday, on the streets of London it felt as if the weekend had already exploded.

After one last deft maneuver past a crowd of young businessmen in white shirts, ties loosened, Nick finally arrived at the small table where Maddy sat.

She smiled—as if she knew how hard it was for a Yank to deal with all this traditional pub mayhem.

"Here you go," he said. He noticed his accent brought a few glances. Didn't get many Americans here, he guessed. And Maddy had already caught a few appreciative looks. Seeing her sitting here, any guy—any bloke!—

would have to be made of wood to *not* notice her. "One pint of London Pride for you . . . and a Guinness for me."

He put the tall glass down in front of Maddy, and then squeezed into the seat next to her. Together, they both took a big sip.

"Lovely," Maddy said. She had to shout to be heard above the din.

Nick looked around. "Romantic kind of place."

Maddy raised her eyebrows. "Oh, is that what we have in mind, hm? Romance?"

Nick smiled. She was so direct, so in your face. There was no bullshit about her—and he imagined that she didn't tolerate any bullshit either.

"Just . . . making an observation."

Then, turning up the heat, she leaned close. She put a hand on top of his, the gesture so direct and physical, unexpected in the rough, smoke-filled atmosphere of the pub. "Now come on, tell me the truth. We're both journalists. We value . . . the truth."

Nick took another sip of beer. Most people in the place were probably well into their second or third pint. He thought of that line from a song a few years back . . . *"pissing the night away . . ."*

He looked around. "I, er . . ." He scanned the room. "Need the loo."

"A convenient toilet break, eh. They're up those stairs, and then towards the back."

"Thanks." And Nick stood up and threaded his way to the stairs.

Maddy sat and watched Nick walk away.

An American. And one with not the greatest track record for loyalty. Maddy sipped her beer, feeling eyes watching her, wondering perhaps if she was now fair game.

But then . . . is there any man that can handle loyalty?

She supposed that they did exist, men so resolute in their love, with such a steely grasp of their sexuality, that nothing could pull them away. They existed.

Maybe.

Would anyone want them? Nick was intriguing, complex, and Maddy imagined he didn't look at all bad when he peeled off his T-shirt.

She smiled at that, wondering what Nick would think if *he* knew the images she let flow through her mind.

He wouldn't. Not tonight anyway. She would take this slow; it could be dangerous waters—even for someone as experienced as she.

She spotted a youngish man who kept looking away from his friends, eyeing her. She looked away—hoping he'd get the message. She dug out her phone and turned it on. The ring was on mute but she saw a mini-envelope flashing, indicating that she had a message. Probably her mother, worried about Paul. She always worried about her younger brother, his climbing, his travels.

She's given up worrying about me, Maddy realized. *Because I'm not the type to worry about or because I can take care of myself?* Maddy wasn't sure. She was tempted to read the message now—

When the young man stood next to her.

"Get you another, doll?" he said. It took a second for Maddy to compute what he was talking about. Then Maddy looked down and noticed that her beer was getting low.

She smiled. "No thanks . . . I—"

The man sat down. "Then how about—" The man fumbled in his pocket, whipping out—of all things—a pack of Marlboro Lights. "A fag?"

Which is when Nick returned. He stopped there, just behind the man. Maddy looked up and grinned, shrugging her shoulders.

"Excuse me, can I—" Nick said to the man.

He turned around.

"Yeah?"

"My seat?"

The man laughed. "Just talking to—what's your name?"

Maddy looked up at Nick. "Maybe we should leave . . ."

Nick looked left and right, as if some of this guy's pals might swoop down and try to remove him.

The man took a slug of his beer. "Bloody Americans. Think they own the bloody world."

Maddy stood up. "We better go." And the uninvited guest stood up, sending the chair flying back violently.

"Hey," he said, "you don't have to go anywhere."

And Maddy looked at Nick. She saw his eyes narrow, and recognized the ancient male surge of adrenaline. *Don't,* she thought. *Please. Sure you might be able to knock his drunken ass on the floor. But why?*

She nodded her head toward the door.

A gesture that said . . . *Come on.*

The man was in Nick's face, begging to be pushed away.

And instead, Nick reached down, took a last sip of his beer, and then walked around the man to stand beside Maddy, leaving the man facing nothing but the pale bluish smoke hanging in the room.

"Let's go," he said, and Nick took Maddy's arm and walked her out of the Lamb and Flag.

Out, into a misty near-rain that—after the hot room— felt refreshing.

Way to go, she thought. A little bit of a test for Nick. He passed—with flying colors.

She leaned closer to him as they walked down the small lane to Garrick Street.

•   •   •

Sophie had to pee.

She thought she could wait until the train finally got to the Glasgow station, and she could find a nice toilet. Not a tight dirty little closet like the ones she was sure this train had.

She had had enough money left over to buy a piece of dry, crumbly cake and a soda. That was hours ago; the soda made her need to pee, and she couldn't wait anymore.

Across the twin banks of seats, a woman watched her with squinty, narrow eyes, looking at Sophie as if she could read her mind.

Sophie looked out the window to the dark fields. The skies had been clear in London but now she saw that here there were nothing but clouds. When she leaned her head against the window, she saw no stars, no moon, just a smudgy blackness.

Sophie turned back to the woman.

Doesn't she have anything to read? she wondered. *Must be something better she can do than look at me.*

The need to pee got worse.

And finally—Sophie had to get up.

She stood up just as the train took a curve and nearly sent her toppling into her seat again. She shot a hand out and caught herself on the window.

Then she stepped out to the aisle and walked toward the front of the train, up to a toilet that had been used for the past three hours. She had seen all sorts of people make their way to it . . . a guy with a leather jacket and dozens of zippers and spiky hair that nearly touched the ceiling . . . and an old man who coughed all the way up the aisle as if he couldn't move without the *chug-chug* of a cough . . . and a mother dragging her noisy little boy who defiantly kept a finger permanently lodged in his nose, planted there, digging, fishing.

Now it was her turn.

She wasn't a germ freak. Not really. But she did like things . . . clean. Nice.

Sophie knew that the train toilet would be neither nice nor clean.

She tried the door latch, and the door didn't open. She pulled down on it again, and then pushed—and finally the door popped open. She immediately smelled the over-powering odor of antiseptic.

She scanned the tight room and then, squeezing in, she shut the door and pulled the latch down, locking the door as the train rattled on.

As Richard stumbled past the crowd making their way to the tube, the trains, to life, he tried not to notice how everyone seemed to veer around him—the disgusting homeless guy.

Of course he knew how he looked and how he smelled. He knew that he made all those people feel uncomfort-able.

Sometimes, that's why they gave him money—to make him go away.

To them he was an anoyance . . . a homeless guy. That's all he was, someone you dropped 50p into a cup for—or you ignored completely. They didn't know or care if he had a name, or if he once had an idea of what to do with his life. Now, he was like a crack in the pavement, inanimate, something you stepped over.

Still, tonight he felt good. He had helped that girl— actually given her his cup—he had done all right! Not even a bloody holiday and he got a good twenty pounds rattling around inside his pockets. Enough for food, some booze, maybe some real fags instead of the dog-ends he usually picked up.

Yeah, a real pack of smokes, a sandwich—it all sounded so good.

He left the station and turned away from the main road

and down King's Road, to a quiet street with some stores that knew him, where he was a regular.

It was strange moving from the rush hour crowds to a deserted street where he was the only person on it.

Except—he wasn't.

He felt someone behind him, and when he turned around, he saw someone, walking behind him, keeping his distance.

Richard walked on, turned a corner, so hungry, and even more thirsty for that first delicious hit of alcohol.

He looked over his shoulder, and the person behind him was closer now. *Weird, it's as if he's following me,* Richard thought. He never saw anyone on this block; he was always alone, always . . .

He looked forward.

The small twenty-four-hour convenience shop was at the corner, not far now and, nearby, there were plenty of doorways to curl up in to enjoy his drink and some rest—after—

A tap on his shoulder.

Richard jumped.

He stopped, and turned around.

The man was there. The street was so dark, the nearest light down near the store. Here was all blackness, and the man's hat hid his face.

"Hi," he said.

Richard nodded.

"Wh—what do you want?"

The man took a step closer. No one ever did that to him. No one ever stepped closer.

"You were in the station."

Richard nodded.

"And I saw you." The man, so much in the shadows, so hard to see the face, took a deep breath. "I *spotted* you . . . talking to that girl."

Richard started shaking his head. He had an idea that

this was going someplace bad, that he was in trouble.

"I—didn't do anything. I just helped her. Gave her some advice. I didn't—"

And the man reached out and touched him . . . actually touched him.

"Easy, friend. I know you didn't do anything. I watched you help her."

Another step closer. Now Richard could smell the man. An odd, clean smell of strong soap, or maybe something in his hair. The man patted Richard's shoulder, his hand in a smooth black glove.

"I just need to know where she was going. I mean, I'm sure she told you—she asked you . . . something. What was it, friend?"

The hand closed a bit on Richard's shoulder. And though he didn't feel any pain there was definitely some pressure, a sudden squeeze.

And Richard thought of the young girl, all alone, heading up to Glasgow. He thought of her being chased by this man in his black trench coat and black leather gloves.

Richard shook his head. "I don't know, I didn't tell her anything." Richard laughed. "Just gave her my cup—told her how to beg for—"

The hand pinched tighter, and Richard felt a sharp pain that ran up to his neck, then straight to his brain. Sparks flared in his eyes.

He moaned.

"No," the man said. "We're sure that's not *all* you talked about."

We're . . . he said we're. Who's the "we"? Richard looked around the deserted block. He could see the convenience store down the road, but no one else was around, no one else here at all.

Richard licked his lips, scared.

Another pinch and now he fell to his knees. Like a doll collapsing, he crashed to the hard pavement. The smack

of his kneecaps sent two more bolts of pain rocketing up
his leg.

The man looked down at him.

"You don't . . . understand. We want to know where
she is going. We want to know everything . . . anything
she told you."

Richard felt his lips trembling uncontrollably. He was
so scared. He had imagined eating some food, smoking,
getting something cheap to drink—and now he knelt on
the sidewalk.

Got to get away, he thought. *I have to stand up—fast.
Then run away, make noise, yell—anything to get someone's attention, someone's help.*

He tensed his muscles, ready to scramble away. The
man's hand was still locked on his shoulder. And then—

He felt warmth.

At his knees. Where his knees touched the pavement.
Warmth. Then a smell, something acrid, burning.

He looked down.

The place where his knees touched the ground now . . .
glowed. A warm yellow glow that made his knees hot,
then hotter, this new pain replacing the throbbing smack
from before.

He went to stand up.

And couldn't.

"Just tell me. That's all you have to do."

The pain bloomed. It was as if he had crouched on a
hot stove, an electric stove, and the twin burners kept
getting warmer and warmer . . .

Tears came out of his eyes.

"Please . . ."

"Just tell me."

Richard moaned, whimpered. He tried to yell, but the
man covered his mouth with the leather glove, muffling
the sound.

"No. I only want to hear what she said."

Richard spoke carefully, the words tumbling out so fast.

"Glasgow, she was taking the train to Glasgow. Had to see someone there. I don't know who. She was alone, scared."

His jaw popped open to scream again—but the leather hand was way too fast.

He howled into it.

The man backed away.

He backed away from Richard a few feet . . . then a few feet more, stepping back, saying nothing.

Richard looked down and saw his legs *glowing* and now the pain obliterated everything as he became surrounded by a small golden pool, a burning yellow pool that had just opened up.

And paralyzed by fear and pain—he watched as he slowly sank into that pool, the molten yellow pool on the sidewalk, glowing with enough brightness that—when he looked up—he saw the man's face for the first time.

And he had had his last coherent thought.

An observation.

That it wasn't . . . a face . . . at all.

fifteen

Sophie pushed the shiny metal button, and a tiny sputter of water shot out. She barely had time to wet her fingertips. She hit it again, and moved her hands under the small spout.

This time she brought her wet fingers to her face, rubbing the cool water on her face. The water was smooth, cool. She shut her eyes.

The train rocked, and the light in the small toilet flickered. On, off, then staying off—as the train wheels rattled below her.

Sophie stood there for a moment, listening to the repetitive sound, waiting for the lights to come back on.

She could see a thin line of light where the door met the floor.

She thought: *There are lights out there.*
But not here.

She looked up, and saw the light above the basin, a small glow struggling to come to life. *Come on,* she thought . . . *why is there no light in here?* And then: Maybe she should just walk out.

Her hand reached out for the door, trying to feel the latch.

She felt nothing.

Wait a second, she thought. *This is a small room. The door has to be* right there. But it wasn't. She moved a bit to her left, and reached out again.

And felt nothing.

Save for a small cool breeze that chilled her bare arms.

Then—as a test—she reached behind her, to touch the wall.

Except there was no wall there.

Impossible. This was impossible. She looked up at the light, and finally it started to glow, the sick, pale yellow growing slowly, steadily brighter until—

It flashed.

Like someone taking a picture.

And in that flash she saw that she was in a room so much bigger than the small toilet ever could be. The room had red walls, bright, brilliant red walls. The basin had been there but in—

Again, another flash!

In the basin—the small faucet—was still there . . .

But now—in the basin—something moved.

Another flash, and her eyes stung from the flash, but not before they could register an image, something larger than the basin, so big, and crawling out.

And now the flashes came faster, like the flickering lights she saw in the clubs on the dance shows on TV. Flickering, capturing each movement, then going dark.

The thing in the basin looked like a crab. But it was so much bigger than the basin. It waved its claws in the air and cut the air with a clicking sound that was even louder than the rattling of the wheels—which now seemed so distant, so far away.

Snap-snap, and the crab sat poised at the edge of the basin, holding on.

Sophie looked around this red room, this impossible red room that couldn't be here, couldn't be real, but felt totally real.

She dared not take her eyes off the basin . . . because now the crab, with such a large, fat shell, a shell curved and puffy as if it were stuffed full . . . teetered on the edge. Sophie saw the twin black eyes of the crab, dark, slimy raisins.

Looking at her.

She breathed in and out fast, her chest hurting from the steady rush of air. She could scream. But it wouldn't do any good, would it?

The flickering light slowed.

That was a bad thing, because now she couldn't see as much.

So—she only *heard* the next thing.

The sound of the giant crab falling to the floor. A heavy *thud.* The sound of shell on the linoleum floor.

She backed up, now touching one of the red walls.

Her hands behind her, feeling the . . . wet wall.

The wall was wet.

The flickering slowed.

Snap-snap.

The sound of . . . movement, just there.

And she screamed.

Nick looked down the tree-lined street.

"Nice," he said. "Trees, shops, cafés . . . a bit of Greenwich Village."

Was it his imagination or did Maddy lean into him a bit? "And Primrose Hill is probably every bit as expensive as your Greenwich Village. Maybe more . . ."

"So the extreme photography business must be going well?"

"Extreme photography? Is that what you call it?"

"Well, I don't know everything you've done—but mountain expeditions, deep diving, and wasn't there something involving a volcano? Sounds extreme to me."

She laughed. And the sound broke the stillness of the quiet street.

"Point made. Let's just say . . . I like exciting things. So tell me, how exactly did your marriage end?"

"Not that novel a story. No innovations there. I had an affair, another journalist. Kept bumping into each other and we just let things happen. Once we went to Dublin for a weekend away. It was fun, thrilling—exciting, you know. Until the hotel called my home, spoke to my wife and said that I left my cell phone charging cord when I stayed there with *my wife*. That was pretty much it . . ."

"So then it was over. You must regret it."

Nick looked up, at the moon, at the shadows on the street, then at Maddy.

"No. It wasn't a good thing that happened—but it wasn't all bad. My marriage had problems. Something would have happened one way—or the other." Nick smiled. "Besides, I'm a great believer in the power of change."

"And stability be damned?"

"A little stability is nice too."

They both laughed.

Maddy stopped walking. And then she nodded at a four-story house with a small tree standing guard out front.

"Well, I'm here."

Nick nodded. "Looks great," he said.

And he wondered. Should he push it and ask for an invite?

But before he resolved the question, Maddy leaned forward and gave him a kiss on his cheek. "I had a lovely day. Thanks . . ."

She backed up, and then—without a thought—he leaned forward and kissed her on her lips. Her response surprised him.

She laughed again.

"Now, no—I don't think, after everything you've told me, that we should jump into things so quickly, hm?"

Nick smiled back. She was just too smart. "Whatever do you mean?"

"Your track record's a bit checkered. I wouldn't want to be just another one of your whirlwind, worldwide conquests—though I'm sure that's not exactly an unpleasant prospect."

"I'm not that bad a guy."

And the smile faded on Maddy's face . . . to something warmer.

"I know. But still—we can take it slow, hm?" The smile returned, and she leaned forward and kissed Nick on the lips quickly—then took the first two steps up to the door.

"Lunch tomorrow . . . at the Russian Tea Room across the street?"

"Russian Tea Room? Thought that was just to the left of Carnegie Hall."

"This one's a real Russian tea room. See you at one?"

"Wouldn't miss it."

She turned and continued up the stairs, and Nick kept watching until she opened the door and disappeared, and the quiet tree-lined street was even quieter.

Sophie called out for help, standing in the darkness, trapped in the darkness, the sound of spiky legs hitting the floor.

Then, shaking, her voice shrinking to nothing when she heard no answer, no rattling of the door that wasn't there, no hum of the train wheels underneath her, she became silent, still.

If I make noise—the thing, the giant crab . . . will hear *me.*

She stood still.

As still as she could. Thinking: *Maybe it won't hear me, maybe it will scuttle away.*

Which is when she felt the bumpy hard touch of something against her leg. It was there, just at her feet.

And now she screamed.

And she heard her scream melt into the sound of the train's shrill whistle, and the light flickered yellow, once, then again, and she again saw the door, the lock bar pulled tight but the handle rattling to let someone in.

Sophie pulled the lock bar free, and the door flew open.

And the woman from her seat stood there, her face filled with concern—so much more concern than Sophie had seen for such a long time.

Maddy closed the building door behind her. *Trouble, that one,* she thought. Smart, funny, sexy—but fitted with the usual male problem. Loyalty. Commitment.

There were times that Maddy knew she didn't give a damn about any of that.

But—she had been trying to *improve*, trying to do better.

At least that had been a recent resolution. Maybe she should have invited Nick in. Wouldn't be the first time that she overrode her better judgment.

She walked up the flight of steps to the door to her flat, stuck the key in and—turning the lock—remembered that she had had her cell phone switched off for the past few hours.

Nothing more annoying than getting interrupted by a stupid call.

And she knew a lot of people who'd call her for work,

to dump an assignment on her, at any time night or day. Especially the magazines from the States. Didn't they ever stop working?

With one hand, she shut the door behind her and, with the other, turned on her Nokia.

It lit up, searched for service.

Then rang.

A message.

Just as she suspected.

She pressed the green button, and held the phone to her ear. A calm measured voice said that she had one new message . . . and then played it.

For a minute the accent threw her. Scottish, thick, deep, and struggling to speak. From the sound, the phone was outdoors, wind whipping around. He identified himself, a police inspector. He asked if she was Maddy Hodge and if she had a brother, Paul.

Maddy looked around the room. The message played without a pause, delivering its information, slowly. Letting her mind absorb it.

Paul had been climbing. She knew that, he was well trained, and the Glen Coe range didn't pose that much of a challenge. Still—

Something happened, the voice said. An accident. But his voice seemed to catch on the word *accident*. Paul and another climber . . . disappeared.

There was only one light on, and it shot a pale yellow light over the small living room. Sickly. Dull. But everything looked surreal now, bizarre. The message seemed impossible. People don't simply disappear.

The message ended with a flurry of names, and phone numbers. The local police, and then other numbers. A Colonel Harris in the army. Strange. Why would the army be involved?

She wrote the numbers down and then hit the number 4 to play the message again.

sixteen

"So, are you sure there's nothing you'll want to eat?"

Sophie shook her head. She felt so stupid having to be rescued from the toilet. Rescued from . . . what? Sophie licked her lips and tried to smile.

"No, I'm not hungry. I just got scared. I couldn't get out."

The woman's eyes narrowed, and Sophie knew this was someone who had kids, probably lots of them, and knew when they weren't telling the truth. She knew something bad had happened. Still, Sophie couldn't tell her.

Could she tell anyone?

"Really? Well—let's hope you don't get . . . stuck anymore."

Sophie smiled for real this time, a shared conspiracy. "So, dear, where are you going?"

Sophie chewed her lip. Another question . . . another lie?

But a few minutes ago Sophie had felt more scared than ever before and this woman, with her bifocals, and pale brown dress, and—she looked down—very simple shoes, had saved her. When you're saved, you have to trust, Sophie guessed.

"I'm going to Glasgow. I have to find someone."

The woman didn't say anything. She paused and looked out the window, then back to Sophie.

"You're arriving kind of late, aren't you?"

Sophie nodded.

"And where exactly will you be staying in my beautiful city?"

Now it was Sophie's turn to look away.

"I don't know. I mean, I have to find this person, a friend of my father's. But it will be late. I—I—"

The woman reached out and touched Sophie's shoulder, a gentle touch—and for just a moment it reminded Sophie of something she hadn't felt in such a long time.

"You need a place to stay."

Not a question.

Sophie hesitated—but then ultimately nodded.

The woman smiled, broadly. "Well guess what, lass? I'm Mrs. Drumlin and I run a bed and breakfast called the Drumlin! And I'm absolutely sure that there will be more than a few empty rooms tonight. And unless I'm wrong, I bet you'll love it. Like pets?"

Sophie grinned. "I do—but my dad is allergic . . ."

She stopped. She couldn't tell her about her father. Mrs. Drumlin—as nice as she was—would have to call the police. Sophie couldn't have that happen.

She couldn't tell the woman what had happened to her dad. That it was just her, she was all alone.

"So, Miss—"

"Sophie."

"Sophie." The woman smiled. "I like that name. Do you want to stay at the wonderful and cozy Drumlin?" She stuck out her hand.

"I'd love to." And for the first time today Sophie didn't feel quite as scared or as alone.

Elaina walked along the road with the setting sun on her back. She had to move tonight, she knew. Though she'd like nothing more than to stay at the sleepy little motel, with Heidi, and get one more blissful night of sleep.

The woman at the reservations desk at Bear Mountain had handed her a bus schedule. She could get a bus straight to Manhattan, then another to the Jersey shore.

Be easier to rent a car.

But she had to avoid leaving a trail. She had seen enough movies to know that credit cards could easily be tracked, like footsteps in the snow.

She shivered. So tired, and still hurting from the crash. A small nap would be nice.

There wasn't time.

Not if somebody still wanted to stop her.

And again she found herself thinking—*What is it on these pages that is so important, so dangerous? What is it that would make someone want to kill me?* It was all from some crazed suspense story. Things like this didn't happen in real life.

A few more steps along 9W and, around a curve, she saw the motel, bathed in the cool shadow of fall.

She stopped.

Something was wrong.

No cars were there. That . . . made sense. After all, it was off-season, and Elaina had seen that Heidi parked her old Jeep Wrangler around the back.

But that wasn't it.

Something else. She stopped, waited, and a flatbed truck, a twenty-year-old dinosaur, roared by with the driver craning his head around to catch a good long look at her.

Did the truck driver slow down with the unbelievable

hope that, yes, they could strike up a relationship? But the battered truck streamed away, curling around a small ridge for parts north.

She looked back at Heidi's.

What was wrong?

The sign. In the gloom, the shadows, and the late afternoon, the sign should be on. But it wasn't. Maybe Heidi was busy, maybe she forgot, or—

No. It wasn't just the wind making gooseflesh bloom on her arms.

Something had happened.

She looked back to the Bear Mountain Inn. She could turn around, walk back there—

She stayed immobile on the road. A van went by, a grim-faced woman at the wheel, a gaggle of kids in the back. The shadows seemed to deepen with every second.

No, she had to go there. To see if what she imagined was fantasy or reality. To try to make some of the demons go away.

She walked across the highway, taking care that no speeding car came around the curve at her. All the time she hoped that Heidi's sign would suddenly flicker to life. But it didn't, and the small motel strip seemed lonelier with each step.

Closer, and she thought—how could she not?—of that other motel.

Twelve rooms, twelve vacancies, Norman Bates said.

It was a line she liked to quote for laughs.

And just as Janet Leigh should have run, gotten the hell out of there before mean Mrs. Bates made sure that nothing happened between her and young Norman, Elaina considered again turning around, walking back to the inn and waiting for the last bus, leaving in a few hours.

Cars whizzed left and right, what passed for the Hudson Valley rush hour kicking in.

The cars—the normalcy—made it seem okay. She

wanted to kill the fear, to learn that nothing was wrong.

Only steps away. The door to the office looked closed. She saw the glow of the old computer inside. Maybe Heidi had fallen asleep; business was kind of slow.

She grabbed the doorknob, gave it a twist, and pushed it open.

The door opened, then stopped, hitting something.

Elaina sniffed. A smell. A sharp, pungent odor.

The office was dark, but she could see the desk, and the broad red smear that ran down the check-in desk. And she saw something that looked like a handprint.

Her stomach tightened, and then she turned to look at what was behind the door, even though every instinct told her to run.

She looked around the door and saw the woman's body, blood still oozing from it. Elaina gagged, backed up, her eyes locked on the body though she knew . . . *she knew* . . . that whoever had done it could be right here.

But she kept looking at the body because she saw the strange way the skin looked . . . peeled back, as if something had exploded inside her, making her a human balloon, popping.

She looked up.

The walls were splattered.

As if she had popped open.

Elaina stepped back again, now nearly outside, and another step, not thinking that anyone would be there.

A horn blared and she jumped.

She spun around as a young kid went by, grinning at her, leering.

She started running.

Maddy threw things in a bag, some jeans, a few sweaters—it was cold up north—then checked her purse.

Not much there—but she could solve that later. ATMs were everywhere.

She tossed in her Mavica and her old Olympus.

She saw her hands shaking as she packed.

She had decided to call the number for Colonel Harris.

And he answered on the first ring. Harris had spoken so slowly, as if he was being very careful what he said to her. At first, he told her not to come—but he shifted when she started talking about all her press connections. And—then oddly—he said that there may be a reason why her coming could help . . . them.

Them? Maddy just wanted to find her brother.

She was only going up there to find out what happened to Paul—and why the military was involved. Harris arranged to meet her in the town of Einbank.

Maddy found a late flight out on Easy Jet, probably half empty at this time of night. If she hurried, she could get to Luton airport, fly up to Glasgow, and rent a car.

Maps!

She walked over to her totally disorganized bookshelf and pulled out the U.K. atlas. She flipped open to the pages covering Scotland.

Where the hell was this place?

She saw the Glen Coe range, and a scattering of towns and villages on either side of it. But then she saw the name of the village mentioned by the colonel.

Einbank.

Sounded more German than Scottish. And it was isolated, in the middle of nowhere. Harris said Einbank was the town closest to where Paul had disappeared.

She threw the map into her luggage and slapped the bag shut.

Funny, it was usually Paul that saved her, whether rescuing her from a party from hell or helping her when her car died in Brighton. He was steady, not easily distracted.

The perfect type for mountain climbing.

He wasn't someone who took chances.

So what had happened now? A climbing accident?

That's not what the colonel said.

"Something happened . . ."

Something. Not a fall.

And then.

"Your brother has disappeared."

That one stopped her cold. Disappeared.

She grabbed the bag and hurried out of the apartment, thinking . . . hoping that this time, she'd get to save her brother.

Sophie looked around the small bedroom, with the bumpy bedspread that looked handmade, and the thick, leaded glass with colored panels on the side. It would all look so pretty in the morning, with the sun pouring through.

"Not our best room," Mrs. Drumlin said. "I'm afraid we have a guest in that one. Still, nice and tidy and homey, don't you think?"

Sophie nodded. "It's great. I love it." She looked right at the woman. "Thank you so much for letting me stay."

"Oh, don't you worry about that. The room would just be empty anyway. Now, I'm very tired—and you must be too. There are biscuits on the shelf there, tea and coffee . . . and we'll fix you up with a great big Scottish breakfast in the morning. Right before you go visit . . . ?"

She hadn't asked who Sophie had to visit.

That question hadn't been asked.

But now—here it was.

Trust, thought Sophie. *I should trust this woman.* Need *to trust this woman.*

And Sophie said, "A professor. He was . . . a friend of my father's."

The woman's eyes narrowed, an all-knowing squint. "And you know where he lives?"

"Aldon Road. I was told it's near the BBC offices. Is that far?"

The woman laughed.

"Sweetheart, not at all. You can walk to it from here. I'll show you in the morning. Now, get some rest, and we'll chat tomorrow."

Sophie nodded, and watched the woman leave.

The room felt quiet and still. She heard a car noise from outside. But then it was quiet again.

And she knew what this place was. Or she knew what she hoped it would be.

Sanctuary.

Such a strong word. She loved . . . strong words. Sanctuary. Safety. Protection.

She looked at the bed. Sleep never seemed more inviting. She ignored the small tin of cookies, and she didn't even take off her clothes, but slipped under the covers and almost instantly fell asleep.

The small jet bumped, and Maddy woke up.

For a moment she was completely disoriented, forgetting how she had raced from her apartment to the Luton airport, just barely catching the last flight to Glasgow. She looked at the garish orange interior of the EasyJet, still screaming and bright though the cabin was dark. The plane was half full.

It bumped again.

She instinctively reached down and fingered her seat belt, making sure it was buckled.

The plane began a succession of quick, jerky bumps, like a car hitting ruts in the road. She looked across the aisle. A middle-aged businessman gripped his seat, his face locked into a grim expression of concern.

Normally, flying didn't bother Maddy, even while hitting bad turbulence.

This felt . . . different.

She looked out the window and she saw that the plane barely floated above a dark bed of clouds. That was the bumpy road—and the jet wasn't doing so well on it.

The flight attendant made her wobbly way down the aisle, checking people's belts. She stopped and looked at the man across from Maddy.

"Are you okay, sir?" she asked.

The man nodded. Then, "Why . . . is it so bumpy?"

Maddy saw the petite attendant, in hideous electric orange, smile. "I don't know. Just a storm. I imagine the captain will say something."

The man nodded again, and the attendant turned to Maddy just as the plane leapt up as though it had run over a sidewalk curve.

Bloody hell, Maddy thought. This was getting out of hand.

"Okay, miss?"

"Sure. Say, could I have a bourbon and water?"

For a moment the attendant seemed to think it was a real request. Maddy followed quickly. "Just kidding. I'm fine. As long as we stay mostly horizontal."

The attendant nodded, and Maddy saw that she was scared. Funny, her job was to make sure everyone else felt okay, everyone buckled up safe. She looked terrified. Another nasty lurch, and the woman's hands flew out to the sides to steady her.

The captain came on the intercom.

"Sorry for the bumps but there's a big storm system from the highlands below us—and I'm afraid we're due to make our descent soon . . . so it won't be getting any better. Please keep those seat belts on and we'll have you down on the ground in about fifteen minutes."

One way or another, Maddy thought.

She tilted her head back, achy, tired.

The plane tilted slightly down, and Maddy looked out the window and watched the gray carpet of clouds rise to meet the plane.

This is going to be fun, she thought.

She thought about the bed awaiting her in the hotel near the airport.

The bus had been fifteen minutes late—and Elaina had gone in to speak to the thin owlish man at the Bear Mountain Inn's desk to ask if it was really coming at all.

He looked nervous, one of those guys who grew unbelievably nervous around women. The prettier the woman, the more nervous.

Despite everything, I must look okay, Elaina had thought, judging from the man's bug-eyed expression.

But as he checked the timetable, the Hudson Valley Coach Line bus pulled up. The bus door opened for only a minute before rushing away with Elaina on board.

The trip through the valley at night, stopping at various towns along the river, took forever.

What a way to travel, she thought.

But, if nothing else, she felt safe sitting in the nearly empty bus, getting farther away from Bear Mountain, from the woman who had helped her, now dead, brutally murdered.

It only reinforced what Elaina knew.

That she stood a good chance of being killed.

She considered stopping at the nearest good-sized town and going to the police. It was their job to protect people. It's what they do—when they're not giving commuters speeding tickets.

Perhaps it was intuition—but she felt better on her own, at least until she could pass off the pages of data to somebody she trusted.

She thought of her father, a simple construction worker, with his hands puffy from grabbing and pulling and banging. Clumsy rough hands that must have been so harsh against her mother's soft olive skin.

Yet, her dad had always told Elaina how important it was to do what had to be done . . . what should be done.

His belief was straightforward: There were times when you had to do the hard thing.

Though he never spoke of it, she had the feeling he had done exactly that many times in the past, whether in the Vietnam war he never spoke of, or in the streets of the Bronx.

His strength fueled her, even now.

She looked out her window and she saw, in the distance, the city. Manhattan—like Oz—loomed ahead, its tall, glittering spires swinging into view, an awesome sight, *still* breathtaking no matter how many times she saw it, no matter what was lost.

She'd be arriving late. Too late to get yet another bus or train and travel to New Jersey to meet Peter, to show him what she had.

She'd have to stay hidden someplace, invisible till morning.

And when the bus pulled into Port Authority, she saw that there were still a few buses and trains to be launched for the night.

She walked into the main terminal and went to the information kiosk loaded with schedules.

She looked up at the tired-looking woman behind the window.

"I'm looking for a bus to New Jersey . . . to the shore."

The woman laughed. "Bit cold for that, isn't it, honey? The schedules are all there. The Green Line runs a few buses . . . to Asbury, Point Pleasant, Lavallette—"

Elaina brightened. "Yes, Lavallette. That's real close."

"Not till morning. You in a hurry for a swim?"

Another big laugh and—despite everything—Elaina laughed too.

She looked around.

"I don't suppose the terminal stays open?"

"Honey, I'm closing up just as soon as you leave. And this whole place is locked up tight by two a.m."

What am I going to do? Elaina wondered. *Try to get a room somewhere—and not use a credit card?*

She looked around the nearly empty terminal and noticed people moving slowly, watching her. The fear came to the surface again. Could any of these people have followed her?

She turned back to the moon-faced woman behind the desk.

"Any all-night places I could go and kill some time?"

The woman looked at her carefully now, reading—Elaina thought—more accurately what might be going on here. Probably not the first time she had seen someone running.

"There's a coffee shop, two blocks south. Not one of those fancy Starbucks places—but it's open all night. They don't care how long you stay as long as you buy their coffee."

Elaina smiled. "Thanks."

The woman smiled back. "And now it's quittin' time."

seventeen

Sophie took a big bite of her toast smeared so heavily with grape jam and butter, a delicious gooey mess. The other guests had long ago eaten their breakfast and left, and now Sophie sat alone in the dining room.

She felt so safe here, with the morning sun pouring through the windows making the small dining room look like a movie set with its silver salt and pepper shakers and starched white linen. The B&B was perfect, and Sophie had to wonder how she'd gotten so lucky that Mrs. Drumlin had found her.

A guardian angel.

Sophie didn't believe in angels—but that was then.

There could be angels. Now, anything was possible.

Another bite, washed down with some orange juice, all pulpy, thick. The door opened and Mrs. Drumlin looked in.

"And how are you getting along, sweetie?"

Sophie smiled. Had anyone ever called her *sweetie*? It

felt warm, like the toast, and the sun in the room. *I could get used to life around here,* she thought.

"Just fine," Sophie said.

The woman walked over to Sophie's table, wiping her hands on her white apron. "More toast and eggs?"

"No, thank you. It's all . . . delicious."

Sophie had long ago dispatched the eggs, but she took her time working through the rack of toast.

Mrs. Drumlin walked closer and then put her hand on a chair.

"May I . . . join you?"

Sophie smiled. "Yes, please."

The woman pulled back the dark wooden chair and sat down.

"I was wondering . . . whether you'd like me to come with you . . . to make sure you find this house, the person you're looking for?"

Sophie wiped her mouth, clearing away a dribble of jelly that sat on her top lip.

"I mean, I have to go out anyway, and I can show you how to get there . . . you say it's on Aldon Road?"

Sophie nodded. She could do that—could have Mrs. Drumlin escort her. Though she had looked on the map in the B&B lobby and saw that the road was actually close, no more than ten minutes away, it would be nice to have company.

Someone to talk to.

But she remembered what her father had said.

If anything were to happen, don't tell anyone—except this one person.

Until then, she had to stay alone.

It was as if Sophie carried around some great weight, some amazing secret that grew heavier. But her journey was almost over. She had traveled from Kent to London, and now to this sunlit room in Scotland.

Dad would be proud.

And in that moment the reality again hit. A real . . . hit. Her stomach tightened, remembering the blood in her house . . . what it meant.

She was almost able to convince herself that it hadn't happened, that her father was somehow alive, only to have the sick truth emerge, again and again, painful, twisting, stronger, nastier.

"Is everything all right, dear?"

Sophie nodded. She forced a smile, though as soon as she did she knew that Mrs. Drumlin wouldn't be fooled by that. No, she was a woman who would know a pretend smile.

"I'm okay. It's just that I think I should go myself. Alone."

The woman nodded.

"I mean, Sophie, I am going out anyway."

Another little smile. "I know. But I should just . . . go," Sophie said. "I'd love to have you come with me." She looked around the sunny room. "And I love it here, so sunny and beautiful. You've been so nice to me."

The woman smiled back and played with a spoon, turning it in her hands.

"Thank you," Sophie said. "For everything. But I should get going."

The woman nodded, accepting the decision as final.

"Well, you can come back here anytime you want to . . . anytime at all. And if there's any help you need, you just ask. Fair enough? Take my phone number. Call me . . . if anything happens."

"I'll come back," Sophie said. "For sure."

A bigger smile, and Mrs. Drumlin stood up. "Now, how about some more toast?"

And Sophie nodded and gave Mrs. Drumlin a big grin, a genuine one this time. "I would love some."

• • •

Maddy stood at the rental car desk at the exact minute it was supposed to pop open for business . . . but no one was there. A full ten minutes later, a sleepy-eyed man with a nearly completely shaved skull appeared behind the counter. He ate a powdery donut and held a large coffee in a paper cup, and didn't even give Maddy a glance. No, too busy getting all his nutrients via a high-speed delivery system.

Another minute, and he still didn't look up.

"Hello, I've been waiting—"

He held up a hand as if he were Dr. Evil from *Austin Powers* . . . *tell it to the hand.* Another bite of the donut, and a shivery spray of white shot out, followed by a gulp of the coffee.

"Not ready yet," he said in a garbled voice.

Maddy waited a beat.

Her brother was missing, and Mr. Donut—who was already late—still wasn't ready.

"Excuse me, but your opening time was ten minutes ago, and I need—"

"Right. Opening. Well, that's the time they'd *like* me to open." He grinned. "And most mornings I get pretty close, luv!"

She wondered what it would be like to grab this over-grown slacker, pull him across the counter, and scream in his ears . . . something encouraging . . . like, *Get your bony butt in gear and get me a damn car!*

Instead she looked right at him.

"I need a car and I need it fast. And you've already wasted way too much of my time." She paused. Maddy had often used her smile, putting on a bit of a flirt to get what she wanted.

This guy wasn't going to get that treatment. She leaned close to the counter.

She lowered her voice. *I wonder,* she thought, *if most guys know what an advantage it is to have a deep voice . . .*

the easy authority it brings. Still, this guy should be able to read the intent in her voice.

"Now, you can start helping me—at your very best speed—or we are going to have a very big problem here."

He paused in mid–donut chew.

He didn't like the word *problem.*

What kind of problem? he probably wondered.

She could hear the creaky gears of his limited intellect and imagination processing that word. *Problem* could mean lots of things, everything from Maddy getting his testicles in a viselike grip, to supervisors and bosses raining down around him. Either way, the word—*problem*—was not something to be encouraged.

He took a moment to make his fatal decision.

"Okay, I'm on it. Don't worry. Let me, hold on . . . there, I'm logged in." He said the computer term as though he were about to do a championship pole vault. "Here. Okay, miss. Let's get you a car. And I imagine you want . . ." Now he grinned. "A really fast car, eh?"

"One with wheels will be fine . . ."

Sophie walked down a big avenue lined with shops—the sidewalk filled with people. Aldon Road should be just here—but she didn't see any roads until the next big intersection, and that was too far away.

But she turned and saw a narrow alley on her left, and then—on the side of a building—the small street's name, Aldon Road. There was no room for cars, but the cobblestone lane was on the map. It was something out of a Dickens story—she could imagine horse carts moving through the lane, vendors selling tin cups, other carts full of freshly caught fish sitting on beds of ice.

The lane had little cafés where, though it was a bit chilly, people sat outside, soaking up the fall sun.

She didn't need to dig out the piece of paper in her bag to find the address. She had that burned into her mind, as though the number ... 21a ... was somehow a secret combination that—unlocked—would answer all her questions.

And did she want all those questions answered?

There was no choice.

People looked at her, sipping their frothy coffees, dipping their croissants. *Do I look lost, confused? I have to lose that look,* she thought.

A breeze tickled the hairs on her neck, and she shivered, turning around to face the gust that seemed to follow her on the winding lane.

Number 21a ... she kept thinking. The house numbers were crazy. Number 37 was a small gift shop on her right, and across from it, the Snail and Fig restaurant—what a funny name—was 139. And 141 was a pub right next to it.

Where was 21a?

She looked left. There was 20.

She *couldn't* have missed 21a. She checked every building she walked past. She had to ask someone—but would that be a stupid thing to do?

But she had no choice, so she walked into the Snail and Fig, empty now, but with rows of shiny blond wood tables with little napkin tents. A young waitress—not much older than Sophie—was erecting the napkin tents on the tables and dishing out the cutlery to every place setting.

"Hello," Sophie said.

"Sorry, we're closed. We don't open for lunch until—"

"I—I'm not here to eat," she said. "I'm trying to find an address ..."

The girl went on putting the cutlery down.

"It's 21a, and your restaurant is 17, and there's a 39 but no—"

The waitress paused. "Oh, I bet I know where that is! There's a little path across the way. Looks like nothing but it leads to a small row of houses. You'll probably find it there."

"Thanks," Sophie said and she left the restaurant.

She found the alley, looking as if it might only lead to a small backyard, but instead it ran up into a tiny court-yard, complete with a birdbath in the center and a single bench painted bright red, all girdled by a row of purple flowers. And just behind the small plaza, a small row of four attached homes.

So cute, she thought,

Like . . . a hideaway.

A hideaway.

Which—she realized—of course it was. Hard to find, almost secret. She walked up the row and saw the num-bers, starting with 18a. The last house was 21a. She walked up the steps to the front door and rang the bell. The wait seemed to take forever as she stood in front of the mystery house on a road without a name.

Maybe—he would be gone. Maybe traveling. Maybe away.

So many possibilities—and then what would she do?

But just as that thought took root, and she was losing hope—

The door opened.

Maddy glanced at the road map. She wasn't used to nav-igating the twisting lanes and hedge-lined rows of rural Scotland. In fact, she felt more at home in the small vil-lages of Central America than the north country of the U.K.

And what countryside?

These weren't the lime-green, lush rolling hills that sur-rounded London.

She saw mountains ahead, real mountains. Not the Alps, to be sure, but she could imagine Paul wanting to climb here. Even the colors and the light seemed different.

Ancient colors, she thought. Everything looks and feels so old. A hedge, she knew, could in fact be a thousand years old, a primitive way of marking off one's personal plot of land.

But she spotted stray boulders squatting near the roadside, dotted with blackish lichen and dark green moss. Stone marbles pushed here and there by the glaciers.

This place didn't feel like the U.K. at all.

The hedges disappeared for a moment when she came to a hill, and she got a glimpse of the crazy quilt of roads ahead. Hitting a momentary straight patch, she scooped up the road atlas. Einbank was at the other end of the tangle of small roads ahead, a small village right at the foot of the mountains.

She thought of what might happen.

She liked to think of herself as an option person. Always know where the exit is, she believed . . . no matter what the situation . . . whether trekking through the rain forest to shoot wildlife, climbing to get a Himalayan sunset, or stuck at a party that was about to turn horribly, interminably boring. Know where the exit is.

Oh, and another rule, know when to call the cab.

And all that meant thinking ahead . . . planning.

Why was she meeting this colonel? And what did Paul have to do with a military base? A climbing problem she could understand. God, even a fall. But this was different. The colonel had said . . . disappearance.

People don't disappear.

She thought about Nick. She had to call him. In such a short time she had gotten good feelings about him. Smart, sexy, talented—what's wrong with this picture?

Easy to answer that one.

He's been married. Cheated. He had trouble with the dumb stick.

Just another man thinking with his dick.

But she didn't feel that way when she was with him.

And there were times when a dumb stick—attached to an intelligent and imaginative brain—could be quite useful.

She picked up her cell phone and, glancing back and forth between the road and the tiny Nokia screen, she found Nick's number among the last calls she had made. She hit the green call button.

Two rings, and Nick was there.

"Good morning, Maddy," he said, his phone telling him the ID of the caller.

"Nick, I can't meet you today."

"Can't?"

"No. Something happened to my brother, Paul . . . something with his climb in Scotland. In fact—I'm here now."

"You're kidding. You had to go up there?"

A sharp curve, and Maddy ignored the phone while she navigated the car down a too-narrow stretch.

"I have to meet someone who can tell me what the hell is going on. A colonel. It's all very strange. Look, I was really looking forward to seeing you again." *Steady,* she told herself. *Don't let him know how much you like him.* "And I'll call you as soon as I'm back."

"Want me to come up? Maybe help you. No reason you—"

Maddy's mouth popped open. A little Fiesta tore around the curve ahead, speeding straight toward her like a bullet. She dropped the phone and pulled her car to the right, into a ditch and flush to a pile of hedges. The Fiesta blithely went screaming by as if she were invisible.

Maddy recovered the phone from the floor of the car.

"—ddy, are you okay? What—"

"Hi. I just lost a round of country lane gladiator. I'm in a ditch now. Nothing terminal—though the rental car's paint job may be a mess. Look, thanks for offering to come up. If I need help, I'll call."

"Promise?"

She was moved by that. It felt good to have someone actually . . . care. It had been such a long time.

"Promise. I'll call you later. Let you know what's happening. Okay?"

"Okay, Maddy—don't you go . . . disappearing on me."

"I won't," she said. "And thanks."

She disconnected the call.

After a few more minutes the farmhouses gave way to a roadside pub, and then rows of houses as civilization slowly began to emerge again. A sign proclaimed "The Village of Einbank," though there was no indication of any village. But in the center of the cluster of small streets, she did see some businesses. A pub—The Speckled Dog—sat at the end of one street.

The colonel had said that there was a small café where they could meet.

Maddy wondered what passed as a café in this wilderness.

She turned down the road and took the first space she saw. She hopped out of the car, noting the scratches on the left side, thanks to the hard branches of the hedges. That . . . would cost her.

She walked down the street, past a tiny post office, then a general store that had—for some unknown reason—planted a three-foot-tall basket of yarn outside. Maybe a special sale?

The door to the second floor led to the Alcohol Counseling Center. "Closed for the Summer," a sign read. Interesting concept—seasonal counseling.

When she got to the end of the block, she was beginning to think that the rumors of a café in Einbank were greatly exaggerated.

Which is when she saw a place with the name . . . Case in Point . . . a wine bar and tea café.

Interesting combination, Maddy thought. Looking in through the beveled glass, she saw full tables, and a man in a uniform sitting toward the back.

She pushed open the door.

The bell rang. The man in the uniform looked up, then stood up.

And his face looked . . .

Scared.

eighteen

Ben Wilson sat outside the office of the head of MI6 as if he were coming to interview for a job.

Ridiculous, he thought. He was the PM's personal representative, a consultant on all sorts of high-tech issues, from genetically modified food to dealing with the ongoing mad cow hysteria.

When the call came from Director Frank McBain to come for an urgent meeting, Wilson had been tempted to say, no, you come to me if you have something urgent that requires the PM's involvement and interest.

And this god-awful building!

The new MI6 stood like an antiseptic eyesore on the Thames, so bold and garish for a building devoted to— of all things—spying.

What would Bond have thought . . . ?

Wilson looked at his watch, and at that moment, a young woman dressed smartly in a sheath skirt and a too-tight blouse came out. Well, he guessed all things Bond-like hadn't faded away. She was a modern-day Miss Moneypenny.

"Mr. McBain is ready to see you, Mr. Wilson."

Wilson smiled, stood up, and walked into the room, following her. The receptionist actually sat in an anteroom outside McBain's office, an inner sanctum for the inner sanctum.

She went to her desk and pushed a button. A subdued buzz, and the door popped open.

"Please, go on in," she said.

Wilson walked in expecting a richly appointed office. Instead, there was a large meeting room and a mammoth table; six people stood around the table, all eyes fixed on Wilson.

What is all this about? he wondered.

Who the hell are these people?

Wilson looked at a giant monitor suspended from the wall on the right. A satellite image sat on it, a bit of a mountain, woods, a structure.

"Mr. Wilson, thank you so much for coming in."

Wilson heard the door snap shut behind him.

Wilson smiled. But no one smiled back. In fact he'd have to say this was the grimmest-looking bunch of men he'd ever seen.

And he imagined . . . in the next few minutes he'd learn why.

The research vessel *Cristobal* rocked in the choppy Pacific. The captain, Paddy Stark, hurried down to the French oceanographer in charge of this mission, Father Louis Farrand.

The fact that Farrand was a priest didn't stop him from using language that any sailor would feel totally comfortable with.

Farrand leaned over the railing watching the efforts of

the giant winch now running three strands of heavy metal cable down to the bottom, miles below.

What Stark was about to tell Farrand . . . Farrand wouldn't want to hear.

"Doucement!" Farrand bellowed. "Easy. Damn it, can't you see the cables are shaking?"

"Father . . ."

Everyone called Farrand *Father*—even though he looked quite unlike any priest, with his blue jeans, over-sized plaid shirt, and three days' growth of beard. Farrand was old . . . well past seventy. Still, the captain would fear for the poor bastard that would cross the priest.

Farrand didn't even look back at him.

Stark stood beside him.

"Father, two things."

"Easy, damn it!" Farrand shouted, turning back to the winch operator. The ship was designed as an ocean re-search vessel, to lower submersibles or, as in this case, to recover one. Farrand had authorized the hydrothermal trip that had cost Ifremer, the French oceanographic institute, and Woods Hole one multimillion-dollar submersible.

He was pissed.

Then there was the mystery. What the hell had hap-pened to Bill Steiner that made the cables snap and left the small submersible at the bottom of the sea? Farrand took the disaster personally.

"Father, we have a problem . . ."

Farrand extended his arm over the railing as if directing the speed of the recovery.

"What is it?" Farrand said, without even looking at the captain.

"The sea—it's much too choppy to be doing this re-covery. We should wait—"

Farrand shook his head. "No. I want it up now, while we have it."

"There's something else. There's a message from the

Coast Guard saying that we must leave the area immediately."

At this Farrand turned and looked at Stark. His eyebrows arched—alarmed, annoyed, Stark couldn't tell.

"And what did you tell them?"

"I said I would tell you and—"

Farrand turned back to the sea. "The sooner we have the submersible back, the sooner we can leave."

With that, the conversation was over. The *Cristobal* hit a big swell, and Stark nearly went rolling into Farrand.

He headed back to the bridge, wondering why the Coast Guard wanted them to stop. And then . . . what would happen when they didn't?

Ben Wilson took a seat at the end of the table.

"I'm afraid I didn't know this was a conference, Mr. McBain."

McBain walked to the monitor. "I asked some people to join us . . . some within the department, some not."

McBain quickly introduced the people, most from MI6 but also two well-known science advisors dating from the Thatcher years. One was a well-known biochemist.

Wilson nodded. "Nice to meet you all. Perhaps we could proceed. Your call mentioned—"

McBain looked around the table as if he were hoping someone else would take the lead and begin talking. There was some shifting in their seats—but no one spoke up.

"Mr. Wilson, there is a division of MI6 that—for various reasons—has been kept secret from everyone except those with an absolute need to know about it."

Wilson laughed. "Doesn't that include the prime minister? I'm sure he'll be glad to hear about that—"

Rangeley, the biochemist, spoke. "All the PMs, I'm afraid—save two, the first one to learn about . . . this thing. And one other."

"And who might they be?"

A moment's hesitation. Rangeley looked around the table. "Chamberlain. And even he didn't learn about it straightaway. He told Churchill. And it was Churchill who decided how MI6—or the division within it—would handle the matter. That included keeping the various prime ministers in the dark unless—for some reason they had to know."

"Well, considering I don't even know what it is you are talking about, I guess I can't really applaud or decry old Winnie's decision."

The moment of attempted levity sat like a dark cloud in the room.

"His decision," McBain said, "was clearly colored by the experience of the war. Information could be dangerous. And England's security, as we had seen with the spy cases like Philby, was lax . . . and that's a charitable description."

"So Churchill made this, er, division secret—even before he became head of state?"

"Secret—only as long as it should be. Prime ministers come and go. The plan was for this division to have some constancy. You see, Mr. Wilson, everyone at this table has pledged to keep the secret and devote considerable time to the project. Gratis. They gained nothing, lost much."

Wilson started to get a queasy feeling in his stomach, the type of feeling he'd get when he discovered that something you thought really didn't have anything to do with you . . . did. And not only that . . . it's bad.

"And now—" Wilson chose his words carefully. "Something has changed with this secret that dates back, what, over sixty years?"

Rangeley answered. This was clearly his meeting. "Oh, yes. Something has changed. That's why you're here, why you will have to tell the PM all about this." Rangeley looked over at Wilson, making powerful direct eye contact for the first time. "Mr. Wilson, do you know the poem 'The Rime of the Ancient Mariner'?"

"Of course, every schoolboy—"

"But do you remember the last line, the very last one of the poem?"

Wilson hadn't expected to get grilled on his knowledge of poetry.

"I don't recall. Something about losing the big bird around his neck?"

No one laughed.

Rangeley shook his head, and smiled the grin of someone about to play a very big trump card.

" 'A sadder and a wiser man he rose the morrow morn' . . ."

Silence in the room for a moment.

Rangeley, who Wilson could now tell was the real leader of this gang of six, looked up at the MI6 director, McBain, and then right at Wilson.

"Prepare . . . to become wiser . . ."

nineteen

The sun warmed Elaina's cheek gently as she became aware it was morning—and then she remembered that she was on the bus.

When she finally forced her eyes open to face the light, she saw the ocean, shimmering blue with a foamy froth at the shore.

The Jersey shore, she thought. She looked at her watch . . . nine-ten a.m. on a glorious fall day. She sat up. Her lips were dry, her tongue felt scratchy. And she felt a few spots on her back that ached from her slumping sleep.

She looked around at the Greyhound bus. Only a few passengers, no beach crowd this—an old couple sitting up front, a teenager who looked like he had had too much Manhattan, a woman with a sleeping baby.

No sun and surf for this crowd today.

Where was she? The bus would stop in Lavallette, a small town that would be only blocks from Peter's beach house. The broad road that was probably packed on a hot

Saturday in summer was now deserted. The gift shops and the Tastee Freeze were all closed, as were the other shops selling unknown souvenir material.

All boarded up, sleeping.

Am I safe here? Elaina wondered.

She doubted anyone could have followed her from Bear Mountain, to Manhattan, to here. In fact—when she turned around—she saw that the road that stretched behind the bus was empty. A ghost road beside a ghost resort.

She looked out at the sea, churning away, tugging at the beach, uncaring if the weather was warm or cold.

She saw a sign on a shuttered shop: Point Pleasant Beach Bungalows.

Lavallette was close. Elaina rubbed at her mouth. She needed coffee, mouthwash.

How did my life get so strange? she thought. *How did it get so dangerous?*

A small sign with the quaint typography of a hundred years ago announced that she was "Entering the Beautiful Seaside Town of Lavallette."

Elaina stretched and waited in her seat as the bus slowed.

Captain Stark held the radio tight.

"Yes, I have told him that we need to leave. But he is a scientist—a priest—"

Stark shook his head. Did that explain anything?

The voice on the other end wasn't happy. He said something about how his hand was forced.

"Forced, what do you mean forced, Lieutenant?"

Stark looked out at the deck, the winch still struggling mightily to haul the damaged submersible out of the sea.

There was no answer from the radiophone.

"I said, what do you mean, forced?"

But the radio was dead; Coast Guard contact was gone.

This is great, Stark thought. *Couldn't be better. The*

Coast Guard is pissed—or worse—and I have a crazy priest who doesn't give a damn about them or the weather.

Stark stood on the bridge, a captain—at this point—in charge of absolutely nothing.

A big clock ticked noisily on the mantelpiece, and Sophie watched the small pendulum swing back and forth with every *tick, tock.*

The living room smelled musty, an old museum smell. But looking around at the mess of a living room, Sophie felt at home here with the piles of books, an open laptop, stacks of papers.

The man, Franklin Cosgrove, didn't look like a professor at all. He was younger than her dad, unshaven, his dark hair sticking up at strange angles. He had deep blue eyes that seemed to study Sophie even as he asked her if she wanted a cup of tea and some biscuits.

He seemed to Sophie like someone who had dropped out of school and didn't do much of anything.

This was the man, though . . . that her father had said she should trust.

"You've made a big trip," he said.

Sophie nodded.

"All on your own. Quite a trip."

Sophie nodded again.

Professor Cosgrove pulled a chair closer.

"Look, I know that something happened to your dad."

And when the man said that, Sophie realized something terrible. For a little while, she had stopped thinking about her dad. That—somehow—she had pushed away the thought, the memory—in order to do this.

Sophie felt her lip trembling.

"What you saw had to be terrible. Your dad was a good man." Cosgrove took a breath. "A good father, and—"

Sophie felt a stinging in her eye, and then one eye was

blurry, the mantelpiece suddenly out of focus. She took a breath and it seemed to hang suspended in her chest.

"But I want you to know . . . you're not alone. Not—"

But Sophie barely heard the words, as her eyes filled with tears, and she sobbed, loudly, shaking, even as she felt the man's spindly arms go around her shoulders.

McBain went to the monitor and pointed to the satellite image on the screen.

"Bear in mind, Mr. Wilson, that everything I'm about to tell you here must be treated with highest degree of confidence. Though I'm sure that will be obvious when I'm done."

"Er, it is briefing the PM that we are talking about."

Rangeley poured a glass of water. "Just get on with it, McBain."

Wilson looked at Rangeley. Yes, he was obviously in charge. So why wasn't he doing the briefing? Unless—

Unless there were even more secrets. Wilson filed that thought away. He'd look into Rangeley's background. Could be he would only hear part of the story. And having come this far, he wanted it all.

McBain pointed at the photo.

"This site, this building here—is located in the Glen Coe range, in northern Scotland. It's situated almost perfectly in a triangular valley made by these intersecting peaks here, and here—"

"He can see that, McBain. He's not an idiot."

The MI6 director paused for a moment. Was he used to taking such abuse?

"Yes. In short, this flat land is girded by mountains with only a single entrance, a natural gorge with a dirt road. You see that here—"

The image enlarged, and now Wilson saw a road, winding in between two rocky cliffs. Natural or not, it looked as though some massive ax head had cleaved the two ranges, creating a narrow path.

"A single entrance. A dirt road. A cold, isolated, inhospitable location. So why . . ."

The monitor image slid up, traveling the road, past a line of Jeeps, a few tanks, some cannons—what the hell was this?—past a chain-link fence, electric wires visibly running away from it . . . to . . . a house.

"—this."

And now Wilson leaned close in his seat.

A house . . .

At least, he guessed he could call it a house. The outer surface looked metallic, as if shiny titanium covered it. And though the layout resembled a Frank Lloyd Wright building, boxes intersecting boxes, there was total strangeness to the structure.

Wilson stroked his chin.

Strange, because he'd never seen anything like it before—in its shape, in its gleaming look. If it didn't look so wedded to the land, he could almost imagine it flying, a gleaming, clunky spaceship.

He shifted in his chair.

"Strange," he said.

"What's that?" McBain said.

"Such a strange building."

He saw McBain look at Rangeley. He guessed that might be an understatement.

McBain turned and looked at the structure. Wilson guessed that he had looked at it many times—yet his face still turned grim staring at it.

The image swelled, and now the monitor was tight on the house.

"The house was . . . um, built in nineteen thirty-seven. We have the name of the man who built it—but we very much doubt it's a real name, Martin Parks. There's no record of a Martin Parks"—he turned and looked at Wilson—"anywhere. And there was no central contractor. Some of the work seems to have been parceled out to various companies, a few from Scotland, others from elsewhere in the U.K., some from abroad. Not nearly enough to account for the size of the structure. No plans exist, no approval, and there is a disturbing thing about a few of the builders."

"They died."

It was Rangeley. Said almost with an ironic . . . laugh.

McBain nodded. "Died. Well, yes. During the construction, or shortly after. Lot of different ways. Fire, crashes, disappearances, domestic violence . . ."

A snort from Rangeley.

"I mean—whole families turned on each other. All that happened soon after construction. But then—"

Rangeley stood up. Wilson saw that the movement was hard for him, that his body had reached the point where the muscles and bones protested the slightest effort.

He walked to the monitor.

"Tip of the iceberg," he said, looking at the house. "The workers dying. Things became more interesting after that . . . Anyone who even went near the place . . . vanished. Classic haunted house stuff, hm?" He looked back at Wilson. "Only you know what, Mr. Wilson? When it's real, people don't leave it alone, they don't just 'stay away.' So more people came to explore the strange house, then the local police. And it was as if . . . as if—the fucking place ate them all alive!" The curse word, erupting from the old man's mouth, was an explosion in the room. "God help us, so many of them . . ."

The monitor changed, and now it flipped through a dizzying display of headshots: men, women, kids, some smiling, graduation pictures, shots that looked as though they were from an amusement park photo kiosk.

The dead, Wilson knew. Or the missing.

And was there any difference?

He was physically chilled now, as if the temperature had plummeted. But nothing had changed.

The slide show of faces stopped on one young man, curly brown hair, a big grin, a modern picture. He wore a soldier's uniform with an SAS cap.

"In stories," Rangeley went on, "the place . . . the bad, dangerous place, just sits there. Stupid really, as if such a place would be ignored. But in reality—" Rangeley turned and took a step toward Wilson. "In reality, Mr. Wilson, such a place would be . . . studied, probed, examined." He nodded, and Wilson thought: *The old bastard is enjoying this. He's got the weirdest story ever and he's enjoying telling it.*

"And when all the probes were done, the studies failed, the scientists disappeared, the toll . . . mounting . . ." Behind him the slide show began again, but now racing, more men and women, lab coats, the faces revealing nothing of their fate, flying by, racing. "When they were done, the army would go in, wouldn't it? The vaunted British army, always ready to face the unknown . . ." Rangeley smiled.

It was sick.

"Tom," McBain said. "I don't think we need—"

Rangeley raised a hand. "Show him."

McBain did nothing. But Rangeley stared right at him. "Show him, goddammit!"

And Wilson watched McBain turn back to the screen as . . . once more the slide show began, and the faces, all people in uniforms now, went flying by, face after face, shining eyes, cocky British smiles, all disappearing into the blitzkrieg of pixels of the monitor until it finally ended. Hundreds . . . maybe . . . thousands.

Wilson felt his stomach tighten, tighten then—uncontrollably—he gagged.

In that moment, he knew: Life, the world, everything had changed for him.

• • •

Nick sat at a glistening metal table of the sandwich and latte chain Pret A Manger, right on a bustling corner of Tottenham Court Road and Goodge Street. Opposing tidal waves of people swirled by, no one looking down at him while he sipped his coffee. The faces were unsmiling, just like New York faces, he thought. Gray, sullen faces that— Nick knew—could explode into crazed joy come Friday.

But for now they were locked into *how the hell do I get through this* mode.

Nick didn't look at the newspaper folded beside his cup and saucer. There had been another train crash, and in a country where so many people depended on trains.

A pretty blonde sat down at one small café table over, making brief eye contact with Nick.

He smiled but quickly looked away.

Because . . . something bothered him. Something about Maddy.

He appreciated her call from Scotland breaking their date. He felt, in these few short days, that they had connected. Maybe she didn't trust him—after all, his record was bad. But there was playfulness in her teasing him. He felt a strong attraction—and he was convinced she did too.

Then she got a call about her brother's climbing accident.

Only she didn't describe it as a climbing accident.

No, something had happened to him, something not a fall.

He took a sip of his coffee.

And it was that something that had her going up there, overnight.

Maybe . . . maybe she had forgotten that he was a journalist. But when that alarm went off in his head, it did so for a good reason.

Instinct, he thought. Some gift. Or maybe a curse. Depends on how you look at it.

Instinct—that Maddy might be dealing with something more. But what?

Another sip.

He had no pressing deadlines. And—he admitted—he cared about her. She wasn't someone who would ask for help even if she needed it. And if she needed help, he wanted to be there.

He had her cell phone number, which he guessed worked in the hinterlands of Scotland. But maybe some old-fashioned snooping might be in order. So he formulated a little plan.

He looked over at the blonde, sipping her latte out of a paper cup of joe to go.

Sweet.

He had a plan and—getting up from the shiny metal table—if nothing else his plan would keep him out of trouble.

Elaina knocked on the door of Beach House 7 on Surf Lane.

The little village of beach houses was arrayed in a miniversion of city blocks; but instead of Sixth Avenue and Broadway, there were Oceanview and Beach lanes, Barnegat Road and Squid Avenue. Most of the small summer houses were closed up for winter, though she did spot one with a laundry line in the back with sheets flapping in the bright sunlight.

She knocked again. *Peter should be here*, she thought, checking her watch. He said he'd be here by the morning, that he needed to gather some material to make sure he really understood what she had. She looked up and down Surf Lane. Totally deserted.

She pictured what this would be like in summer: gaggles of kids traipsing up and down in bare feet, stepping lightly on the superheated tarmac of the narrow road, racing to the shady spots, heading lemminglike to the dunes and roaring surf.

She looked into a cottage window, covered on the inside with a sheer curtain. All quiet. She opened her purse and found an old ATM receipt. A bit more digging produced a Rolling Writer. She pulled the cap off with her teeth and wrote a note.

"I'm here . . . going up to the beach. Find me!"

She wedged the thin receipt into a window lintel. The small breeze made the paper flap in some irregular rhythm—but it looked firmly lodged.

The same wind blew her hair. She could use some coffee, maybe even a real breakfast, some deadly eggs and bacon . . . home fires. But she wanted to stay close for when Peter came.

It would be so good to have someone to share this with, to finally not be alone.

She started walking up the lane to the main dune that separated the beach homes from the beach and the ravages of storm season. A weird slat fence held together with wire cut a path through the dune, a sandy valley allowing access to the surf.

Coming through the other side, Elaina saw the ocean. Large waves broke on the shore—three-, four-foot waves rearing up and then crashing down and shooting a jet of water rocketing up the shore.

She walked to the water, her feet digging into the sand, the progress awkward. She reached down and did what she remembered doing when she was a kid.

She slipped off her shoes.

Somehow her bare feet made better progress, the arch and the toes somehow able to get better traction in the sand.

Or maybe it only felt better.

Now the wind blew steadily off the water, and the sound of the waves became a rhythmic beat growing louder with each step. To her left, a few herring gulls walked around pecking at the sand as the water receded. Probably digging for small sand crabs near the surface.

To her right . . .

She saw someone sitting right near the surf.

An old woman, sitting legs out, wearing a faded flower dress, her gray stringy hair blown by the wind but not moving, more like a stagnant piece of coral.

Strange, Elaina thought.

As she came closer, she looked over at the woman—and the woman looked back.

"Good morning," Elaina said.

For a moment the woman didn't respond. So strange, she thought. Then she realized what made the scene even more odd. The woman looked a bit like Bette Davis from *Whatever Happened to Baby Jane?*—the hair, the dress, God, even the beach. That film always stuck in her mind. Elaina always joked . . . *I hope I don't turn out that way.*

She turned back to the sea, to the steadily churning surf.

"You know—"

It was the woman, her voice raised high enough to be heard over the wind and the sea . . .

"They're *out* there. That's why I come down here. Because maybe . . . maybe if someone watches, they won't come out. Come out for you."

Elaina turned back to the woman.

O-kay, she thought. *I don't need this.*

"Didn't you hear me?" the woman said. And now Elaina—polite girl that she was—couldn't ignore the crazy old person.

"I'm sorry?" she said, looking again at the woman sitting with her heels facing the giant Atlantic.

"I've seen them before. Right here. In my dreams. Have for years. Call them dreams, though that's not what they are, not really. Seen them, down there, waiting, planning, plotting. And this—"

Elaina now watched the woman, as she made a big pointing gesture at the sea, accusing it, challenging it.

"—is not the only place they are. But maybe—maybe if I watch, they won't sneak in."

Elaina looked at the woman's bare legs—and even from a distance she could see how they were pockmarked with bumps and bruises . . . maybe bites. Sand fleas could be so nasty. The woman's wrinkled face was ruddy, leather brown. Did she come here every day, a psychotic version of the Coast Guard?

Elaina didn't know what to say, but now the woman had turned back to look at her.

"We don't want them sneaking in. Not now." She shook her head, the gray hair shaking. "God no, we . . . we . . ." The words faltered, then the woman lowered her chin and she . . . was sobbing.

Elaina looked out at the sea.

But then this pathetic sound bubbled from the woman's lowered head, a steady, sad sobbing, and Elaina wondered if she should do something.

When a hand touched her shoulder.

She spun around.

The sun sat square over the head of the man next to her—and she blinked.

"Elaina, I got your note. Sorry . . ."

Peter. Finally.

"Thank you. I mean. I've been so scared. And this woman—"

She turned to the beach.

Elaina expected the crazy old woman to be gone. She was still there, but the weeping was over. She had her head raised up, looking straight out at the sea.

The woman made some more jabbing, pointy gestures at the sea, this time without saying anything.

"A new friend?" Peter asked, grinning.

"No. Just some . . . woman. Lonely." She lowered her voice. "Crazy. Not what I needed this morning."

"Let's go back to the beach house," Peter said. "And we'll see exactly what you have."

Elaina nodded, and followed Peter back to the first big dune and the cut-through.

twenty

Colonel Harris greeted Maddy at the door of what appeared was the unlikely combination of tea room, café, and wine bistro. She looked around the odd place and saw someone in tartan shorts and kneesocks holding up a glass of red wine, and tilting it left and right.

"Maddy Hodge—I'm Colonel Tim Harris."

Maddy shook the man's hand. His face was lined, cracked from years of weathering. A career military man, someone who could be forty, fifty, sixty . . . hard to say. His handshake was strong, reassuring, confident.

She looked again at the man in the shorts.

"He's the owner. The new Beaujolais is in. Cause for excitement, I imagine."

"And some early imbibing, it would seem."

Harris led Maddy to a small table near the back. "Yes, he's been urging a glass on me since I've come in. So far, I've resisted." He looked around. "Just about the only quiet place in this rather odd town."

"Odd?"

The colonel smiled. "You'll see . . . if you walk around. Everything's just a bit . . . off."

They sat down, and in a minute, the owner, whose hair looked an unnaturally dark black, sat beside them.

"Now, General, now you must try some of the Beaujolais nouveau. This is an occasion."

Colonel Harris looked at Maddy. "Would you?"

Maddy laughed. "I usually wait till lunch. At the earliest."

"It's a pity. If you change your minds, I will be right over there." The man pointed to his little Beaujolais station.

He's in his cups, Maddy thought. The whole room was an *Alice in Wonderland* tea party, with the proprietor as Mad Hatter.

"Just tea for me," Harris said, "and Ms. Hodge?"

"Maddy. Tea would be lovely."

"And some toast?"

Maddy nodded.

"Sure," Harris said, and the man went away, whistling something familiar. It took a second for Maddy to recognize a shrill version of the *Ride of the Walküre* by Wagner.

So . . . weird, she thought.

And unreal—it made her apprehensive about what she was about to learn about Paul.

"My brother . . . you know, I've always supported his climbing. Clears his system. He can get so angry."

"Yes. And there's some beautiful climbing around here. Especially this time of year. Tough climbs too. Most climbers, well . . . they know that there's a big stretch of the Glen Coe that's off limits here."

"Off limits?"

The owner brought over a small teapot and two cups, accompanied by a tiny creamer and a bowl of sugar cubes.

No calorie-free pink or blue stuff in sight, and Maddy guessed that asking wasn't the thing to do.

The colonel put a strainer up to the tea spout and filled the two cups.

"Yes, a good portion of the range, especially where this valley leads into the range, has been closed for—" He hesitated, and looked up at Maddy. And there was that look again. Something in his eyes that seemed to show him fighting to stay steady. It seemed absurd.

Everything here—despite the wackiness—was so peaceful.

She wanted Harris to cut to the chase. What had happened to her brother? But she sensed that eventually she'd know it all. And she'd know more if she forced herself to be patient. Harris seemed to be watching her, gauging her reactions.

"Closed, since the late thirties. The locals barely pay attention. They just know they can't go too far up certain roads before they hit a checkpoint, then a gate, then a massive fence, surrounding the whole area."

Fence? Maddy wondered what could be so secret that it was fenced off.

Harris took a sip of his tea.

"Electrified. Twenty feet tall." He smiled. Letting the simple words paint the picture. "A major fence."

"Why?" she finally asked. "Why such security?"

Harris looked at her while he blew on the too-hot tea. "I know you have been to some incredible places, taken some amazing photographs and film and video in Sarajevo, Kosovo, and in the mountains, and well—I just know that you don't blink at fences and barriers . . . and weapons."

Maddy squinted. "What—do you have a file on me?"

"Yes."

The doorbell sounded. Someone else came into the shop, another victim for the Sargasso Sea of the mad

Beaujolais man. Maddy looked over and saw a startled-looking white-haired lady actually take a glass.

"Looks like he found his mark . . ." Harris said. "The man's dangerous."

"So you know my work. But what about Paul?"

Harris looked left and right, making sure that no one was within earshot.

"We know this: He came here to climb . . . two days ago. He didn't stay in town, just drove up with a friend—"

"Simon Anders," Maddy said.

"Yes. And they entered the range on the western side of this part of the range. Nasty cliffs. Nearly unclimbable. Or so we thought."

"My brother is good. He likes a challenge."

Harris nodded and hesitated as if absorbing that information, building a mental profile on her brother.

"He tackled a western cliff—wait, let me show you . . ." He dug out a small folded map that showed the area in amazing detail. Maddy saw the white-gray line of mountains, the town of Einbank, and the narrow valley that ran between the cleft that separated one chain of mountains from another.

Her eyes were drawn to the flat yellow of open space . . . surrounded by the mountains.

She read the words. *U.K. Military Reservation: Off Limits.*

Harris pointed to a mountain toward the western end of the map.

"They climbed here—as I said, a tough, damn near impossible climb. But they did it, and got to this area here . . . and then they kept on going. It would have made sense for them to turn back, get to the ground while it was still light. But I imagine they were feeling—what's the word—'pumped.' So they kept on going."

"That's not like my brother. Once he's made his target, he likes to get down, think, plan. Not a spontaneous guy."

"This day he was—"

"And here we are," Mr. Beaujolais said. "Toast with butter and jam, and—anything else? I can whip up an amazing omelet!"

The man's eyes glistened with his early morning buzz. Wouldn't want him breathing too near a stove, Maddy thought.

"Not for me."

"We're fine," Harris said.

The man's smile evaporated, and he turned back to his other customers.

"He's going to be loads of fun at lunchtime," Harris said.

"Lots." Maddy looked back at the map. "So you're saying . . . he hit his target turnaround point . . . and then kept on going?"

"Yes. Maybe they saw a pinnacle and they thought it might be the topmost point in the area. Anyway, they continued a small, gentle trek until they got to where this other large outcrop joins this severe cliff. Another damned hard climb. Don't know how they had the energy. But they climbed it . . . to about . . . here."

Maddy looked at where the colonel's finger pointed, near a mountain that encircled the flat area—the off-limits army site.

She looked up.

"And then . . . ?"

Harris took a breath. "You know, now that you've seen the map, maybe we should leave . . . walk around . . . while I tell you the rest. This place is getting full—and it looks like a few people are taking the proprietor up on his offer to sample the nouveau."

"I have to tell you, after talking to you, Colonel, I'm beginning to think I might need a glass before long."

"Both of us might, Maddy. Both of us."

And he turned to the owner and made a signal that he wanted the check.

Stark watched the hoist labor to pull up the submersible. Every roll of the *Cristobal* made the job that much harder, as the tension eased up with one roll of the ship only to immediately snap back.

We should just drop it, Stark thought.

Come back some other day—or let Farrand travel around the world and raise money for a new mini-sub.

He looked up at the darkening sky. He wanted out of here. Then he looked down at the radio, now turned off. More warnings from the Coast Guard kept coming—and if he wasn't going to obey them, he had to shut the annoying radio off.

After all, what authority did the Coast Guard have here? They were in international waters.

Out on the rolling deck Farrand—an old man who moved as fast as any of the crew—dashed from one side of the hoist to the other, checking the cable. From the looks of the spool of cable, there could be no more than another twenty, thirty meters there.

In only a few minutes, they'd all see what happened to Dr. Bill and the submersible.

Probably a pressure leak, Stark thought.

Things could happen when you have the equivalent of a few tons bearing down on a centimeter of metal.

Bad fucking things happen.

Stark dug out Rizla papers, removed two sheets, and poured some tobacco into the paper before rolling it into a compact tube and sealing it with a lick.

Rolling cigarettes was his way of cutting back on his smoking.

He thought it worked—but did those rolled cigarettes ever taste sweet!

He lit it and then opened the bridge door out to the stairs.

Might as well be there when the prize came aboard.

He walked down the metal stairs, the clank of the metal echoing. A stiff breeze blew from the east, and the sea had turned into all chop now, little frothy whitecaps everywhere.

All eyes were riveted to the spot on the sea where the hoist cable disappeared.

Another big roll, and Stark shot his hand out to steady himself.

The starboard railing tipped nearly low enough to touch the water.

Stark reached the deck. He heard a sound. An engine, not his ship's engine, but that was quickly lost in the shouts of everyone on deck. Then—breaking through the whitecaps, a small, smooth surface.

There were cheers.

One for the home team. The mini-sub recovered.

The hoist engine groaned. Perhaps that's what he heard, he thought. Groaning, to finally bring the submersible out of the sea. Groaning, struggling.

Now more of the submersible's dome popped out, looking perfectly fine. Nothing wrong with it at all.

But Stark had seen the video. Something very wrong happened down there. And the whole point was to—

The hoist moved slowly now, moving a heavy object from the buoyant sea to the full weight of gravity. Higher and—

He saw the first signs of destruction. He leaned over the railing, slowly, puffing on his needle-thin cigarette.

As the sub emerged, Stark saw the top of the passenger dome slope inward as though it had been in a car crash. Higher, the smashed slope continued, and now a large ugly gash—a foot in diameter. Jagged, rough. Like a bullet wound, or as if some shell had ripped into it.

What the hell happened down there? Stark wondered.

Higher—and now the gash widened, and bits of the inside cabin could be seen, water racing out as the hoist lifted the submersible up. The inside cabin, exposed by the opening of the now meter wide gash.

No sign of Bill Steiner.

Nothing.

No corpse.

No blood.

No compressed and imploded body. Did scavengers get in and pick it clean. Yes, that's—

Higher, and the submersible was nearly totally out, the undercarriage exposed . . . the twin sledlike rails used to give it a perch on the bottom.

When someone shouted.

And pointed.

To that undercarriage. Something was there. Not a body. It looked like a cable, except thick, a foot, maybe more. More shouts, a giddy excitement, confusion. Stark felt his cigarette burn his lips and he tossed it over the side.

And as he tossed it, the wind gusted from the other direction, and he became aware of that sound again, audible over the excited shouts, the pointing, the yelling. Stark looked this way and that . . .

The hoist groaned.

Groaning—as if it were too heavy. As if . . . there were something heavier than the submersible attached. Stark turned around.

Dots in the sky.

No, not dots. Against the gray clouds, the dots moved. They weren't planes. They were *helicopters*, the noise resolving itself every few seconds as the wind blew toward the ship, becoming more clear.

Helicopters. Coming here. Four of them. Right for this ship. Why is that, what could they possibly want—

A loud noise erupted from the railing.

And when Stark looked back there, everyone had backed up, away from the submersible suspended over the east. Back against the wall of the upper deck.

Everyone, that is, except Farrand. The old priest stood there at the railing, only meters from the undercarriage, from the long, thick cables that trailed from the carriage, into the sea.

The cable *moved*. The end at the front of the undercarriage seemed to tip up, sensing the air, and now Stark saw what everyone else already knew.

It was alive. Twenty feet long, and that was just the part they could see, not knowing how far it extended into the ocean below.

But the color . . . a creamy white ribbon with red, a deep, full red even under the dull light of this sick gray sky.

"Drop it," he whispered.

But he knew that he had said the words too quietly. Less an order than a wish.

He looked back. Like the madness from *Apocalypse Now,* the choppers were close, bearing down on the ship. And Stark—in that quick glimpse—could see that they weren't any little weather helicopters. They were massive, military helicopters.

Stark didn't understand. But he knew what was going to happen.

He ran to the railing and turned to the hoist operator whose face—like everyone's—was riveted on the show unfolding above the choppy surf.

"Drop it!" he screamed, gesturing to the man at the controls.

A quick look back, and now the cable, some living thing dragged from the bottom—coiling, twisting, tasting the air for the first time—started stretching toward the ship.

"Farrand," Stark screamed. "Get the hell back."

But the old scientist didn't move. Did he know what he was seeing, what this could be?

"Farrand!"

In that instant, the swirling living tube moved with blazing speed right for Farrand. Stark heard a tremendous *whoosh* of air—and then Farrand was raised above the deck, screaming. That was the true horror—he screamed as though the thing had grabbed his insides, sucked onto him, and fed off the old man's screams.

It wasn't real.

Yet nothing had ever seemed *so* real.

Back to the hoist operator, signaling him . . . *let it go, let it—*

But the copters were there, and when Stark looked back he saw the guns, and under them, rockets, and he wasn't surprised . . . when in unison, all those rockets fired.

He had a second to consider their smoky path to the ship.

Less than that to think that what they were doing . . . was right.

And then, no sound, no explosion to be aware of, just the intense flash of blistering, sunlike heat, and it was over.

twenty-one

Sophie didn't know how long she had sat in this book-filled room, sobbing, feeling like she was a little girl again who had fallen off her bike, and this nice old man had found her, helped her.

He didn't say anything. Just a strong arm, a weathered hand on her shoulder.

She watched the dust motes float through the air, a steady stream falling onto the man's oxblood carpet.

Finally she took a breath and straightened up.

"Get you something, Sophie?"

She shook her head. But then realized that it was a reflex. She was hungry. Very hungry.

"Yes," she said. "Maybe something now."

"I have some fresh tuna salad . . . on some nice seven-grain bread . . ." Professor Cosgrove smiled. "Or maybe it's eight-grain. I better check."

"That would be great."

Sophie watched him walk into the small kitchen and open the fridge . . . and she decided to follow him.

"I like your place," she said. "It feels homey . . . like my house. All my dad's books."

Cosgrove looked over his glasses.

"We love our books, your father and I."

She took a step farther into the cramped kitchen. The clutter of the books in the living room was easily matched by the chaos here. A small table overflowed with boxes of cereal, condiments, an open jar of jelly with a knife still stuck in it. The sink was full to the brim with dishes.

Was now the time? she wondered. Tell him now . . . why she had come here, what she had to tell him?

"Professor," she started hesitantly as he spread the creamy tuna salad mixture on the bread.

He looked over again, his busy eyebrows rising above his glasses, making him look comical.

"I want to tell you why I came here."

Cosgrove nodded. "I knew you'd get around to that . . . because"—another glance—"you know I will have to call the police soon . . . let them know where you are. It's something . . . we must do."

"I know. But first . . . I needed to get here in case . . . they tried to stop me."

Cosgrove put the other slice of bread on top and then took the knife and cut her sandwich in half. He turned and handed her the plate.

"A bit of apple juice maybe?"

She nodded. The sandwich looked delicious.

He poured her a tall glass of juice.

"And we can eat out there—I've given up on my kitchen, as you can see."

She smiled. He seemed so patient, waiting to hear what she was going to tell him. Then she had another thought. Patient . . . or scared?

Out in the living room she sat down with the sandwich plate balanced on her knees. She grabbed one sandwich half and took a bite. And it was the best thing she had ever tasted. She took another big bite before she grabbed the juice glass and washed it down.

"Easy there . . . you're demolishing that poor sandwich."

She grinned. "I guess I was hungry."

Cosgrove watched her.

Another bite. Another swallow.

And then she continued. "My dad didn't tell me everything; he said . . . I didn't need to know it all."

"All. You mean—"

"About the house. What he said they call a house."

"A house . . ." Cosgrove made a shallow laugh. "Yes, they didn't know what else to call it."

"He told me how it was surrounded. Nobody went in there anymore, not after everyone—"

"Vanished? He told you about that?"

"Only that they tried to find out what was inside. He didn't tell me what they saw . . . if anything. But that you and he worked with the other scientists, with the army."

"If you can call it working. After they lost so many, after they had seen the pictures—"

Cosgrove looked up. Sophie didn't know there were pictures. Her dad hadn't said anything about that. Pictures. Showing the inside. Showing what had happened. But how did they get them out?

"He said you left . . . before him?"

"Yes. I knew that what they were doing—if anything— was provoking . . . it. If you can use that kind of word. God knows what might happen to them despite all their cannons, and their giant fence. It would all mean nothing. I felt I could do more, maybe learn more . . . here."

He looked at Sophie again.

"I'm scaring you?"

She shook her head. Have to be brave, she thought. Her dad had told her that old Franklin D. Roosevelt was right. The only thing she had to fear . . . was fear itself.

Be afraid . . . of being afraid.

But now she knew all too well that it wasn't true.

"No. I won't be scared. I know a lot, Professor. My father told me. And that's part of the reason I'm here. But . . . anyway . . . you left. And he kept working. He tried to tell the army about everything you and he worked on."

"The quantum biology theory? The basic principles of quantum physics applied to life?"

"Yes. I mean, I didn't really understand it all. Except I understood this . . . that everything we see . . . feel . . . taste . . ." She looked down at her scrumptious sandwich. ". . . is only one of many real worlds."

Cosgrove laughed. "He spoke to you about the multiverse? To you? Amazing man."

She could see that he wished he hadn't laughed.

"Sorry, Sophie . . . just such extraordinarily complex stuff to tell someone so young."

"Yes. I didn't understand it all. It made me dizzy. But he worked alone after you left—"

"We spoke on the phone a lot."

"Yes. And he would have stayed. Until something happened."

She stopped. Now she took another bite. The bread was turning a bit soggy from the salad, still tasty, but not as sweetly fresh as only moments ago.

"Something happened?"

She nodded. "We lived right in the valley. Only minutes away. And then—I was only five or six . . . and I started having the dreams. I dreamt of places at first, empty, big . . . brightly colored as if drawn in a comic book. And then—I was in these places. I could feel things, the air . . . more like water, and smells. In those . . . dreams, I smelled things I never smelled before. I told my dad—he listened—but he was always so busy. And night after night, I'd be there, first one place, lush and green and dark, with the smell of living things everywhere, then someplace completely different."

Cosgrove leaned forward. "Go on."

"But I didn't see anything living there. It was as if . . . the picture wasn't complete. Then. One night. I was there. And *they* were there."

"They?"

Sophie looked away.

Be afraid of . . . being afraid.

"I—I can't describe them. I could draw them maybe. But . . . in one place, filled with strange-colored rocks and boulders, I'd see heads of things rise up, emerging from the stone itself . . ."

"Yes."

"Looking at me. Standing there. Seeing me. Feeling the air swirl. The smell growing stronger. Until that place was filled with them."

Sophie took a breath. She looked away. This was so hard. Impossible. So crazy to tell someone . . .

"They made a noise. Like screaming, howling. In my dream . . . I thought my ears would burst. And then some-how—I knew that it wasn't screaming, It was laughter. They looked at me, laughing. I felt . . . contaminated."

"In your nightmare?"

Sophie looked back at Cosgrove—right at him, at his bloodshot eyes, his leathery face. And she shook her head.

"No. Contaminated. Because I knew—when I woke up—I *knew* . . . it wasn't a dream." Another breath.

The dust motes continued to fall.

"It was . . . real."

Wilson walked briskly across the Westminster Bridge, the file folder from McBain and MI6 held tightly under his arm.

He wondered, what would happen if he lost the folder and it fell into some hands of some tabloid?

The most amazingly lurid cover stories, he imagined.

Lurid . . . unbelievable.

Still, he'd never felt so nervous in his life.

McBain, with the old scientist's blessing, had given him printouts of a timeline—the history of the place in Einbank from 1937 till now. And just to add a little power to the dry facts, some photos. Some a few decades old, others taken only five years ago.

And lastly, the reports from MI6's contacts around the world . . . "a small, select group of what we call 'monitors,' " McBain had said.

All together, it painted a frightening picture.

He hadn't booked any time with the prime minister, but he knew he could, on the fly, get five minutes. And if he got five minutes, then he'd use it to make the PM cancel the rest of his damn schedule for the day. For the week.

This folder would help.

And then what?

That was easy to imagine. The PM would look up, brow furrowed in a thoughtful mode as opposed to the smiling media darling he usually presented to the world— and he'd ask Wilson two questions . . . "Ben, how the hell has this existed—and I didn't know?"

No good answer for that one, except that the information was so . . . insane, that it couldn't be trusted to an elected official who could be booted out at the whim of the people.

The second question—that was even harder.

"And what the hell do we do now?"

Good one. What the hell do we do *now*? Wilson shifted the folder in his hands. He let the black cabs stream by. He needed this walk to think about everything.

What the hell do we do now?

Leave the country? Hide?

A grim joke.

But then again, maybe not a joke.

McBain had said that the scientists in Einbank were theorizing. Making up scenarios.

It all sounded so ineffectual.

Wilson came to the steps that led from the bridge's footpath down to the street and the Underground, teeming with people, so many people unaware that the rules for life on this planet might have changed.

Might? No . . . *have.*

Unaware—but for how long?

Elaina rubbed her shoulders as the wind rattled the beach house's single-pane windows. In winter, it would probably be just as cold outside as it was in. Now the rattling seemed more of a threat, the angry sound of fall slipping into dreary ocean winter, gray skies, gray sea, and the loneliness of a beach town when there were no more hot sunny days to have.

The crumpled pages she had carried all the way from the Hudson Valley seemed almost pathetic, spread out on the tabletop.

Peter rubbed his eyes, looked at one sheet, then another, back and forth. She almost hoped that when he was done he would look at her, laugh, and say, "Do you know what this is . . . do you really want to know?"

Then, still laughing, he would tell her the simple error she had made, the wild assumption. Although she worked for GenTech as a research scientist, her understanding of the human genome was imperfect at best, her background in gene replacement not so hot. She could have thought that she saw something in these pages and pages, in the endless lines of code—that simply wasn't there.

But then—why did they try to stop me?

Why did they kill the motel owner? If this wasn't all . . . something. And she knew that her faint hope was a total fantasy.

The windows rattled again. Wasn't there any heat in

this little cottage? Doubtful. Why put heat in when no one would ever be here when it was cold? She walked to the window and looked out.

And someone stood just outside the cottage.

The old woman from the beach. Standing there, her mouth agape, just staring at the cottage. Elaina quickly looked away and pulled the sheer curtain closed. But when she looked back, she could still make out the shape of the woman out there, on the street.

"Holy shit," Peter said.

He looked over at Elaina.

"What's wrong?" he said, obviously seeing her distress.

"That crazy woman. From the beach. She's standing outside."

Peter nodded.

"You found something?"

And now she took in Peter's face. Had it turned ashen or was it just the diffuse light in the cottage?

"How did you get these? And, God, how did you get them out?"

"Nobody saw me print them. I think the whole file was supposed to be protected from my level—somehow, it wasn't. My password worked. I was looking for something else . . . and . . ."

She stopped.

"Peter, what is it?"

She had her own . . . theories, ideas. Fantastic plots, equal mixes of mad eugenics and a genetically modified food program spun out of control.

Except she knew that this code wasn't for any food she knew.

As for eugenics . . . must be mighty strange eugenics.

Peter looked down at the pages again, almost as if he couldn't believe what he was seeing.

Then he gathered them up into a pile. Elaina thought that maybe he would hand the pile to her.

Please.

But Peter held them.

He tapped the pile with the index finger of his left hand. "Here's what I think they could be." He looked up at Elaina. "What I think you saw in them too. It's a nearly full code."

"That's what I thought."

He nodded. "For a goddamned organism."

She nodded again. That much she had picked up. But what? There were whole strings there that seemed completely out of place, others missing, and the size of it . . .

The human genome wasn't an amazingly long or complex code, no more than any other mammal—and some mammals were much larger.

This was easily twice the size of the human code.

"It's the code for some . . . organism, an animal of some kind. And it has markers and indicators for traits"—he shook his head—"Jesus, I can't even imagine what they could be."

Then: "I don't even want to imagine."

Elaina took a breath.

She had rocked Peter's world. Not an easy thing to do. "Where is it from?"

Peter laughed. He stood up. "Where is it from? Where the hell is this from? Elaina, I don't have the slightest clue where it's from. I can only tell you this. Whatever this . . . thing is, wherever the hell it came from, it isn't here." He repeated it as if to bring the point home even more strongly to himself, to hammer it down. "It isn't the hell from here."

More rattles. She had to get out of here. This place, supposed to be safe, a place to hide, had her spooked. *Where next?* she thought.

"Then where, Peter? Where is it from?"

Now he walked up to her. He looked as though he might stick the sheaf of wrinkled pages in her hands and say, *Here, take these—and pretend you never saw me.*

Instead, he walked up close. "There are only two . . . explanations. One, it's something cooked up in some amazing genetic experiment. Amazing, because the scope of this would mean years of work, decades, building something that never existed." He looked Elaina in the eye. "But why?"

He paused.

"Or?"

"Or . . . or the code was taken from a . . . a specimen."

"A specimen? But you just said that this organism— whatever it is—couldn't be from here."

Peter nodded. "Precisely." He laughed. The absurdity of it was amazing.

Elaina didn't know what to ask next.

There was silence.

Then—

They both heard the sharp rapping at the door, shocking, startling, terrifying.

twenty-two

Nick walked up the steps to Maddy's apartment.

The door was locked, but he had worked his way through enough locked doors to know how to jiggle this one open.

He took out a straight paper clip and—bypassing the lock—he used the thin wire to push back the locked latch. Depending on the mechanism, it could be hard to move . . . but in this case, he could push it back just enough.

Then he moved into the room quickly, as though merely another tenant in the Primrose Hill building. It was getting late—the streetlights had already started glowing to life—but he was ahead of the rush home.

He went up the stairs, smelling of countless meals cooked in the flats: beef and fish, cabbage with asparagus, a spicy tomato sauce now turned sticky sweet in the closed confines of the hallway.

He walked up steadily. Maddy lived on what the Brits called the first floor . . . but there were two flights above her; he didn't want to run into someone coming down, looking at him curiously, asking questions . . .

He got to her door.

Another look at the lock. This was even easier. A simple credit card inserted in the crack, and the door should pop open. This was no single woman's apartment in Manhattan.

He dug out his trusty CitiBank ATM card, slid it along the crack, and the door popped open, swung open in that almost archetypal way doors swing open in horror movies. Too easily, beckoning you in to have your head cut off.

He stepped in and oh-so-quietly shut the door behind him.

What am I doing? he wondered. *Why do I have the right to spy on her?*

Which is when he knew that somehow Maddy had gotten to him. He didn't want her to vanish—and something told him that her sudden disappearance meant that she was playing with something dangerous.

He walked around her apartment.

He saw her small living room, a book on an end table. He picked it up. *Kitchen Confidential.* Right, Nick had heard about the book. The chef who spilled all the nasty beans about what goes on in the kitchens of the world.

She was halfway done.

Strange thought then . . . being halfway through a book, a lifeline to her world here. Something to come back to.

He moved to the small kitchen area. A wineglass half filled with wine. Some dishes in the sink.

Where did you go, Maddy?

He turned back to the living room . . . and on to the most private room . . . her bedroom.

The comforter was a twisted mess. She had obviously bolted without getting her bed straight. Or maybe she was the kind of girl who didn't ever make her bed.

My kind of girl, he thought.

He saw a pad by the bedside phone. He walked over to it. Half the pages gone.

But he could see the faint impression of what she had written.

He picked up the pencil from the bedside table, put it on edge . . . and began rubbing.

A few letters appeared, and Nick smiled. *It really works.* But the letters . . . *Ei . . . ank . . .* Then some numbers . . . *785.255* . . . Frustratingly incomplete. Nice trick— if it had worked.

"What are you doing?"

The voice made him spin around in the room, already shadowy gray in the twilight.

Nick stood there for a minute. Was it Maddy?

No, too short. The voice thinner, younger.

"Er—"

Nice answer, he thought. Nerves of steel.

"I'm going to call the police."

She was a shadow—all outline, dimly backlit.

"No," he said. "Listen." He took a step. A mistake.

"Don't. Don't take another step. One push—and the police are here in three minutes."

Nick doubted they could respond that fast—even in London.

"I'm Nick Fowles. I'm . . . a friend of Maddy's. And she took off to help her brother. And I'm worried."

"So you broke in here?"

"Guess you could say that. And is that what you did?"

Now the woman took a step closer.

"American?"

"Yes."

Not only was he a clumsy breaking-and-entering guy; he was, God, American to boot.

"So did you break in too?"

"No. I have a key. I stay here sometimes." She paused

a moment. "And I'm worried too—but not just about Maddy."

Nick nodded.

"We should talk."

She could help him, maybe at least put his fears to rest that Maddy wasn't in the middle of some uprising somewhere shooting impossible pics for *Time* or *Newsweek*.

"Okay. There's a coffee shop down the street."

"Lead the way," Nick said. And he brought the pad with him as he followed her to the door, the stairs, and the dark street below.

Maddy walked alongside Colonel Harris, holding her leather jacket tight against her.

Winter was already knocking at the door in Scotland. And Harris was right, the town was odd. They passed a walk-in psychotherapy store—it actually said *store*. She pointed it out to Harris.

"See," he said. "I told you so. Strange village."

And then, just down the block, what looked like some kind of general store. But it had the strangest assortment of items in the windows, toys that had a thick patina of dust that would be about as inviting to a child's eyes as a rock. Outside the store, right on the sidewalk, they walked past a barrel filled with random kitchen utensils.

"For that impulse buy . . ." Maddy said.

Harris laughed.

She could tell he was waiting until they had walked somewhere that people weren't passing every few minutes. They turned a corner and faced a small church, easily five hundred years old and nearly all steeple. A tiny graveyard sat right out in front—another odd thing.

Harris pointed at a bench off to the side of the small graveyard.

"How about—if you're not too chilled—over there?"

"Fine."

Harris opened the latch of the metal gate and the gate emitted the most prolonged, exaggerated squeak.

They sat down facing a gravestone where all the words had turned into a soft-focus blur, unreadable save for the date . . . 1794.

"Colonel, I need to know what happened to my brother."

He nodded. "I know. I'm trying to explain. What we know, what we think . . ." He looked at her, and for the first time Maddy felt a funny feeling in her stomach. She had been prepared for almost anything. Paul in the hospital with broken bones all over the place, or even worse, her brother dead. You don't have a brother who climbs and not deal with that, live with that fear.

To some extent, she could accept that.

But everything that Harris said, now sitting here, and the look he gave her, seemed even scarier.

"It's something else, isn't it?" she said.

"What do you mean?"

"This . . . is not just about my brother, or Simon, or a climbing accident."

Harris looked away. "God, no. Would that it were. If your brother had been hurt—or worse—up there, we wouldn't have to talk. It is, as you say, something else."

"And Paul is all right?"

Harris looked back at her, held the look. "Maddy, we don't have a clue."

She shook her head. "How could that be? Either he's—"

Another squeak, and the big oaken door to the little church opened, and a youngish clergyman looked out, tufts of hair pointing in strange angles as if he had rolled out of bed with his cassock on, opening up the door, ready for business.

To open the church *store*.

He nodded to Maddy and Harris, and then quickly disappeared into the dark church.

When Maddy looked back, the colonel had a photo in his hand.

Maddy took it. It was a picture of something like a high-tech museum, lots of curves, covered with polished metal. But the building was clearly surrounded by mountains. If it was some modern museum, it had landed in a pretty desolate spot.

"What . . . is this?"

But Harris handed her another photograph. The same place, only now from farther back, so Maddy could see the fence that surrounded it, dozens of soldiers, and, to the side, what looked like artillery and—God—even a SAM setup.

All pointed right at the "house."

She flipped photos back to look at the building, and now—having seen the previous picture—the very shape . . . the Möbius-like curves, the jutting points . . . looked dangerous, sinister.

She looked back to the colonel.

"This place. It's inside the military reservation?"

Harris nodded.

"And are you telling me . . . Paul is in there?"

"He might be." He took a breath. "No. We think he is."

She stared down at the picture again.

"I don't understand. Why . . . why . . . don't you go get him then?"

Harris looked away. Maddy held the photographs tightly, a connection to her brother.

"Colonel?"

Harris looked back. "Well, we're hoping that that's something you might help with. Only one more theory, Maddy. We had the idea when you called . . . because of your background, your connection to your brother. I was going to ask you. To come with me. To go in there . . . and find your brother."

Now Maddy felt flush, angry. "I don't understand. Can't you just go in there yourselves, all those damn soldiers, and—"

Harris shook his head, exasperated. "No, we can't. We *can't* just go in there. And even if you do go in, with a connection to your brother, you may not find him . . . you may not come out, and—"

A giant raven, the size of a fat tabby cat, landed only feet away from them, perhaps expecting a crumb of bread, something.

Harris took the photos from her.

"I need to tell you everything we know. Then you will decide if you'll go in and—"

"I'll do it."

"You'd best hear what—"

She stood up. "I said . . . I'll do it. And I see no point in waiting."

Harris looked up at her, and Maddy could see that he wasn't surprised by her determination. Of course they had a file on her. They probably expected her to respond like this.

He stood up.

"Let's go. You need to hear everything anyway, and there's equipment we have for you."

And Harris led the way out of the pocket graveyard, out to the narrow street, with Maddy wondering . . . where the hell was she going?

Sophie sat in the oversized chair very quietly while she watched Professor Cosgrove walk to the window, pull aside the curtain, taking his time.

He was thinking, just like her dad used to.

Walking around wrestling with a problem.

Until he turned around.

"I think," he said slowly, "that you're not telling me something."

Sophie chewed at her lower lip then stopped.

"I told you everything. What I saw, and—"

"No." Cosgrove took a step forward. "I think"—he took a deep breath—"you're not telling me something because it frightens you."

Sophie shook her head. "But I told you about what I've seen, and my dad knew that you'd understand, that you could tell."

Cosgrove knelt down next to Sophie. And when he got that close, she could see that he was scared. His eyes looked . . . glassy.

"There's another reason your dad had you come to me."

And Sophie wanted to leave.

Because when Cosgrove asked that question, she knew there was an answer. That—in fact—the answer was the real reason she came to Scotland, had to come to Scotland.

And finally Sophie nodded. For a moment she thought she would cry—so much had built up. But she couldn't . . . because she knew it was only beginning, that this was only the start for her.

"Yes," she said. "There is something else." It sounded as if she was trying to make it a small thing, nothing important. But then she knew it was vital.

"Go on," Cosgrove said.

"He knew—my father knew that I went there. In my dreams." Now she took a breath. "That they could reach out, and *make* me see. They could use me. That's why . . . that's why he wanted me away. And for a while the dreams stopped. Things got better. But then they started again, and got worse. I felt—"

She looked away to the window. This room had felt safe. But not anymore. There was no "safe." She had to accept that, live with that.

"What did you feel, Sophie?"

"It felt like they had found me. That they could use me again. My dad wanted to move again, but I didn't want to leave my school, and he was involved in his work—"

Now she cried. There was no way to stop it. The guilt that maybe she was the reason her dad was killed. A single gasp, and the tears erupted; she heaved and then felt Cosgrove put his arm around her. And just when she thought that the tears might end, more bubbled up, and more . . . until, eventually, somehow, she felt drained.

The drying tears left salty patches on her cheeks.

"Can I get you something?" Cosgrove asked. "More biscuits, tea?"

Sophie nodded. Hot tea and sugary biscuits. And maybe the world wouldn't seem like such a scary place.

She sat quietly while Cosgrove got the kettle whistling again and opened the tin of cookies. Neither spoke, knowing that the only thing to do was carry on the conversation.

In minutes he was out with a fresh pot of tea and a tray of cookies.

"Have a biscuit," he said, smiling.

And she did. One disappeared. Then she knew she had to start again.

"My dad knew . . . that I could see this other place, see them. And he told me once that if they ever got out— those are the words he used . . . *got out*—that I might have to help."

"Help?"

Sophie nodded. She sniffed the air through her still-runny nose. "Yes. Help. Tell people what I see, what's happening, so maybe—maybe they could be stopped."

"Maybe?"

Sophie nodded. "Because he told me he wasn't sure— he didn't want to scare me—but he said he wasn't sure . . . they could be stopped."

"And you think you can help?"

Sophie nodded again. She felt so small in this room of dust motes and books.

"Yes. That's what Dad said. He gave me this."

She zipped open her backpack and handed Cosgrove the thumb drive.

"What's this?"

"All my dad's work. His notes. All his theories and experiments. He said it would help."

Professor Cosgrove nodded and then, sitting across from her, leaned forward. "And can you, Sophie? Will you help?"

She knew this question was coming.

The answer wasn't easy to say.

But she had prepared herself for it. She knew she had to say it.

"Yes," she said. And the shadowy room seemed to eat the single word with a long silence.

twenty-three

Wilson walked out of Ten Downing Street feeling as if he were on LSD—not that he had ever tried the famed drug of the sixties. The pavement, the street, the cars and buses—all seemed surreal. He had this thought: *None of these people know the truth.* About their world—and just how things work.

He walked down the steps, past the guards who didn't look at him at all, and turned left. What did he want . . . a tube station, a cab, or maybe to walk?

Did it matter? The PM had completely lost it, tearing into Wilson, and threatening everyone connected with the project. But then Wilson handed him the file with the big U—for *Unidentified.*

He had sat there as Prime Minister Edward Hogue, the Labour Party's latest and brightest, flipped through the decades of reports, the obituaries, the photos. Wilson offered the video—but Hogue had declined.

Good thing. It wasn't long—but it was the stuff of

nightmares. The photographs, some taken from the video, were compelling enough.

Still Hogue had wasted no time; he called Einbank and let the "team," as Wilson called them, know that he was in the loop. Then he spoke to others who knew of the compound, a retired physicist in the Bahamas whose voice—on the speaker—shook with more than age.

Maybe he had figured that living on Abaco he was far enough away.

Then Hogue tore into Wilson. In the middle of the PM's tirade, about the irresponsibility, the absolute reck-lessness of not informing the goddamned head of the gov-ernment, Wilson flashed on something.

Hogue was scared. This had just been dumped in his lap. And not only the Einbank compound but also the reports from around the world, all the grisly, bizarre sto-ries that were creating the strangest newspaper headlines. The team monitored those incidents, "incursions" as they called them, Wilson explained.

But for every one they knew of, there had to be others they didn't know a thing about.

Wilson came to a busy corner and stood there, indeci-sive.

People passed him, bumping into him, annoyed that he took up some valuable, navigable chunk of the sidewalk.

And when the tirade was over and Wilson's ears thor-oughly pinned, ringing from the dressing down, Wilson had finally told the PM the plan.

It sounded so pathetic.

He told him about the photographer . . . and her brother. And what it meant. An opportunity, perhaps, to get some information.

Because, Wilson had told the prime minister, merely waiting and watching and containing all looked as if they weren't working anymore.

And after that, Hogue sat down, quiet. Letting it all sink in.

On the street, still feeling dizzy, Wilson waited for the light to turn green again, and then moved with the sea of people moving across the street. The tide of people streaming toward the tube bumped against him while Wilson didn't have a clue what he was doing.

A young woman cut in front of him and Wilson inadvertently bumped into her.

She looked back and scowled.

"Sorry," he whispered.

Then a man to his right jostled him. Wilson felt drunk, wobbling among the crowd.

He looked to his right.

Someone was looking at him as they walked together. A man with a black fedora, a dark trench coat. The man smiled at him. *Do I know him?* Wilson wondered. *Is this someone I know?* He smiled back.

Which is when he felt something. Just a bit of pressure on his right side, below the rib cage. Pressure, then a sharp feeling—like a stray pin from a new shirt somehow *jabbing* in.

Wilson kept walking—even with the pain—but his hand went down to that spot, to his side, where he felt something.

The smooth feel of a leather glove.

Moving away. Moving away from him.

The feeling—the tiny pinprick—bloomed. Like pain spreading over a surface, the pressure turned into pain and spread throughout his right side.

Instinctively he looked to his right—but the man had picked up his pace, and was now well past Wilson, then lost to the crowd—

Because now Wilson doubled up as the pain splashed against his chest, waves of pain breaking over him. Then down to his midsection, up to his throat. He started to say the word *help,* staring down at the pebbly mosaic of the pavement.

He only gasped, trying to suck in the air. But that was like trying to suck in stone, to drink molten metal.

Someone from behind bumped into him and Wilson went flying to his knees; his thighs were on fire. His arms broke his fall, but then they wobbled as the pain covered his face, a chemical fire burning, tearing through him.

My folder, he thought. *U.* The reports. He looked left and right as he tumbled forward, his head in agony, blotting out all other pain as it smacked hard against the sidewalk with a hard *thwack.*

A fence of legs formed around him. He tasted blood, salty, so much of it.

The feeling, the intense agony, captured his brain.

He'd scream, howl out a protest at the torture. But all he could do was lie there, his mouth bubbling as the blood gushed out.

Until—not anywhere soon enough, death not coming anywhere soon enough, a final brilliant spike of pain flashed, and he felt nothing more.

Nick waved at the waiter and, with a shrug, the waiter came over to the small table.

"What would you like?" he asked Emma.

"A latte," she said.

"Make it two," Nick said.

"Two lattes," the waiter said, confirming the very complex order.

Emma waited until the waiter had retreated.

"My brother Simon adored Paul," Emma said. "They climbed together every chance they got, but there was always this competition between them. To show who was the best climber. I worried about him."

"Two trained climbers—they should have been okay."

"But then—he didn't call."

The waiter appeared.

"Two lattes," he repeated.

Must like the sound of the word, Nick thought.

"And we could use some sugar . . ." Nick looked at Emma. "Or maybe some pink stuff?"

The not-so-happy waiter shrugged and sailed off again.

"There's a guy who loves his job." Nick said.

Emma smiled.

"So, your brother would normally call?"

"Yes. He knows how I worry. So he'd call just as soon as he got to a place where he could use a mobile phone. But yesterday he didn't . . . so I came to Maddy's. She lets me stay whenever I'm in the city."

"And Maddy was gone?"

"Yes. And she seemed to vanish so fast. I was afraid that something had happened to the two of them and Maddy knew."

"And you called her?"

"I think—she's ignoring calls."

"I know. I tried a call after I spoke to her, but could only leave a message."

Nick took a sip of the coffee. Scalding. McDonald's hot. *I can sue,* Nick thought. *Where's the damn "really hot coffee" warning?*

"So what are you thinking?"

"Here—" Emma dug out a small folded map. "Here's where they went to climb, in the Glen Coe range near Einbank. Right here. That's where they were. Maddy probably went up there, to where they had been climbing. Maybe we could go there—"

Nick nodded. Precisely what he was thinking. He didn't know the two climbers. But he knew and cared about Maddy. Novel feeling, that, especially for someone who he hadn't slept with.

Perhaps—that was it. She was, so far, unattainable.

"You're right. Going up there is a good idea. But not

for the two of us. If Maddy's keeping something secret, best I go alone." Emma seemed disappointed. Nick smiled. "Don't worry. I do this stuff all the time. I'm not, er, Nick Danger . . . but to get my stories I have to do some risky, strange stuff."

"I'd like to come with you."

"I'll call. Every few hours. I promise. I'll find Maddy in Einbank, find Paul and your brother if I can. You know it's probably nothing. But we'll both feel better knowing for sure."

A cloud suddenly blotted out the sun, and all the light faded from the chrome tables of the café.

Nick took out his wallet and dug out a five-pound note.

"And I better start now. Keep your phone charged. And don't worry."

Funny expression, that, Nick thought. *Don't worry.*

As if words could make someone's concern, their fear somehow smaller. Words are powerful . . . but not that powerful.

He put the money down.

"We'll all go for some beers and laugh about this when I come back. Wait and see."

"Shit," Elaina said. "That woman—she's still out there."

Peter looked up from the printout. "Want me to tell her to go peddle her poison apples elsewhere?"

"No—it's just that she's giving me the creeps."

Peter put a finger on the printout. "And this is giving me the creeps."

"What the hell is it, Peter?"

"It's either the most amazing practical joke, or, or— it's almost ridiculous to say it."

"Go on."

"If someone didn't just make this up, it's off the chart. Unknown. There's hardly any sequence in the whole

damn genome that matches anything from the earth pool.
I don't want to use the A-word, but—"

"A-word?"

"*Alien*. The whole sequence is so fucking alien, I mean,
you saw that yourself."

"Yes, I thought that maybe GenTech was doing experiments on living specimens, something strange, experi-
mental, possibly dangerous."

"Strange is right. And you stole it."

"I don't know a lot, but even I could tell that they were
doing something that no one had authorized them to do—
whether with a living specimen or something of their own
making."

"Your dad would be proud."

Elaina smiled. "Maybe. Dad was always one for standing up, no matter who or where."

Peter laughed. "But I don't think they are experiments,
Elaina."

"Then what?"

There was a rap at the window. The old woman was
there, her eyes bulging out, froglike. Her face a saggy fold
of wrinkles.

"Christ," Elaina said.

"That's it—I'm getting that crone to move onto the
next stop in her homeless tour."

Peter went to the door and opened it.

"Hey, you. Spooky lady. Get over here . . ."

Elaina went to the door and stood behind Peter. She
saw the woman walk over slowly.

"Now, listen—do I have to call the shore patrol and
have you put in beach jail—?"

The old woman's hand shot out and latched on to Peter's wrist.

"I told you that they are here . . . just"—she looked
back to the sea—"out there. Why are you still here?"

Elaina chewed her lip. The old woman's words should mean nothing.

But the stuffy beach house felt bone cold.

Peter snapped his wrist free.

He laughed. "They're out there? Who, the aquatic boogeymen? I think—"

The woman looked past Peter and right at Elaina. When she spoke, dried spittle made gummy threads between her lips.

"*She* knows. She knows what I'm talking about."

Elaina shook her head, thinking, *Go away, old woman, take all your spooky jabber and just—*

"Leave now," the woman said. And her eyes turned filmy, sad, almost loving. "Leave, before they come. Hide. They know about you. They will come—and take you."

"Okay, that's it. I gave you fair warning, so now it's police time. Probably be the first good night's sleep . . ."

Elaina came closer to the woman. "No. Wait a second." Her eyes locked with the old woman's eyes.

She got a chill. There was something in those eyes. She looked at the woman . . . nearly her height.

And then at the face, so old, wrinkled. Eighty . . . ninety.

She looked at her clothes. The swirling blotches of colors on a dress that was ten, twenty years old.

Elaina almost whispered the question.

"What . . . is your name?"

Peter looked back at her. "Why would you want to know that—"

Elaina tapped his arm.

The woman looked so sad now. And she did the most unexpected thing. She reached out—and touched Elaina's cheek.

"So . . . beautiful," the old woman said. "What a terrible . . . thing time is."

Elaina felt her eyes filling, the thought . . . crazy, resisting it, impossible, yet— The woman's fingers on her cheek felt like her mother's. Like her mother's. But a little different. If anything, more knowing.

"Who are you?" Elaina said, fighting back the hysteria. And now the old woman smiled.

"I think . . . ," she said slowly, "you know who I am. Why I'm here. And why . . . you must leave. Take"—the woman looked into the room at the stack of printouts—"that, and do what you have to do. You're so close."

Peter took a step forward. "Look, what 'that' is is of absolutely no concern to you."

The woman looked at Peter. And then Peter stopped.

Elaina wondered—did he just flash on the same bizarre thought, with the woman standing so close next to her?

Elaina nodded. The woman's fingers pulled away from her cheek.

"There is still time."

Elaina looked down from the woman's face to her neck, the simple silver necklace. Just like the one Elaina's mother had—and then had given to her. To always wear for protection.

Elaina dared not touch the one around her own neck.

Couldn't . . . bear that.

"Don't go. Not yet."

The woman shook her head. "You have to hurry." She looked back to the beach. "And I do too . . ."

Elaina nodded. The wind blew through the window, and the printout went flying across the room. Elaina and Peter turned back to them, grabbing the pages as they flew.

And when she looked back to the doorway, the woman was gone.

As Elaina knew she would be.

And then, helping Peter, unable to really explain what just happened, she started crying.

twenty-four

Maddy looked out the window as the car swerved through the deep forest, climbing higher to the base of the mountains.

Some clouds rolled in and that, and the fog, cut off any view of the mountains in front of them. But Maddy knew they were ahead.

And though it was only fall, as soon as the military Jeep started the climb, the temperature dropped. Now, a steady stream of heat shot out at her from the vents. The side windows grew foggy, and Maddy wiped the windows to look out at the thick—and now gloomy—forest.

Harris had asked her to wait until he told her more at the reservation.

Maddy repressed the urge to ask questions, but every now and then one popped out—like some thought bubble escaping.

"You mentioned . . . equipment?"

Harris nodded. He drove so slowly. The road was slick with a thin coating of rain. She saw him chew his lower lip. Anxiety over the drive or what was to come?

Or both.

"Yes. There are things we'd like you to carry in. Mini A/V receivers. We'll be able to see everything you see, and you can also plant some mini-cams as you move through the place."

Maddy laughed. "How long do you expect me to be in there?"

Harris looked at her. A quick glance. The type of look a father might give a child as if gauging . . . *How much can I really tell her?*

"Not sure. We—" Harris hesitated. And Maddy knew from years of being around public figures that Harris was conflicted—wanting to hold something back and yet wanting to tell.

"Go on," she said. "I can handle it."

Harris nodded. "We're not sure how long you'll be in there. Looking . . . exploring. More to the point"—he took a breath here—"we're not sure that time works the same way. Once you're inside."

Maddy nodded. *Nothing out of the normal there, now is there?* Another forced laugh. "Does it run backward?"

For a second she had the horrifying thought that her question—a joke—was a reasonable one . . . at least in the universe that Harris was taking her to.

"Damned if we know. Just that things are—well, all the evidence we have shows that things are very different once you walk through the door."

Maddy had another question she had to ask. But she felt she had best digest that answer first.

"As for the other equipment, you will be able to talk to us. We're also giving you some long-life tungsten lamps. Very bright, last for hours—"

"We are talking hours . . . ?"

Harris nodded. "We will want you inside for only a few minutes at first."

She had to ask the other question.

"Colonel, what the hell is this place?"

He took a sharp, near hairpin curve.

"Damned if we know, Maddy. But—" He paused as the Jeep looped around, his two hands locked on the steering wheel. "We know this, though. We have to find out. Now."

She looked right at him.

"Because—?"

"Can we wait? Please. Till we're inside?"

She took a breath. "Sure."

And as the road grew narrower, the grade steeper, Maddy thought of London, her cozy flat in Primrose Hill, and—amazingly—Nick. A bit of reality she could use now.

The stage-effect fog seemed to roll down from the mountains like a gray puffy blanket, eager to cover all.

Elaina sipped a cocoa at the Toms River bus terminal.

She could have waited for the bus by the side of the road in Point Pleasant. But one look at how deserted it was there, and she asked Peter take her to the terminal.

"You could come back with me," he had said.

But Elaina was still chilled by what she had seen. The warning. It made no sense, but then nothing had ever since she left GenTech.

Hide, the woman had said. *Before they find you.*

At least here she felt strangely protected, amid the bright fluorescent lights, the odd travelers shuffling about.

She knew where she would go. Her brother worked in Washington with FEMA . . . the government flood people. She wouldn't stay with him, not if people were looking for her. No, but he had friends, and she was sure that he could find someone that would put her up.

Until—

When?

When would it be safe?

Or would it *ever* be safe?

Another sip of the dark rich chocolate.

She had to think what to do. There were people she knew who worked with the government's genetic think tank. As soon as Peter knew more, she could call them, let them know what GenTech was up to.

Let them figure out what was going on—

Let them stop it. But first she had to get the information—checked by Peter—to them.

Every paranoid Hollywood movie flashed before her. What if *they* are working with GenTech? What if the government wanted her dead because she broke ranks? That's the way it would be in a film.

In a film, she reminded herself. In real life, things weren't so pat, so crazy.

Besides, she had no other choice.

She looked over at the bank of pay phones. She wanted them all to be completely vacant so that no one would overhear her.

One old man stood at a phone nodding, talking . . . been there for about ten minutes. Looked like he might be a permanent fixture.

Come on, she thought. *Say goodbye. Good. Bye.*

She looked to her left. A New Jersey state trooper walked in, surveying the evening crowd. Though reassuring, in a film even the tall, lean trooper could be working with the other side.

The other side. Now, who the hell is the other side? Who wanted me dead, stopped? More important, who's playing with genetic code that . . . that didn't come from here? And why?

Dad, she thought—*if ever I needed you with me it's now.*

She looked down at her two hands holding the cocoa. A slight tremor.

Good, she thought. *Physical fucking evidence that I'm scared.*

Finally, the old man hung up the phone. But he didn't move from the bank of phones. Instead he lingered there and dug out a fat cigar, and a lighter, and lit it.

Still, he didn't move.

Then Elaina saw the trooper walk over to the man. The old man looked up from his cloud of puffy blue smoke. The trooper pointed at a nearby No Smoking sign, then to another, and another.

The old man shook his head, and tossed his cigar to the ground. Now the trooper shook his head.

Littering, the old man was littering!

And I can't get to the damn phones!

She watched the old man bend over and pick up the cigar and storm away, watched by a smiling trooper.

Who then noticed Elaina.

No, she thought. *Don't come over and ask me how I'm doing . . . what I'm doing.*

The trooper hesitated for a minute, just looking. Elaina took another sip of cocoa and then looked away, staring anywhere but at the trooper.

She looked back and he was gone.

The phone banks were empty. She stood up and walked to them. She saw a young mother with a toddler approach the phones, then turn away, as if changing her mind.

I wonder, Elaina thought, *what kind of stories you find in bus stations?* People running, people hiding, people going home, meeting people, losing people.

She got to the phone, picked up the handset, and quickly punched in her brother's number and then her calling card information.

"Hello?"

"David, it's Elaina—"

"Whoa, what's the occasion, E? I haven't heard from you since—"

Elaina looked around. The trooper had reappeared, walking by the newsstand, then the donut and coffee shop, on a trajectory to be next to her in a minute or two.

"Listen, David, I have a problem. I need a place to stay—"

"Sure, I mean if you're coming to Washington, I've got—"

"No. They—I mean, I need someplace not connected to you. Some friend."

"Elaina, what's wrong?"

"Can't tell you now. Please. My bus gets into Washington at one a.m. Can you have a friend—a good friend—meet me?"

"Bus? One a.m.? What the hell is this?"

The trooper turned away from the coffee shop and saw Elaina. Now he walked right toward her.

What am I scared of? she thought. *He's a trooper, a cop, serve and protect . . . and—*

"Just tell me you'll have someone there—and you'll have someplace for me to stay."

A slight pause at the other end before he answered.

"You got it. I can wait for the story . . ."

Elaina hung up. She recovered her cocoa from the little ledge of the pay phone. She took a sip as she walked away.

Cold cocoa. Too sweet now, sweet, sticky.

And she had to wonder . . . Did she just put her brother in danger?

Peter hit the brakes and parked—illegally—in front of his apartment on West Thirteenth Street.

Fuck the ticket, he thought.

More than anything he wanted to start playing with the numbers Elaina had given him, the lines of code that he knew couldn't be anything he had seen before, or anyone else working on any known genome.

What the hell is it?

He bolted up the stairs rather than wait for the ancient elevator to sleepily make its way to the ground floor.

He opened his apartment and his fat calico cat, Oscar, meowed a hungry greeting.

"Hey babe, sorry . . . hang loose. Food coming soon."

Oscar was way too fat anyway, he knew. A fat tabby, a city cat that needed to be on a diet.

He ran into his living room, where his desk threatened to take over the whole room. He turned on his computer and waited for Windows to kick in with its reassuring and soothing chimes.

And while it booted, he went out to the small kitchen and dumped some crunchies into Oscar's bowl.

"Here you go, fattie. Don't say I didn't warn you."

Then back, in time to see his cable modem activity light blink. The program was automatically getting his mail, sweeping for viruses.

He'd check his mail later. He sat down and opened up his pirated version of the GenTech D-Code program. With D-Code, he could play with any known genome, altering strands, and seeing what the possible implications would be for reproduction. The Brits had used this type of program to create Dolly, the cloned sheep, and GenTech used it to show how genetically altered fruits and vegetables were—*almost*—identical to the original, save for the tiny detail that no bugs would go near them and they didn't bruise.

Otherwise, just peachy!

Dig in!

Small changes for better produce was the pitch.

Peter didn't buy it. He knew that a full genome was links, more like dominoes. You couldn't simply yank one bit of strand, rewrite it, and then expect it would have no other implications.

But in these heady days of gene fever, that's exactly the claim that was made.

The program was loaded.

Peter spread out the copies of the sheets that Elaina gave him.

Oscar meowed again.

Peter didn't look at his cat. "Can't be hungry, baby . . . so what is it . . . need a bit of love? Sorry . . . I got work to do."

And with lightning fingers that his mom, the piano teacher, said were wasted in science, he started hitting the keys.

twenty-five

The trees seemed to close in, the pines arching over the narrow road to prevent any life-giving sun from hitting the pavement, wasted.

Not that Maddy thought that they got much sun up here. The higher they went, the more this area of the Glen Coe range seemed perpetually shrouded in fog.

Romantic? Perhaps—but she found it more disconcerting, and she saw Harris slow the Land Rover to a crawl.

"Visibility is horrible up here," he said. "And it's a constant problem. Some days . . . you can't see five feet in front of you."

"And Paul climbed in weather like this?"

Harris shook his head. "No. He was on the western face, just this side of the fog. On a good day—and it was a good day—he'd have blue sky, sun, clear climbing weather."

Maddy wondered whether she should ask the next question. The big one.

Did she want to hear the answer?

"So . . . what happened to them?"

Harris didn't answer. He took a breath.

"Can you wait? We're almost there. I'd like to explain it all. As much as we can. There are some scientific people who can help."

"You make it sound as though Paul turned into some kind of lab experiment."

Harris said nothing.

Enough questions, thought Maddy.

For now.

The fog bank did indeed thicken, and Harris slowed even more.

If another car took one of these curves fast, Maddy couldn't see how they could avoid a collision. But then Harris beeped the horn, a little warning as he took a hairpin.

It's like we're driving blind.

The side window fogged up, and Maddy put a hand against it and felt the cold. Already it was winter up here.

Harris looked over. "Cold? It can slip below freezing—even now. The climate . . . is strange . . ."

Strange, forbidden, dangerous. Maddy had spent enough time around the base of Everest and K2 and even Mt. McKinley to know that weather, at altitude, was a living thing. Heartless, cruel, suddenly a nasty killer. High-altitude weather could rise up and show humans that nature, in the end, called the shots.

And though she had done a lot of climbing getting her best pictures, it never became routine.

"Hold on," Harris said. And in a moment the Land Rover started bouncing up and down.

"What's that?"

"Security measure. We're close to the gate. These would slow any terrorist attacker, and infrared cameras would pick up the vehicle for an ID."

"Even in this pea soup?"

"Oh, yes. The heat-sensitive cameras can pick up the shape, model, the year of any approaching vehicle, match it to our database, and spit out a positive ID. If the vehicle doesn't pass, they'd walk into a closed fence—and behind the fence, a riot of firepower waiting to blow them off the road."

"Hope it recognizes us . . ."

Harris tapped a small green light on a black box sitting below the dash.

"Already has. Green means go. No missile launchers will be waiting for us."

Harris took another tight turn and then slowed. The Rover creeped ahead . . . and out of the mist rose a fence.

Twenty feet tall. The biggest fence Maddy had ever seen.

"God," she said. "That's amazing."

Harris stopped the car. Some shadowy figures moved on the other side as the fence opened.

"Amazing? I'm afraid the really amazing stuff lies ahead . . ."

Peter Friedman sipped the herbal tea . . . Sleepytime tea, he thought—that is, unless he had simply stuffed all his herbal teas into the empty box with the drowsy bear on the top.

He licked his lips.

Entering the code, trying out possibilities with the program, could take days, even weeks. He didn't have that amount of time. Not with Elaina on the run and GenTech, the crazy fuckers, up to who knew what.

His hands entered more lines of code, a big strand of DNA, which he then began placing into possible sequences. It was trial and error, but having played with genetic code he could guess where a sequence might fit— and what it might do.

It was strange playing with the building blocks of

something, wondering . . . is this part of the nervous system, perhaps the brain, the muscle structure, or—?

His tea was gone, and he got up for a refill.

"Oscar?" He whistled. Where was that fat cat? Ate his fill and curled up in the bottom of the small linen closet for his favorite activity, sleep?

Peter filled his cup with tap water, tossed in a reddish tea bag, and threw it in the microwave.

And then—standing there—he thought of the material he was working with. And a light bulb went off in his head. A breakthrough.

I have it all wrong, he thought. The basic structure . . . all put together wrong.

He ran back to the computer and quickly started typing, moving the strands around. And now they seemed to fit, to flow. Nothing familiar of course, he didn't expect that. But there was logic. Now he could couple whole blocks, millions of chromosomes, and put them into place.

"Okay," he said. "Let's see what we have here."

Even as the program built the genetic structure, another part of the program tested the Pentium 4's capabilities to construct . . . a model.

A model. Of what? Peter's heart raced. This would be extraordinary if it fit together. If it worked, he'd get a construction of—

And then—a new screen popped up.

The imaging screen, and something began to draw from the head down.

Taking up almost the entire screen.

He guessed it was a head. But then—

"No. Shit, I fucked up. Can't be."

More of the headlike structure came into view . . . more like a misshapen planet, almost rocklike.

Peter's first thought: *I got it wrong. This must be some program glitch.*

But then the strange planetoid on the screen narrowed

to something resembling a trunk and then the program drew branchlike "arms" coming out.

The program finished, then it rotated the figure . . . which had been displayed from the back.

And he saw an opening.

If pressed, Peter might call it a mouth, but it was more like a jagged hole lined with razors, both outside and in.

"God," he said. "Were they making this, or designing it, or—?" He took a breath. "Wait a second, how big is it? Size. Damn it . . . how big . . ."

He hit some keys, and there it was.

Peter leaned forward toward the screen.

"No way." At over two tons, the thing, whatever it was, was gigantic, as large as the very largest creatures known to have lived on earth. That is, if it was a creature.

The program could also reconstruct the movement of the creature.

But do I really want to see that? Peter thought.

He quickly typed an e-mail to Elaina's Hotmail account.

Say hello, he typed. He attached the .jpeg image file, then clicked Send.

He sat back.

He looked around the room. Things were getting creepy.

"Oscar? Hey, buddy . . . come keep me company."

There was no answer. No plaintive . . . *meow.* Funny, Oscar was almost doglike in his response to a call.

Then—Peter heard something.

A sound from the bedroom.

"Yo, Oscar, get your lazy butt in here."

Still nothing—but now he heard the sound again. He glanced at the image on the screen. It was freaking him, this genetic creation, whatever it was. Maybe just some theoretical experiment gone wrong . . .

The sound again! Peter tried to place it.

And then he remembered . . . a year ago his condo had had a mouse problem. Whenever he worked quietly, very quietly, he would hear the mice come out of some invisible hole in the kitchen and start nosing around . . . looking for crumbs, getting into Oscar's bowl. Oscar proved useless, snoring away on an old terrycloth towel.

Peter had thrown a shoe at the first mouse he saw. He didn't see that there were three or four others lurking behind him, hanging out by the toaster oven.

He'd hated it.

Now—more sounds, small steps, and Peter knew that he had mice again. Though the super sent an exterminator around every month . . . the guy probably just pretended to squirt fluid at the mice.

Peter looked around the room for something to use as a mouse weapon. A broom would be nice, but that was in the kitchen . . . the mice would scatter. He saw his silver steel attaché case.

Perfect. Designed to take any abuse baggage handlers could dish out, it would be a nasty weapon against the mice.

He stood up as quietly as he could and then slid over to the attaché. It was open so he had to gently close it . . . slide the latch shut, making it a heavy metal brick.

He picked it up and walked oh so slowly into the small kitchen. The light was on, so if the mice were partying he'd see them.

He peeked in to get a view.

But there was nothing. No mice on the countertop, or beside the micro-dishwasher that held about six plates, or near Oscar's bowl. *Did they hear me?* he thought. *Maybe the mice are smarter this year.*

No. There was the sound again, but he was wrong. It came from his small bedroom.

Okay, he still had the opportunity of surprise. And he was even madder now. Stupid mice.

He was just glad they weren't rats. He saw rats in the street a lot. But he figured there was way too much good eats on the sidewalk for them to bother climbing up the four flights to his one-bedroom.

He passed the small linen closet between the bedroom and the kitchen. He looked down to Oscar's familiar bed.

Except Oscar wasn't there.

Well, that happened too. Oscar sometimes got carried away with himself and slept in Peter's bed. Though he would reluctantly abandon the bed when Peter yelled at him.

But it wasn't like a dog where you could make them feel guilty by saying "bad dog." Cats had no guilt.

Amoral little furballs . . .

He was at the bedroom.

God, mice in his bedroom, gave him the creeps. What if they came out when it was dark . . . climbed onto his bed? They obviously could climb, having breached the fortress of the toaster oven counter.

Another small, quiet step, and he looked in.

For a moment—he didn't understand what he saw.

Something here, and there, and *there*—grayish, furry, then . . . across the bedspread . . . a big smear of red.

Peter felt his heart beating even faster, and he started breathing heavily. He could smell what he was looking at.

Oscar, ripped into pieces, his hindquarters toward the right wall, a big chunk of—what, his chest—near the foot of the bed.

He could smell the blood.

The first thought was stupid, illogical. Rats. Some king rats got in and tangled with Oscar and—

But there had been no loud yelping, no scream from the cat, and what the hell kind of rat could—

He waited for another hypothesis. But it didn't come. Only a question.

Where's Oscar's head?

He took another step into the room, walking over a small furry chunk.

All I heard, Peter thought, *was those little mouse noises, tiny sounds—*

Another step, and there, on the other side, he saw his cat's head, lying square on the wood floor. Had it been neatly severed from his body—so fast—so that there was no sound, and, and—

A step back.

Because even in those very few precious seconds before Peter learned what was happening, he knew . . . he knew . . .

I have to get out of here. I have to back up, turn around, and—

Another step . . . the charnel house of his bedroom disappeared.

Another backward step—and his foot brushed into something. Something right there, at his foot level. He didn't want to take his eyes off the entranceway to his bedroom, but he turned around, looked down—

And there he saw a shape in the darkness of the hallway. His eyes adapted from the bright light of the bedroom to the darkness of the small hallway and the barely lit living room, glowing only from the computer screen.

But as they adjusted, he saw something at his feet that he recognized.

The rocklike head from the computer screen. More like a piece of molten rock. And legs, so many, not six, not eight, not even twelve—and—

The hole. Call it a mouth. Must be a mouth.

Not two tons, he thought.

Must come in all sizes and—

More sounds, the mouse sounds from within the living room, and he looked up to see them . . .

A dozen of them . . . perched on his chair, beside the

computer, on his worktable, on his small couch, a few just lined up on the floor . . . and this one right at his feet.

Had they been here waiting? Did they come in? How did they come—

And the one at his feet made a noise, a sickening, screeching, scraping sound, and a few of those pincerlike legs went flying, *jabbing,* into Peter's feet, and through his feet, right to the floor.

Peter screamed.

But there was worse, even as he felt an insane burning billowing up from his trapped feet.

A few of them on the floor leapt up, flying four, five feet, landing in front of Peter, their mouths . . . looking up. Could a mouth look? Because that's what it seemed like.

The pain, fiery, beyond resisting, hit his thighs, then his midsection, when—the sounds swelled . . .

And then two of them squatting in front of him leaped up—just like jumping spiders—right at him. Peter tilted backward but he was only inches from the wall.

The two things landed, one wrapping itself around his right arm, the other clutching his chest.

And Peter remembered having this weird thought . . .

At least they didn't land on my head . . . or my neck. That's a good thing. I can still see, and breathe, and—

He heard a howl. A constant, endless, sirenlike howl that filled his small apartment.

He was doing it. *He* was making the sound. Couldn't stop, as a matter of fact.

Not with those legs—so many—opening and closing, as if tightening their grasp, getting a better hold. Opening and closing, while all the time the mouth . . .

Gotta be a mouth, Peter thought.

The mouth . . . attached itself to him, one to the arm, the other to his chest, and then—such a weird, sickening sensation—he felt the razorlike lips begin to move.

Not up and down. Not chewing. Of course not. We chew . . . here.

Not where these things come from.

The razor lips spun, twisted, turned, boring into him.

He howled. Loud. Louder. Until.

He couldn't howl any more.

His last thought: no blood. Not a drop escaped those mouths.

And those bumpy rocklike bodies.

Oh, how they swelled, ticklike, fat, plump, as the drilling, boring went on . . .

Harris drove through the open gate, past a line of soldiers fully armed with machine guns, helmets, camouflage gear.

Looks like Afghanistan, Maddy thought.

A war zone. To either side, she saw rows of armored vehicles . . . tanks, mobile cannons, SAM launchers.

"Lot of firepower you have here."

"There's more," Harris said. "We have some heavy missile deployment just beyond those bunkers over there."

"Ready for anything," Maddy said lightly.

Harris didn't take it lightly.

"Ready for anything? Not sure about that . . . Ah, here we are."

He pulled up to a squat building that resembled a World War II Quonset hut.

"Not very fancy, I'm afraid," Harris said. "Dates back to the beginning of the project. We haven't put in any big-budget items for construction up here. Gets too much attention. We added some troop quarters. Some bunkers for the science team. The original headquarters . . . suffices."

Harris stopped the car. "Ready?"

"You tell me."

He smiled and got out, and Maddy followed him. As soon as she was outside, she felt the cold air.

"God, it's freezing."

"Gets a lot worse come January."

Maddy looked around . . . where was the house?

"Oh, you can't see it from here. See that outcrop there? The old road continues around there . . . and then you can see the house. About five hundred meters past it. Kind of nestled in this circle of granite. Hidden."

"And you have more . . . soldiers, cannons, whatnot . . . over there?"

He nodded. "Some. But there have been . . . problems. We don't let anyone do two consecutive nights in close proximity to the house. And every bit of heavy artillery requires two soldiers to operate."

Maddy shivered. This grew crazier by the minute. How could this have anything to do with Paul, or herself?

"You sound like you're ready for an invasion."

Harris tilted his head. "Invasion? Good choice of words. Well, if you're ready, everyone's waiting for us . . . inside. Just one word of advice."

Maddy blew out a puff of air, making a little steam cloud.

Cold. Scared.

"What's that, Colonel?"

"Doesn't matter whatever you've been thinking, imagining . . . brace yourself."

She nodded.

"Good." And then Harris led the way into the curved building.

book three

wonderland

twenty-six

Molly Berger didn't like the late night. All she wanted to do was get home from her cleaning job, watch a little Conan, have a nice cold beer, then fall asleep.

But each night the subway became a circus train. Bad enough with the wobbly homeless people riding the train to wherever . . . there were also loud punks blasting their boomboxes and kids drunk or stoned.

Even the occasional businessman in a suit looked strange, sitting so straight—as though they could ignore all the craziness in the car.

Molly couldn't ignore it.

No. Because the subway car was just like her dreams.

No—not dreams. Nightmares. She didn't tell anyone about them. How can you complain about dreams? But they woke her up, dripping wet every night, sweating and sometimes crying from the fear.

No matter how much she drank, or if she took Tylenol PM, nothing mattered . . . the dreams always came.

And each night, her subway car seemed like it was just

the dream . . . continuing. The weird faces, the rubbery lips, the bulbous eyes—the grabby hands holding on to railings, picking at noses. Even the signs on the train began to look like they came from her nightmare factory. Signs in Spanish she didn't understand . . . cartoons about AIDS, and ads for colleges, and ways to earn $$$ now!

She felt as though she couldn't stand it.

But as bad as the train was . . . it wasn't as bad as the nightmares.

She thought—just the other night—of not sleeping. That would be one way to stop them. If I don't sleep, I'll have no dreams.

But then—around four a.m.—she finally succumbed, the TV blaring, a fresh beer by her side, the sky outside picking up that first little bit of dull gray light . . .

She fell asleep.

And now it would be like punishment. The nightmare had to make up for last time, the *missed* nightmare . . .

It was as if some giant gate had been opened. Opened, and then they came out—

They . . . she called them. Some she knew from other dreams, the strange creatures she spotted in different places . . . in a children's playground, walking through a hospital, slithering out of some sleepy lake . . . so many scenes, flipping, flipping . . .

But always there would be new ones. And not just the things she saw, the creatures, the—

She looked up. A big black kid with a tight bandanna was laughing, then he happened to see her face. And his smile evaporated.

He kept on listening to his friend—but whatever he saw in Molly's gaze made him freeze.

She looked away.

She didn't want to be thinking about this . . . not now, not here. This ride was bad enough.

The train stopped. The doors opened. And old Hispanic

couple got on . . . looked left and right looking for seats that would place them away from all the noise.

They spotted some space to the left of Molly.

And the small little man with the tan wrinkled face steered his wife with her Coke-bottle glasses toward the seats.

Not here, Molly thought. *Don't sit . . . next to me.*

She looked away from them as they sat.

Yes. Just like people getting into the subway, there would always be . . . new ones appearing each night.

New . . . monsters.

The word was so silly. *Monster.* A kid's word.

Until you've seen them. And she saw them every night. *Monsters.*

She shook her head, thinking—not for the first time—*I need help.*

Harris held the door for Maddy and she entered a plain meeting room filled with men and one woman, some in uniforms, others in academic-looking sweaters and corduroy pants.

They all looked up at her—and Maddy got a sick feeling.

They're looking at me as though they feel sorry for me.

Their eyes barely met hers before they looked down again.

It was an older woman in a wheelchair—perhaps sensing her distress—who spoke.

"Thank you for coming. We hope this hasn't been too upsetting for you."

She was an American. Maddy didn't know what to say.

"No. I just want to find my brother."

A man at the end of the table stood up. "We all want that, Ms. Hodge." He extended a hand. "I'm Dr. Pollack, and everyone here has been working with this . . . project for a long time."

Harris took her arm and gestured toward a seat.

Maddy sat down. She looked at the other faces. She guessed introductions weren't forthcoming—no one made an effort to tell her who the other people were.

She scanned the room and she saw maps . . . the United States, Eastern Europe, and even one of the Pacific Ocean floor. All of them had little pushpins stuck in them—pushpins all over the world.

A media station occupied the front of the room, with a computer, VCR, DVD, and a big NEC monitor.

"Colonel Harris . . . said I would get some answers."

Dr. Pollack nodded and smiled. "As many as we can give you. Which—sad to say—isn't a lot."

"But that isn't to say"—the American woman rushed to speak, as if to cushion the other man's words—"that we don't know *some* things. Perhaps—"

Pollack continued. "I want you to know that the U.K. government—at the highest level—is now monitoring what we are doing here."

The prime minister?

And Maddy thought: *I'm in over my head.*

Pollack held up a hand. "Let's start at the beginning. But we'll be moving fast. You see, we don't think we have a lot of time." He laughed. "Time to do what? you must be wondering. We'll get to that too. As I said—fast—

"First, this . . . house, this— Colonel, if you wouldn't mind, the first screen—"

The house appeared on the screen.

"—has been here since nineteen thirty-seven. I say 'been here' because though some work was done by various local builders and contractors, they didn't build it."

"It just appeared?"

Pollack smiled. "We don't know. You'll hear that answer a lot. And, when the locals started to nose around, bad things happened."

He gestured at Harris, and some still images began to appear slowly on the monitor screen.

Maddy had seen enough battle scenes and the aftermath of skirmishes not to blink at what appeared on the screen. Still, these were hard to take. The black-and-white images showed massive wounds all over people's bodies.

"These are the ones who made it out. Barely made it out, dying shortly after. Others didn't come out. Vanished inside. So of course, the local authorities got involved . . ."

An old picture of the building surrounded by vintage cop cars and police came onto the screen.

"The results—the same."

More bodies, these in uniform.

"In twenty-four hours, the locals knew that they were in over their head. When they notified the military—every possible hypothesis was flying. The OSS and MI6 got involved, especially due to the imminent state of the world. War was . . . inevitable. And there were those who conjectured that this place was some kind of foreign invention. Some trap, a distraction—" He took a deep breath. "That was until the first fence went up, the first quarantine was put in place, and then the first troops went in."

Maddy looked at the screen. He was going fast, and Maddy found that her mind, her understanding of what was happening, couldn't keep pace. She didn't have a clue what she was learning.

The next image showed a few Jeeps, troops, leaders arrayed outside the house.

"The full platoon went in. All of them, save for one radioman. Amazingly, once they were inside, the radio signal worked. There was some thought that maybe it would be shielded by the metal outside. But—for a while at least—that radioman heard them. Inside."

"Gerald, not so melodramatic please . . ." the woman

said, then looked at Maddy. "The facts are horrid enough—without embellishing."

"Perhaps, Mary, you'd like to carry on," Pollack snapped.

The woman didn't respond. And Maddy became aware that the room was thick with tension. *They must be at each other's throats.* And the reason: *They're scared.*

"No tape was made. Didn't exist at the time. So all we have is the radioman's report, a bit of transcript. We have it in the files. Suffice it to say, that everyone inside sounded mad. There were screams, horrible screams that— the radioman reported—made him cringe, even cry. And then a few demented soldiers inside spoke about what they saw. One said . . . something key. He said, in a shaking voice, 'It's all in here. Everything. All here.' And then he said . . . 'Tell them—it's all real.' "

" 'It's all real'? What did he mean by that?"

"Not too sure. We'll get to it. To what we think at least. Later, when Dr. Richards takes over."

The woman nodded.

"Dr. Pollack, we have scheduled her equipment briefing in just twenty—"

Pollack turned to Harris. "I'm hurrying as much as I can . . ." He turned to Maddy. "They all vanished. More soldiers, bigger guns, more weapons. I guess you can figure out the rest."

"Nobody escaped?"

"Yes. And then the first big fence went up, the first quarantine began while the nation went off to war . . . it wasn't until after the war that the first experiments began."

"Experiments? To find out what was inside?"

"Inside?" Again, another private smile. "You could say that. There would be special armor, just radio communication, and cameras—no video, still a decade away for that. But a real . . . incursion was planned. And out of that . . . a mess. It truly was a mess—so many people lost—we got a few things. A survivor . . . for a brief time anyway, and some radio recordings of the squads before they ended, and—"

"Gerald—can we save that?"

"Right. I'll save that till the end. So, we heard more madness, some squads in rooms where the normal rules of physics simply . . . vanished. Others opening a door and finding themselves someplace else, desolate places, or in bizarre jungles. We heard only brief descriptions before the gunfire broke out and they were attacked—by something. Gunfire, the screams. Always the same."

"You said . . . someone survived."

Maddy was thinking of her brother. Someone went in, and got out—and lived.

"Briefly. Either he didn't get too far in, or he somehow found a way out. But he stumbled out—and not only that—he came out with a camera. We got to see inside." Pollack came close to Maddy. "Hope you're ready for this . . . still rocks me every damn time I see it."

The monitor flickered.

To show: An image.

Inside. Something that resembled . . . a hospital waiting room, or more like a foyer.

Again—

An open door, and on the other side, some dark shapes huddled over something.

Maddy realized they were soldiers on the ground, and these things, still hard to make out, were perched on them, pulling, tearing.

Image: Another room. Only there were soldiers on *every* surface—the floor, the ceiling, the walls, crawling like babies, weapons forgotten. Like some trick picture created by a surrealist painter.

Image: a tilted, chaotic picture, the camera at a crazy

angle, catching a meters-long curved grayish hook slicing into . . . a soldier. The hook alone was easily twice as long as the soldier.

"You see, the camera was picked up by another soldier. Whoever took these pictures never got out. But they told us a lot and—"

"Dr. Pollack, we *have* to get Maddy to an equipment briefing . . ."

Maddy turned to Harris. "I'm a little confused. You said equipment. I mean, what are you planning? I just want to find Paul."

Now everyone looked around the table at each other, the floor, the walls, anywhere but at Maddy.

"There's reason to believe . . . that is, we think—"

Dr. Mary Richards came over to her and put a hand on Maddy's shoulder. "I know it sounds crazy. Why we want you to go inside . . ."

The subway car was *filled* with monsters.

Everywhere Molly looked, she saw them . . . hanging from the straps, slouching in the seats, leaning against the doors. Their faces all rubbery, the veins under the skin so clear like they wore a mask of red netting.

And they were all looking at her.

Soon, she knew, they'd turn exactly into the monsters from her dreams.

Then she would feel the horror of being in that place when it was daylight, when she was awake.

Or was she?

Had she lost her mind so much that she didn't know whether she was asleep, awake?

Again the thought . . .

I need help.

The man next to her slid against her, his sleeping dead weight hitting her shoulder.

Molly jumped up. Everyone watched her do it; they stared at her.

Again she squeezed her eyes shut.

This is no dream, and they are turning to monsters, all of them, and I'll never get home again.

She opened her eyes.

The next subway car was nearly empty. She could go there; maybe the horror would stop.

She looked to her right. And an old woman with white hair and thick glasses opened her mouth. A long, dry tongue snaked out as if it wanted to touch her as she stumbled by, walking to the other car.

The rocking train made her wobble back and forth, and she held fast to the handholds above the seats.

She couldn't look at the passengers. Seeing them would only make her freeze, maybe break down and fall to her knees and cry. She squinted, stumbled, close now, only a few more feet and she'd be at the door between the cars.

What if the door didn't open? she thought.

What if the door was stuck—and everyone saw her try to escape and she failed?

A few more feet . . . but then she heard the screeching of the train's brakes, and then the bright light of a station. As the train flew past people waiting, slowing, stopping, she saw that there were new monsters waiting to board.

No, she thought. *Not more.*

She reached the door and turned around.

She watched the people come on board, all with the same rubbery fun-house faces, all stumbling into the car. Did their eyes look hungry? They were always hungry in her nightmares. Always hungry—as if eating were constant. Eating, devouring . . . *constant.*

She turned back to the door. Okay, all she had to do now was pull down on the latch, pull open the door, and walk into the other car.

She pushed down. The handle didn't budge.

No, Molly thought. *This is too much like a nightmare. But I'm awake. It's never been this bad, never been like that world was . . . suddenly . . . here.*

She gagged.

As if something were stuck in her throat. The monsters in the car all looked at her, curious.

Another gag, then she vomited onto the floor. She was dimly aware of groans, curses, even some of the monsters shuffling away. Another heave, but that didn't end it—as now her midsection felt as though it were on fire. Burning. She wanted to tear her clothes off, so hot.

The train roared through the tunnel again. Lights flickered off, and Molly was thrown to an empty seat, slipping on her own greenish vomit.

The burning grew as though someone held a torch to her stomach. She clawed like an animal at her clothes, and she heard this strange groaning.

In a moment, she realized that *she* was the one groaning.

Then, when it seemed like the burning couldn't get any worse, the pain any more intense . . .

She felt something in her midsection that was almost like a paper cut. A thin, subtle cut. Only—she was aware—this cut was *inside*. Where the burning was.

She closed her eyes. This would only get worse.

But when she closed her eyes, she was there, in that strangely colored jungle, kneeling in some greenish, sticky clay, her hands palms down on the stuff while they walked around her . . . the monsters, their eyes so hungry.

She opened her eyes.

The paper cut . . . exploded. She screamed, as a giant gash opened from her chest down to her pelvis. She cried. She looked around. They were people in the train now. Not monsters. That had been fantasy, madness. This, though—was real.

And she watched as her split body opened up, tugging on the skin of her neck where it hadn't been cut, hadn't split—at least not yet.

While something emerged.

Something attached to her.

She had seen something once like it in a pet store. Some kind of underwater plant . . . or a feathery coral waving in the tiny currents made by the bubbler, glowing under the bright fluorescent light.

This thing—all sickly colored, dotted with blood and other fluids—started to come out.

It was in her, she knew.

Part of her.

They were together.

And then—

Another important thought.

I'm the monster.

The people in the subway car screamed, and backed away, running to the far end of the car, huddled, yelling. Molly heard the sound of brakes. Someone hit the brakes, and stopped the train. The wheels screeched—but the train kept moving.

Why would they do that?

They were scared. And it probably seemed like a smart thing to do. Stop the train. *There's something in the car with us.* But somehow the brakes didn't work.

Molly looked down at the thing now perched on her chest.

Blood filled the floor. But still Molly felt alert. The pain had amazingly vanished. It did that, she guessed. Stopped the pain, stopped the screaming.

And each small tendril of the thing opened, revealing smaller tendrils, like a box within a box. The smaller tendrils waved—like leaves of grass on a wind—but Molly knew.

They were ready.

They started to stretch out of her, stretch, lean—

She knew where they would go. How each tendril would tear through these people. She had seen how it happened. So fast . . .

Molly looked at the door to the other car.

She reached for a railing and pulled herself up.

Already the tendrils had stretched out of her and fallen to the floor, picking up speed as if sensing she was going to do something.

She nearly fell onto the latch—then pressed down hard. This time it opened, and the noise of the rocking train was deafening.

One of the tendrils turned, looking . . . at the open door, then at Molly.

Maybe it could come right out of her, she thought. Come out, fall to the floor, and kill them all.

She looked at the open door and the gap between the two cars.

Then to the sides, at the few thin strands of chain link that offered the only protection for falling onto the tracks.

Molly looked back, down at the subway car floor, completely covered by a pool of blood.

I have no blood, she thought, *I have nothing*.

A tendril reared back as if it were about to lurch at Molly's skull, as if they had neglected one small detail in . . . using her. Because she knew that's what they were doing . . . using her.

To get here.

They were using so many.

Molly looked at the opening between the two cars and then she threw herself over the chain-link barrier.

Her foot caught as she fell forward—but only for a moment. She slipped down, landing on a rail that went flying by, before she seemed to stick to it—and then the subway car's wheels went screaming over her, right over the strange thing that had erupted from inside her, slicing it into a hundred pieces.

twenty-seven

Harris led Maddy out of the administration building to the courtyard.

"It's late now—I'll have a meal brought over to you, along with all the information—not much, I'm afraid, that may be helpful. Then tomorrow—"

"I'll go into the house?"

"House? If that is what it is. If so—it's a haunted house. No creaky doors, no rumors and whispers. It's the real deal. Something that we've watched for over sixty years—watched, contained—and now it won't stay contained." He dug out a cigarette and lit it. "Will you need anything else for tonight?"

"No," Maddy said. She smiled, trying to put on a brave face. "I doubt . . . whether I'll even need . . . a wake-up call."

The late-night plane dumped Nick in Glasgow . . . where he had had to sit and wait . . . till the city lumbered awake.

He knew every hour was another hour Maddy could

slip farther away. Finally, the city awakened—but he was still trapped.

"What do you mean, you don't have any cars?"

The cow-eyed woman at this latest car rental place just shuffled some papers, barely awake. "I don't see anything on my lists . . ."

"Listen, I just flew here, I called ahead—"

The woman's accent was thick, and Nick had to strain to catch the meaning as he lost the odd word or two.

"Sorry, sir. But the last gu-rll"—the word *girl* suddenly acquired a *u* and what was an infinity of *l*s at the end— "didn't keep any good records at all. And all my vehicles are rented proper and—"

Nick rolled his eyes and looked out at the rental lot.

Not a car in sight—but he did see a small flatbed truck.

"Wait a second, is that truck for rent?"

The girl at the counter turned around slowly.

"The lorry? Yes, sir. But that's for a farm rental or retail, not—"

"I'll take it."

The girl froze. This was so American, he knew. Doing something that just isn't done.

"But I just explained to you that the truck—"

"—is for rent. And I want to rent it."

"But it's for retail, sir, or farm use only."

"So I'm going"—he leaned close, smiling, but adding just a hint of baby-don't-push-me-or-I-will-crack—"to use the truck for retail."

The girl froze. Then she nodded.

"Very well. Then fill out this—" And magically she produced a form that would require him to specify the retail use.

"No problem."

Nick started filling it in . . .

• • •

Maddy had been awake for hours before Harris appeared at her door.

"Ready?"

She nodded, and stepped out of the room.

"You had some breakfast?"

"Couldn't eat a thing."

"Not surprising. We're heading over there, where we keep all the equipment."

Maddy nodded. All of this seemed like some fantasy, though the bright afternoon sun beating down made everything stand out in brilliant relief. The hard part was, it seemed only a theory that somehow her brother had ended up in the house . . . someone else who had vanished.

"I could still say no. Right?" Maddy said.

Harris turned to her, slowing his pace, but not stopping. "Yes. You could. I mean, there's not a person here would blame you. It's only a guess on our part that your connection to your brother—if he's in there—could help. In fact—" Harris was about to say something, but then stopped himself.

"But I won't say no," she said. "If my brother's in there, then that's where I'm going."

Harris nodded. And Maddy saw that he wasn't thrilled with the prospect of sending her in.

They reached the supply building; Harris ran ahead and pulled open the door and Maddy walked in.

Harris, just behind her, said, "First door on the right . . ."

Maddy opened the door and walked in.

The room seemed more like a warehouse, with rows of metal shelving, large metal trays on large steel tables, and TV monitors everywhere.

Three people, two men and a woman, stood uneasily at a table filled with equipment.

"This isn't the command room. But we have monitors

here so everything can be seen. The more eyes watching . . . the better."

Harris gestured at the three people behind the metal table. "And these nice people will get you ready."

Maddy turned to Harris. "Can I ask some more questions—?"

"Well, there will be a briefing . . . just before you go to the house. And then—"

"No, what really makes you think Paul is inside?"

"We don't know for sure. Not really. We know he was climbing on the mountain, he came close. And we know that his gear was found with no sign of him. He vanished. Like others have vanished from around here. It's one of the reasons we need to act fast. Whatever is going on in there has gotten stronger. It's no longer limited to the house." He took a breath. "They have allies."

"Allies?"

"People that have been contacted . . . that help them."

"But my brother may not be in there?"

"Yes."

"And—what do you want me to do in there? What do you think I can do? What will I see?" She took a breath. "Just a quick heads-up."

Harris took off his hat. He looked at the tech people and Maddy wondered if maybe she was asking about things that they weren't supposed to know about.

"Here's the short version, Maddy. We know that things are happening outside the structure. And not just here . . . all around the world. Some kind of critical mass has occurred. We need to see what's going on. Or as much as we can . . ."

"So why not send in more squads of soldiers with—"

"We tried that. You've seen the pictures. We believe that because you have a connection to someone inside . . . that you might be able to find him—and"—he took a breath—"maybe get out."

"Maybe." She shook her head.

"You can still refuse . . . but we need to know more, see more, and perhaps—using you—and I'll be honest, that's exactly what we're doing—test it."

Maddy nodded.

Harris had a sick look on his face.

And Maddy thought: *I remember being on the Hillary Step and seeing nothing as the top of Everest became shrouded in an icy fog.* She had felt frozen, immobilized, with precious minutes needed for the climb down seeping away.

But then her fear had just become another element, like the wind, and the fog, and the ice, and she had taken that fatal next step, then another, along the razor-sharp ridge.

She got up, and she got down.

As for this, she told herself, she'd get in—and she'd get out.

"Okay, let's get started," she said.

The young man behind her cleared his throat. "Ms. Hodge?"

Maddy turned around.

The man continued. "We have a lot to show you, your equipment . . ."

The woman beside him added, "And weapons."

Harris put a fatherly hand on her shoulder. "I'll come back in thirty minutes to take you over to the entrance point, okay?"

Maddy nodded.

One step. That's all it takes, she thought. *Then another.*

"Okay, show me what you've got . . ."

Nick stopped on a corner and watched as two old women holding walkers made their way torturously toward him.

He thought: *If it's a race, ladies, I'm winning.*

Then he immediately felt guilty making a joke—even

to himself—about the two women. *My day will come*, Nick thought.

For now, he had been through this town looking for some sign of Maddy. He had asked at the gas station and the local newsagent's about a pretty woman, short brown hair—but he drew a blank every time.

What was he thinking? That he could just come up here and wander around Einbank until he spotted her? She could be anywhere. He'd have to call Emma soon and give her the bad news.

The two women were only meters away. *They move slowly, but they do move . . .*

Nick smiled at them and stepped off the curb.

"Good morning," he said. Together they looked up at him. He expected a nice grin and a smile back. Instead, with lips pulled tighter than the drawstring of a purse, they looked up and—if that was possible—adopted a more sour look.

Careful, ladies, he thought, *hate to kick your aluminum struts away from you.*

They moved on. Slowly, human turtles, while Nick stood on the pavement.

When he noticed a shop across the street. He thought it was a liquor store, but now he could see sandwiches and tea advertised.

Case in Point, the place was called.

Wouldn't hurt to ask there, Nick thought. He walked across the street and went into the shop, setting off a tinkling bell.

A man wearing lederhosen and a bright yellow shirt with puffy sleeves pounced on Nick.

"Well, good morning to you, sir. Would you like breakfast, or a bit of the nouveau—"

Nick looked at a little table outfitted as an altar to the apparently just-arrived Beaujolais Nouveau.

"Maybe some coffee or tea?"

The man gestured at the wine table. "Really? Never too early to sample the nouveau, I always say."

From the man's florid cheeks and vein-splattered nose, Nick imagined that was quite true, for him at least.

"Er, no, I'm actually—"

"Ah, an American. No drinking before five, isn't that how it is in the States? Such a big puritanical country . . ."

Nick rolled his eyes. As if this character outfitted as an extra from a Tyrolean nightmare had any grounds to complain.

"Yes, well actually, I'm looking for someone. A woman."

Now the man rolled his eyes. "Ah, *cherchez la femme*? A runaway I suppose, girlfriend, or—?"

"No. A friend. She came here yesterday. Short brown hair, medium height, from London—"

The man snapped his fingers.

"Why yes. They were in here yesterday morning."

"They?"

"A young woman, yes, very beautiful, and a military officer. Talking . . . very seriously."

"A military officer?"

"I imagine he came from the reservation."

"A military reservation?"

"Yes, at the foot of the Glen Coe range not far from here. Strictly off-limits, all hush-hush, you know. Tell you though, I can't imagine that lady . . . and that man . . . well, you know what I mean."

Nick nodded. It was a clue—and it came from somebody who seemed completely crackers. "Can you tell me how to get there?"

"Certainly! Just take the road out of town until you get to the petrol station, make a right, then follow signs for Old Carrath Road. Once you start climbing, you'll see signs announcing the military base—and warnings too. It is a restricted area. Nobody goes there. Nobody. Those military people can be so . . . stuffy about such things."

"Thanks," Nick said.

The man grabbed his glass of wine from a nearby table. "Sure you won't—?"

Nick smiled. Crazy guy, and a crazy town—but at least he had some idea where Maddy might be.

And—maybe it was instinct—he had a chilly feeling as he walked back to his rental truck, ready to drive to the base—restricted or not.

Maddy tried shifting on her feet. She looked down at the outfit she wore, shiny reflective material that, the tech guy told her, would protect her.

From what? Maddy had asked.

Oh, radiation, heat, any surface abrasions.

Maddy thought: *I'm just going into a building, aren't I?*

But she knew after everything, that whatever the structure was, it was not just . . . a building.

Then there was a helmet that covered her entire face. She could see well through the visor, but small microphones and headphones in the helmet would pick up sounds from her outside as well as relaying audio from the command center.

But the woman tech, Brigitte, had told her, "We don't know how far the audio penetrates into the structure."

The past "incursions" had had only ten, fifteen minutes of two-way audio. Then nothing.

They were still wiring up the headset video cam and checking the audio when Harris came back to the equipment room.

He looked up and down at Maddy. "You okay with all that gear?"

She smiled. "You should have seen my Everest ascent.

Between my pack, crampons, and oxygen tanks, the stuff weighed as much as I did."

Harris nodded. "No weapons, though, I imagine?"

She looked down at the gun by her side, a massive handgun surrounded with a belt of clips. She was told it was a Mauser M2, a powerful .45-caliber that was easy to operate . . . just pull the trigger, and then stick a new clip in when out of bullets. An automatic laser sight had been added.

So comforting.

"It's kind of ridiculous," she said. "Who am I supposed to be . . . Lara Croft?"

"Lara . . . who?"

She reached up and felt the camera attached to her helmet. There were actually two cams, one strictly for a series of stills, the other for streamed video direct to the center.

"Remember, Maddy. After twelve minutes, no matter what you see, you stop and turn around. And get out."

"Not an easy task. Or so I've been led to believe."

"No. But you are one person—and we think the fact that you are related to someone in there may make a difference."

She looked at him. "You've said that. Why?"

Harris looked away. "When others have gone in, people close to them . . . got glimpses . . . saw what happened. The human connection seems to matter."

They reached the winding path that led to the structure.

Maddy, suddenly aware of what she was about to do, turned back to the command center. "Don't we need to check in there, any last-minute instructions?"

She noticed a group of heavily armed soldiers appear beside her, obviously coming from the gate.

"Time . . . is of the essence. If you can get in, and get out—and God, I hope with your brother—"

"If he's in there—"

"Then we will be able to plan some action against it. Up to now everything has been useless."

"And maybe this is . . . too."

Harris said nothing.

Nick stopped the car.

He looked at the road map, a sprawling mess on the seat beside him. Did he miss a turn? Did some small road appear and fly by, without him noticing?

He looked up at the tiny sign on the road ahead.

Old Forest Way.

Damned if he could see it on the map. He brought it up close. His reading vision was perfect, but this map would test anyone's acuity. No Old Forest Way but then he saw . . . a tiny squiggle, and the small letters *O.F.W.*

O-kay. That's helpful. He then saw that he hadn't hit the turnoff, but it was just ahead.

He put the map down. And there, by the side of the road behind a rusty barbed fence, was a big cow, chewing and looking.

And though it didn't look mad at all, the cow certainly did look curious.

The tech people stood back as though admiring a work of art. The woman nodded at Harris. He looked at Maddy. The soldiers stood at attention.

"Ready?"

She nodded. "Lock and load. Or whatever it is they say in those noisy, violent American movies."

"I'm going back to the command center. I'll talk to you from there, watch the monitors. I'll be right with you."

Sure, Maddy thought. *Right with me. Safely inside.*

But she had no one to blame but herself. Step by step, she had agreed to everything. Maybe the same crazy ambition that sent her from mountaintops to jungles to the sea bottom, had brought her here.

If it meant she might see Paul again, that was enough.

"Thanks, Colonel, for giving me this shot. I'll do . . . my best."

Then Harris did something strange, almost comical.

He saluted. Maddy nearly laughed. A first. She just smiled and turned around.

The soldiers' faces were impassive. Their hands, holding machine guns in front of them, spoke volumes.

"I'm ready."

And she walked away, flanked by the four soldiers.

Nick took a corner as the winding road grew narrower, almost hostile, with the dark pines so close to the roadway that they threatened to scratch the car with every swerving turn.

And he began to doubt that there was anything like a military base up here. Hard to believe there was even a little shack located at the end of this particular yellow brick road.

Unless there was another way there.

And he thought: *If I were building a top-secret military base, I would certainly make sure the main drag that led to the base wasn't on any map.*

Another corner, and even at a mere twenty miles an hour, the tires screeched out their protest.

Perhaps—this is a dead end.

A mountain road to nowhere, or to a nice view of the Glen Coe range and the wacky village of Einbank.

A hairpin. He cut the wheel hard, and then saw a small car pulled off to the side of the road. A man stood over an open hood, with a young girl beside him.

I should keep on going, Nick thought.

As he got close, the girl—twelve, maybe thirteen—looked up at him. Her dark eyes seemed to lock on Nick's.

Damn, he thought, *what the hell are they doing out here?*

He hit the brakes. He stopped the pickup beside the other car, a Toyota, well advanced in years. Nick pulled up the hand brake and got out.

"Hi. You guys need some help?"

The man looked up. He had a scraggly beard, thick black-rimmed glasses, and the befuddled look of an academic dealing with the real world.

"My car—the engine just seized up. I called in town for some help . . . but they haven't promised anything."

Nick nodded.

"Mind if I ask . . . where you are heading? I thought this road—"

He saw the girl shoot a look at the man, then back to Nick.

"There's a military base ahead. I used to work there."

Nick nodded. He had a funny feeling about these two. Why were they here?

"I'm going there. That's where I'm headed."

Again the girl looked at the man, then at Nick. She spoke. Softly, but with amazing power for a young girl. "You could take us there."

"Yes, I suppose I could. But I wonder"—he looked at the man—"you worked there. Are you going back for a reason? What do they do there?"

The girl took a step closer. Eyes locked on him.

"My dad—my dad was killed. He used to work there too. And I think—we think—I know something that my dad found out. Something I have to tell them."

"Sophie," the man said, "I don't think you can—"

"Okay. Tell you what. I think a friend of mine is there," Nick said quickly. "Someone I care about. That I'm worried about."

The academic nodded. "You may have good reason to

worry. Okay, if you take us, we'll tell you what we know. Only"—and he put his hand on Sophie—"if Sophie is right, we don't have a lot of time."

Nick nodded. "Get in. We'll talk while I try to get up this mountain . . ."

twenty-eight

The path curved around and Maddy got a clear view of the building, gleaming in the afternoon sun. She stopped.

It wasn't like anything she had ever seen. Because of the way the metal—if in fact it was metal—reflected light, she couldn't tell how big it was.

And she understood why some people called it a house. In outline it looked a bit like those low-lying American ranches, the ones that all the sitcoms take place in.

Only—there were no windows. She thought she saw lines on the metal that suggested openings.

"You okay?" a voice in her ear asked. Harris. Maddy remembered that he could see everything she did.

Maddy nodded, then added, "Yes. Just—well, there it is . . ."

Two of the soldiers had walked to an interior gate, only about twelve feet high, also electrified she saw, with a big warning sign posted on the gate.

"Still time for you to pull out, Maddy."

It sounded as though Harris was almost hoping that

Maddy would rip off the headgear, the camera, and say—
Sorry. No way in hell am I going in there.

And now for the first time she felt the fear ratchet up to a physical level.

Maddy knew fear. Not the way—she imagined—most people knew it . . . as that occasional feeling that popped up at the oddest moments, usually over something inconsequential, something later discovered to be harmless.

No, she knew what it meant to feel real fear over something that could, quite easily, kill you.

Slipping on the ice and dangling over a crevasse.

She still had nightmares where that figured prominently.

Or when she was in the Caribbean for a feature when Hurricane Floyd decided that it was going to rip the island apart.

She had watched her small cabin lose its windows, its door, until it seemed the storm wanted to pry her out.

But there was a difference—in both those cases she knew what she was afraid of.

What was she afraid of here?

All of it unknown.

"Maddy, do you see the entrance?"

"Yes. I mean, it looks like a doorway . . ."

"Yes, odd, isn't it?"

"A door to a meat freezer." As soon as Maddy said that she realized how horrible that sounded.

Harris didn't respond. "The soldiers will stay at the gate. From here, you're on your own. Remember the time limit. Out in twelve minutes, not a minute more."

"Oh, I'll come out. Trust me on that one, Colonel."

She looked at the big, heavily armed soldiers. She knew why they wouldn't accompany her. So many soldiers had gone in before and vanished. Why send more?

"Okay. I'm ready."

And she started walking toward the door.

• • •

Harris watched the two monitors, one showing streaming video from Maddy's head cam, the other sending stills refreshed every fifteen seconds.

Then he turned back to the room filled with scientists.

"I think we should have told her. About MacDonald. The other . . . events around the world," Harris said.

Mary Richards wheeled up to Harris. "Told her that it's maybe not an accident that her brother might be in there? Tell her that it's no mistake she's here?" She gave Harris a withering stare. "I don't think so."

"We don't know what the hell she'll face in there. The more information she has going in—"

The woman shook her head. "Not that information. Not the fact that she may already be connected to the structure . . . through her brother."

Pollack cleared his throat.

"It's only a theory anyway . . ."

The woman turned to him. "For which we have good evidence. And if she—"

The loudspeaker crackled to life.

"Er, I'm there. At the door." Maddy's voice interrupted them.

All eyes turned back to the monitor. "The place is— huge. Gigantic. It almost seems—"

Harris saw Richards look at her colleagues . . . as if she knew what Maddy would say . . .

"Too big—too big for this site."

"Right." Harris waited a beat. "We know, Maddy." He didn't tell her that it had gotten bigger, changing over the decades.

Now he wished she knew everything. She should have seen all the photos of the piles of bodies. Everything . . .

"Okay," she said. "Cameras rolling? 'Cause I'm going in."

Harris didn't say anything as he watched on the screen

as Maddy pulled on a protrusion from the structure and a doorlike opening swung open, easily, silently.

And they saw once again—the disarming view just beyond the threshold.

Maddy looked at the open doorway; then, behind it, she saw a bit of the wood floor, and what looked like marble pillars in the background.

She knew this wasn't the place to hesitate.

She stepped in.

One step, then another.

"You still there, everyone?" she said.

"We're here, Maddy."

She turned and looked at the room. *It's almost a foyer*, she thought.

Down to the polished wood floor, and the pillars, and the bare, lime-green walls, and then more doors in the back—wood, metal, each door different.

It was almost someone's impression of a foyer.

"This is what you've seen before?" she said.

"Yes. So far. This is pretty much all we've ever seen live. Twelve minutes, Maddy. Remember, you can always go in again. Could you do us a favor and look up?"

"Sure."

Maddy looked up.

Her heart stopped.

Up . . . seemed infinite.

More doors, then a spiraling swirl of endless levels, some with doors, others with gates, others just bands of brilliant color, shining steel, flashing light, on and on—with no end.

"Oh, God . . . oh sweet God . . ."

Instinctively she spun back to the door to the outside.

It was still there, still open.

The yellowish sand of the outside courtyard was still visible.

Then she looked back up. She almost expected it to be spinning, the coils, the rings, the doors, the bands of amazing color rotating.

"Colonel. What is that? It's impossible. So huge."

"Yes. We've seen it before. Never the same, though. The colors, the doors different—"

As she looked, she saw the doors above her burst open, actually explode outward as if a massive explosion had erupted inside and sent them flying open. Then she heard the howling sound of wind, first just a tremendous gust, but it built in intensity, turning into the roaring scream of a gale.

Her hand touched her gun.

Ridiculous, she thought.

A gun.

"Ten minutes, Maddy. And I have to ask you something."

"G-go on."

"If your brother is in there, you may have to try and—"

Harris hesitated. Maddy flashed on the truth right away. There's something they hadn't told her.

"Yes?"

"You may have to try and *sense* where he is. You got that, Maddy?"

"Sense him?"

She looked around. And one of the doors on her level seemed to glow a burnished color.

The wood turned from a deep cherry brown to a golden color, then almost glowing.

She had to say . . . what she felt.

"I'm scared."

"You can come out."

She shook her head and then stopped herself from doing the stupid gesture.

"No. Do y-you see that door?"

A pause. "We do."

Truth, or were they lying? Was this a place where only the person inside could see things?

She remembered the picture of a body on the very floor she stood on. The dark, sprawling body. A photo that somehow somebody had gotten out and—

She felt it—

Behind her.

She turned slowly.

"Maddy, you okay? Are you going to the door? Is there a—"

But she was barely listening. She didn't know if the voice had turned more distant, or if it was just her edgy imagination—but Harris's voice seemed so far away. And now there was definitely something behind her.

She kept turning. Another blast erupted from above her. But she didn't look up, had to keep turning, until—

Maddy saw the soldier on the ground.

Only now—only now she could really see him. The massive punctures in his body, great gaping holes. And how it looked as if part of his face was—hanging off.

She groaned.

"Maddy!"

"Do you see that? God, do you people see that?"

Another quick look at the door to the outside. Still there, still open. There were birds outside, and grass, and puffy clouds waiting to turn purple in the setting sun.

But in here . . .

"Yes."

"It wasn't there before. It—wasn't—there!"

"The door, Maddy. You said it was glowing."

It was as if Harris was prodding her to stay focused, to get her back on track.

"Nine minutes, Maddy."

She thought the dead soldier might move. Stupid thought. Dead for so long. How old were those pictures? Ten years? More?

She turned back to the door. It glowed brilliantly now, bright, the glow now filling this room. Maddy walked over to it. It had . . . a very ordinary handle. Maddy reached out—and brought her hand close, attempting to feel if it was warm.

But it gave off no heat. Her hand closed on it, and she twisted the handle. The door opened inward. All was dark behind it. Of course, she thought, it could simply appear dark due to the brilliance of the door.

"It's open," she said.

"We see it. Eight . . . no, seven minutes, Maddy. Be careful."

She pushed the door all the way open . . .

twenty-nine

"Jesus."

Nick looked at the girl—Sophie—and then at her companion, Cosgrove. He still caught himself swearing around his own kid. "Sorry," he said. "I don't understand what you're telling me."

Cosgrove looked back at Sophie and smiled reassuringly. "Welcome to the club. But unless we're very wrong, every minute is like gold, eh? We have to get to the base—and inside—as fast as we can."

Nick had to keep his eyes on the road as he came to a series of twisting turns.

"You think they'll just let us in? Just like that?"

"They better," Cosgrove said.

"How much farther?"

"A few minutes."

And Nick thought of Maddy inside. Inside—and if Cosgrove was to be believed—who knew where she was . . . right now.

• • •

Harris looked at the video monitor as the golden door opened.

"We should get her out. Enough of a test. Already she's gone farther than a lot—"

But Richards shook her head. "Steady, Harris. You gave her a time limit. Let it run."

Besides the video monitor, there was the computer screen, refreshing the image every fifteen seconds. Each high-res image was then evaluated for any information missed from the streaming video.

"Colonel Harris," a technician said, sitting beside the computer monitor. "The heat readings on these images is totally off the chart."

Harris looked at the biofeedback terminals to his right. They showed all of Maddy's vitals. Her core body temperature and the surface temperature were all within normal range.

"Not showing on Maddy," Harris said. "Check again."

The technician stuck to his guns. "I'm telling you, the place is bloody hot."

Harris hit a switch on his microphone. "Maddy, you okay? Feeling any temperature change?"

There was no answer. She seemed halfway over the threshold, moving so slowly.

"Yes," she said. "Yes. Definitely."

The technician nodded.

Then Maddy said something that surprised both of them.

"I'm cold."

Nick pulled up to the gate. He spotted the twin cameras pointed down from giant perches, aimed right at the gate entrance. And the gate was actually a series of three fences, one electrified fence girded by two nonelectric, all topped with big spirals of razor wire.

Looked strong enough to keep Godzilla in there.

"Amazing," he said.

"Look lively," Cosgrove said. "We have company."

Two soldiers came out of the gatehouse, machine guns pointed right at the car.

"You'll 'ave to turn around, sir. Immediately."

The man had a thick Scottish burr. Nick almost didn't understand him. Cosgrove leaned over.

"We must talk to the base commander."

"Colonel 'Arris is not available. Now, use that turn-around—and head back where you—"

"No."

It was the girl, Sophie, from the back. And the voice gave Nick chills. A command from God couldn't carry any more power.

"No," she said again, and now Sophie popped open her door.

"I have to talk to them. They don't know. They don't . . . know." She waited a bit. Nick saw that the soldiers were rattled by her display.

"They don't know—but I do."

Sophie stood beside the soldier. She could smell the gun, the thick smell of oil. And then, out of the car, the woods, the musty smell of clothing worn too many times before cleaning. The soldier's helmet let her see only a bit of his eyes, the square jaw, thin lips. Another soldier, also holding a weapon, came up beside him.

"I have things to tell them. Inside."

"You must turn around now. This is a restricted area."

Professor Cosgrove got out of the car and stood beside her.

"I used to work here—and this"—he put a hand on Sophie's shoulder—"is Ian MacDonald's daughter. He was the head scientist here. Before he left, before—"

"They killed him," Sophie said. And she knew when

she said that . . . that nothing could get her to move from this spot before she got inside.

One soldier seemed to lower his gun, and the other one tapped his partner on the shoulder. On the other side of the fence Sophie could see more soldiers lined up, and then beyond the tanks and guns.

The man, Nick, who had picked them up—and Sophie knew that was no accident—spoke.

"It won't hurt. To call. To ask. Whether the commander will speak with us."

Sophie knew that was no accident. No. There were no real accidents. Things happened for a reason. And things also *didn't* happen for a reason. There were reasons for everything.

And she knew why that could be so bad.

The two soldiers talked together, then one of them finally turned away and walked back to the small gatehouse while everyone waited.

So dark . . .

Maddy walked in slowly, tentatively. She felt the chill. For a moment she thought that the wind from the endless levels above now blew through here. But no, there was no great wind, just a chilling cold.

The darkness began to clear, like a mist clearing, the black turning to gray, then she could make out things . . . first the ground she stood on—the cool gray of granite, then—a few feet beyond that came into view—and she saw a rocky wall, curving to the left.

More clearing, and another wall to her right, some boulders, loose rock, and—

A pack.

Her heart leapt. A pack. Paul's pack?

But it wasn't Paul's. She knew his gear, and his bright red pack was dotted with the patches marking all the mountains he had mastered. So this pack might be Simon's—still a reason to be hopeful.

For a brief few seconds, Maddy didn't question the fact that she seemed to be standing on a rocky outcrop, on a mountain . . . inside this structure.

The mist rose a bit more, and there were clouds, and the top of a mountain.

Impossible, she thought. *Completely, totally impossible*.

"Ma—ddddd-y." Harris's voice in her earphones came through distorted, twisted around. He was under the sea, gargling.

"Do you see where I am? Can you see this?"

No answer for a minute. The ending of a word . . .

"—sssssssss. Don't—"

"Don't what?" she said.

She looked back to the golden door.

There was no door there. What did she think, that a door could be here too? She was on a mountain, near this pack, and—

She heard a scream. She turned and saw—

Paul's friend Simon.

He was half buried in the stone, mired in it—as if the rock had turned into liquid that had turned hard again, trapping his body. His hands protruded pathetically, and he clenched his fingers. His head was held fast into position, but he kept screaming.

"Simon," she said.

But his eyes gave no awareness that he heard or saw her.

Am I a ghost here? she wondered. *And is this what happened to Paul? Is this place showing me what happened to Paul?*

Another sound. A different voice. A voice she knew.

Paul.

Just around the rocky outcrop.

She looked at her watch. Two minutes left. But what did it matter? The door was gone, there was no way back—and somehow, now—she might see her brother.

She hurried toward the outcrop.

Harris turned toward the techs fiddling with all the black boxes.

The video monitor was blank. And the still monitor kept showing the last, fuzzy, degraded image—what looked like some mist-covered granite outcrop.

"Is she gone?"

No one answered.

"Is she gone, damn it? Will someone answer me or I'll have their bloody butt."

Finally Brigitte turned around.

"All signals are gone, sir. Audio, video, vitals. At exactly the same time. All we have are her last words, and that last image. We're analyzing it now."

"Analyzing it? Christ."

He turned to Richards. "I *told* you ten minutes was the limit. No one has gone twelve."

But Richards wheeled closer to the monitors and then she turned to the table of scientists.

"But look—look at this! We have never seen that. Maybe it can—"

"That woman has vanished for a damn 'maybe'?"

But Harris soon saw that he had hit a hot button. "Harris, do you want to speak to the PM again? Hear it straight from him? Or maybe you want to see the event reports again, the photographs from around the world? The Pacific Rise video, maybe? That makes for fun viewing."

No, Harris didn't need to see them again.

He had tried to warn Maddy off. It was a stupid gamble, a spin of the roulette wheel. And what for? To drop another pebble down the well? Someone else to join the list of those who had gone inside the place, to disappear, to be gobbled up?

"So—what now?" he said. "What the hell now—"

"Colonel—the gate is calling."

Harris turned to his aide, a reed-thin lieutenant.

"What is it?"

The lieutenant's eyes looked even bigger than normal behind his thick glasses.

"I think you better speak to them."

He handed the phone to Harris.

"What is it?"

He listened to the name.

Cosgrove, persona non grata at the base. He was someone eventually deemed dangerous to the security of the project. And some American was with him.

But he also had a young girl with him.

"Who is she?" Harris asked.

The soldier answered. Sophie MacDonald.

Harris hesitated. Ian MacDonald was dead. It was assumed that his daughter was dead too. Gone—who knows where. The possibilities . . . were endless.

But here she was . . . alive.

Then the soldier told him. "She says she has a message from her father. That it's important."

Harris cleared his throat.

"Bring them here. And fast."

Maddy ran around the outcrop, around the giant boulder sitting on top of the flat mountaintop.

She saw Paul.

She yelled his name.

And this time—he turned.

Just as he was about to touch a flat piece of stone. Only Maddy could see—the stone wasn't just a piece of granite, some rock.

It was something *more*.

"Paul," she said. "Don't." And it occurred to her that she was only . . . a few seconds too late.

Because already his fingers had touched the stone.

She imagined he would become like Simon, mired in this rock, melted into it, trapped on some kind of human flypaper.

But that's not what happened.

Instead, Paul's arm went into the stone, pressed right into the shimmering rock that apparently was as penetrable as a cloud.

One arm, then his other arm, disappeared as he turned away from Maddy, as the stone *pulled* him close to it.

"No!" Maddy yelled.

She ran to him, thinking crazily that she could pull him out.

Not even trying to rationalize what was happening, what might be really occurring.

She went to grab him, and watched as—in a flash—he vanished into the stone.

The stone stood before her.

"Harris, can you hear? Can you see?"

She looked around.

She was alone. Clouds flew above the sky.

Nobody could see, nobody could hear.

She thought . . .

I came here to get you. I came here to find you.

She took a breath.

She raised her fingers to the stone. A millimeter away. She felt nothing. The stone was mere rock. A millimeter away—and she hesitated.

I'm mad. This place has made me mad. None of this is real.

She touched the stone.

And a massive bolt of heat ran into her hand and up her arm. She felt the pull, her other arm went flying to the stone in a reflexive action to stop the pull. Reflexive and futile.

Then she faced forward as she braced herself to experience just how real this really was . . .

thirty

Four soldiers, guns at the ready, escorted them to a squat building at one end of the compound.

As they walked there, Nick got a brief look at . . . something in the distance, something silvery and shimmering.

"That's it," Cosgrove had whispered. "The 'house' . . . as they call it."

But the gap in the mountainous cul-de-sac was narrow, and soon Nick lost view of it and they reached a small building. One of the soldiers opened the door.

Nick looked down at Sophie. Older than his son, she seemed to have a steely confidence that was . . . incredible.

"You okay?" he asked.

The girl didn't smile. But she nodded.

"We're okay, hm?" Cosgrove added. He patted her other shoulder.

"Go on in," one of the soldiers said.

They walked into the building.

Sophie looked around at all the people and the equipment. Some of the faces she knew . . . they had visited her father, trying to get him to come back. They said hello to Sophie. *I wonder if they remember me,* she thought.

Then she looked at all the equipment. Sophie could guess what it was all for. They want to see what's in there.

They want to capture it . . . control it.

They couldn't do that, she knew.

But what she'd tell them would help.

The secret. Her dad's discovery.

He had never wanted her to come back here, close to the place.

She saw a man in uniform come over and talk with Professor Cosgrove. He acted upset. Then he turned on the American.

Sooner or later he'll talk to me, she thought.

I can wait. I waited a long time.

She thought of her dad.

Her dad. The real reason she was here.

She could never tell them that. Not now.

Maybe not ever.

Finally, the man in the uniform stopped talking and tuned and looked at her.

"Sophie MacDonald," he said.

Sophie nodded. He seemed ready to ask her a question, when one of the people by the equipment called out.

"Colonel—we have something here, sir. Can you come over?"

And the colonel turned away.

Sophie was here—so close.

I can wait, she thought.

Nick had asked about Maddy—and the close-lipped Colonel Harris said she had been here.

"Had been? And now?" Nick asked. "Where the hell is she now?"

Harris got close to Nick's face. "I will tell you. For now—you will wait here."

Right, thought Nick. *But not for long.*

Harris walked back to the instrument bank where Pollack was examining two photographs.

"What is it?"

"Look at these."

The images were close-ups.

"What are they? Just more stills from Maddy's headset, separated by a few minutes; what—"

"No," the woman said. "This one is from Maddy's headset. But this is a surveillance photo from the surrounding mountain range."

Harris took both photos in his hands. There could be no doubt that they were the same place.

"They're identical. That's crazy. She went in there—and somehow she's back"—he gestured with his hand—"somewhere up there?"

"Apparently so."

"It's mad."

Harris felt someone at his elbow, and turned to see Cosgrove—one step from being a traitor in his mind.

"Mad, but true, Harris. And if you talk to Sophie—and hear what Ian learned—you can get a better understanding."

Sophie looked at the image on the TV screen.

It didn't look like any of the places she had seen in her nightmares. It just looked . . . like a mountain.

It looked like a mountaintop—but it could be anything.

She looked around the room at the people sitting around the table, reading papers, talking quietly.

Then—loud voices from the front of the room—the American was angry. Someone had gone into . . . that place. He wanted to get her.

Sophie walked to the front of the room and waited until they all stopped and noticed her.

Cosgrove turned to her. "Sophie, are you okay?"

She nodded and then looked at Nick.

"You can go in. You can get her. I can help."

"Not possible," the colonel said. He looked right at Sophie as if he were explaining some complex idea. "We can't send anyone else in—we don't know what's happening—"

Sophie took a deep breath. "They made a mistake. Inside, they made a mistake. That woman's not supposed to be in there. They need her outside. They can make mistakes—and they have."

" 'They'?" Nick said. "Who are . . . 'they,' Sophie?"

"There are so many . . . so many of them. They were here once, and now they can come back and take everything, destroy everything. Because—that's what they do." She looked around. Everyone in the room was looking at her.

"Because—that's what they do?" Nick said.

"Still—no one can—" the colonel started.

"Sophie," Cosgrove interrupted, "tell them. What you told me. Show them—"

Sophie pulled out the piece of tinfoil.

"My dad knew that my nightmares were more than dreams. I could see into their world. And they could see that. They could use it—use me—to come into this world. So my dad took me away from this place. But there were others around the world, like me, who can let them out. But that wasn't all they needed."

The colonel took a step, took the tinfoiled thumb drive, and unwrapped it.

"What is this?"

"M-my dad's experiments . . . showing how all the worlds can be here, all the time."

"All the worlds?"

Cosgrove turned to the colonel. "The multiverse, Colonel. It's what the slit-scan experiment suggested. MacDonald proved it. God, he proved it—"

Nick looked at them. "Look, what is this slit-scan experiment? I need to go in there—get Maddy out now." Cosgrove turned to him.

"A beam of light shines into twin slits, breaking it up, creating twin intersecting beams. The light waves should double in certain areas, cancel each other out, like waves. But they *don't*. The twin slits create two independent light sources . . . the light . . . suddenly exists in two places at once. The very act of . . . measuring it changes the light, multiplies it. It exists in two places at once."

Sophie remembered her father explaining the crazy idea to her. So . . . crazy, so incomprehensible. She saw the same look on the colonel's face.

"There's not just this one world, but—my dad said—endless worlds. Imagine it, he said, and it's real."

Such a scary thought, Sophie remembered.

Imagine it . . . and it's real.

Harris didn't say anything for a moment.

Then . . .

"Endless universes . . ." The woman in the wheelchair repeated the words. "Where all rules of science can exist—or not exist. He proved it?" She looked right at Sophie.

No one said anything for a moment. Then Harris turned back to the monitor and looked at the screen, the last view from Maddy.

"If it's true—if that insanity is true—how does it help us?"

Cosgrove shook his head. "Only in this, sir—" He turned to Sophie. "Want to finish?"

Sophie rubbed her arms. Was this room cold? She felt the picture in her back pocket, all crumpled from her sitting on it.

"They use people like me. If they can get someone in-side . . . and someone is outside . . . connected to them . . . it's like a—like a . . ."

"An anchor?" Nick said.

Sophie nodded. "Yes, a bit like that. An anchor to our world."

"So"—Harris shook his head—"that's what's been happening. They've been finding ways out, to, to—"

"Destroy it all," Cosgrove added. "All of . . . this uni-verse is based on life. Their universe feeds off chaos, de-struction—"

"Enough," Nick said. "Enough." He turned to Sophie. "What do we do?"

"They have a connection . . . to the outside. But I have a connection to their world. If someone is in there, I can—help them."

"Help them?"

"I can see inside there, tell them where to go."

Cosgrove looked at her. "And there's the other thing. Sophie?"

She nodded. "My dad said that maybe . . . somehow . . . it can use your own mind against you."

The woman in the wheelchair rolled up to Sophie, shak-ing her head.

"Is that all? All the theories of quantum physics sud-denly true, and any imagined universe . . . could possibly be real? Is that all of it, young MacDonald?"

Sophie hesitated.

"No." She licked her lips. "They're getting ready to come out. Soon."

Maddy vanished into the rock.

For a moment, the cold vanished and she felt a syrupy warmth cover her body. She had her eyes shut tight as if she were on some hellish theme park ride, the type she hated when she was a kid.

The feeling of warmth vanished, but she still felt the breeze, neutral, just a steady flow of air.

She opened her eyes.

She was in a room, a long room that stretched so far into the distance. She stood on the bright red floor, indistinguishable from the walls or the ceiling.

"Paul," she said quietly. Then louder. "Paul!"

Her voice echoed in the empty chamber just as she imagined that it might.

She took a step—and when she did she fell forward, into the wall, as if gravity itself had twisted, and now the wall was the floor. She landed with a painful *thud,* the side of her head smacking against the wall. She knelt up.

What is this place?

Slowly, she brought herself to a standing position. Maybe she had only imagined what just happened.

There was only one way to test it—she took another step and now flew off the wall-turned-floor and crashed into the ceiling.

Another hard smack slammed her helmet against her head.

Wait a second, she thought.

She remembered this feeling . . . from a childhood dream she once had. Not a dream, though—but a nightmare where her bedroom lost all gravity, and her toys and childhood furniture tumbled to a wall, then the ceiling, sometimes passing her, and other times crashing into her as she joined the free-falling jumble.

It was . . . just like this.

Only this was no dream. It was real.

She looked down at the other end of the room, so distant. She saw an opening—a small rectangle of light. She started to crawl, thinking: *Maybe if I crawl nothing will happen.*

But she had only slid a few inches forward when she

rolled into the right wall, which had once again turned into a floor.

The room would continue to batter her, toss her around, play with her. There was nothing she could do.

She knew that now . . . as she inched her way closer to the light.

"Good," Nick said quickly. "I'm going in."

"No, if anyone goes in, it will be some of our SAS people. You don't—"

"Richards, don't be such an ass." Nick watched Harris glare at the woman in the wheelchair as she positioned herself at the center of the group.

"Didn't you hear what this girl—" he looked at her . . .

"Sophie."

"What Sophie *said*? The connection between people is somehow important, a lifeline for whatever is inside. He knows Maddy; it can only help. If anyone goes in to get her out it should be him."

Nick saw that the woman cradled a pack of cigarettes in her hand. "All right then. Not that it matters, not that I think anyone can come out of that damned place."

Nick turned to the woman. "I can try." He turned back to Sophie. "And you think—you can help me?"

She nodded.

"It's like . . . I can almost see it now," Sophie said.

Harris turned toward Cosgrove. "Can you check Mac-Donald's notes? There might be something there to help." He stopped and looked at Nick. "Okay, if we're going to do this, let's get started."

Maddy smashed into another wall, landing hard on the small of her back.

But she had gotten closer, actually made progress.

Good, she thought. *And I'm not dead. Wherever this is—I'm alive.*

She heard a noise. A low moaning sound, followed by something breaking, crashing.

She turned around, and she saw the room behind her ... imploding, as the walls, the ceiling, the floor closed in on each other like a giant throat closing, gulping.

Back to the rectangular light.

Not far now, not far. I can make it, I can get out.

And she hurried now, kicking forward, flying through the air of this room where gravity shifted with every leap.

They quickly suited Nick up and strapped a gun on him.

And he thought of the last time he'd used a gun—how pathetic his stand was in Sierra Leone.

Now he had a chance to do better.

Did he really imagine he'd get in and get out?

He didn't know what he believed.

The helmet had a camera on it—though Nick knew that Maddy's signal had vanished after ten minutes.

Sophie said she'd help him. Did he really believe that was possible?

Anything's possible, he imagined. *Isn't that what Cosgrove said quantum physics is all about?*

Before he knew what was happening, Harris and the others came to get him from an equipment room. Sophie stood in the front, watching the whole thing.

"You all set?"

Nick nodded.

Harris explained how they would watch everything on video. And Nick thought: *Just like they watched Maddy disappear.*

"Well then, let's go."

Nick nodded, and as he walked outside, Sophie came up beside him ... walked beside him.

"Something you want to tell me?" Nick said.

Sophie nodded, and spoke quietly. "Just before you go in, I want you to do something for me."

Nick smiled. "Depends. If it involves getting out, then sure."

"Okay. I'll tell you—just before you go in."

Nick walked across the courtyard to the inner gates.

He thought of that expression . . . good money after bad.

Then a children's fable . . . "Chicken Little" . . . how each bird followed the fox to its doom, one by one . . . except for Henny Penny.

And that was only because she was a really stupid chicken.

Except—thought Nick—*this time, the sky really was falling.*

They got to the inner gates, and Sophie grabbed Nick's hand and pulled him away . . .

thirty-one

Elaina stood under the big clock in the Washington, D.C., terminal.

The giant space had thinned out and she didn't see anyone who might be looking for someone . . . looking for someone like her.

Her brother had promised that someone would meet her there and take her someplace safe.

Elaina knew what she would do. She'd call a lot of people. A few key senators, like Hatch and Luger, both interested in all things genetic. This would get their attention right away. Then maybe a few private watchdog agencies dealing with genetic research—they'd also be interested.

In an hour she'd have GenTech—and whatever it was up to—spread over a dozen different agencies, private and public—throughout the capital.

She looked around.

Still no one.

Could . . . something have gone wrong?

She had used a public phone—still, her brother's phone could have been tapped. *They could have done that, couldn't they?* she thought. In which case, they'd know she was coming here.

And just as she had that thought, she looked around and she saw someone in shorts and a bright Hawaiian shirt walking in her direction. Whoever it was looked like a college student trying to prolong summer.

He made a beeline toward the clock, toward Elaina.

She shifted on her feet.

In moments he stood beside her, smiling. He was tanned, his close-cropped hair bleached a snowy yellow from the sun.

"Elaina?" he said.

"Yes."

"I'm a friend of your brother's—Mark Weintraub."

Now he looked over Elaina, taking in her tired, sunken eyes, and probably checking the ill-fitting jeans and her general disheveled appearance. She almost wanted to say: *I can look better.*

"Well, *mi casa . . . su casa.*"

So funny . . . his use of Spanish.

"Gracias, señor," she said, smiling.

"De nada," he said. "Come on. I'll take you there." He leaned close to her. "Your brother said that it was important no one saw you. *Mission Impossible* stuff, hm?"

She nodded.

"Well, wait till you see me drive. Anyone who tries to tail us will be dead meat . . ."

Elaina reached out and touched his arm. "I'll have to use your phone. To make a lot of calls. They could be dangerous."

"Now I'm really interested."

"Do you have a fax . . . or scanner, because if not—"

"Hey, don't worry. I got them all. And white wine and pretzels and all of life's essentials."

And for the first time she had started this, Elaina relaxed—but only a bit.

Sophie pulled Nick away. Nick looked up to see Harris start to follow, but Nick held up a hand, indicating that he should stop—and wait.

"Okay, Sophie. What is it?"

The girl looked at Nick. "There's a secret about the place. I just wanted you to hear. Because it's very dangerous."

"A secret about a place you've never been to?"

She nodded.

"What is it?"

"My dad said . . . if you think of something, it becomes real."

Nick paused. "You believe it?"

She nodded her head vigorously.

"Anything else?"

Another nod, and this time she swung her backpack around to her front and unzipped a small pocket. She pulled something out of it.

She handed it to Nick.

One more look around at the others.

And then she leaned close, whispering something that made Nick's eyes sting, his nostrils pinch, as he felt Sophie talking to him, heaving against him, knowing, now, why she had really made this great and terrible journey.

Harris looked over at the young girl talking to the American, a crazy American apparently willing to vanish down the rabbit hole where Maddy had just disappeared.

"What is she telling him?" he asked Cosgrove.

"Probably . . . telling him how she will try to feel him in the inside . . . and help him."

"And you think she can do that?"

Cosgrove looked at Harris.

"For all our sakes, we better hope she can."

Harris watched Sophie after she finished whispering to Nick, as she turned back to everyone, her eyes puffy, her cheeks tear-stained, whipping at them with her sleeve.

Harris looked at the soldiers at the inner gate and gave them the signal to open it.

One of them hit a switch, and the current running through the inner fence was cut off as the hinged gates swung open, and the way to the house, the shining silvery structure, swung open.

Elaina used every trick she could to speak to a real person.

Though it was late, she got assistants, and secretaries, and other assorted people. And when she told them what she had—proof of a dangerous genetic experiment—they listened. She faxed and e-mailed copies of the code.

Better, she thought, *the more people that had it*.

Companies, politicians, and eventually she checked her Hotmail account for a word from Peter.

There was some e-mail with an attachment, from early in the evening, when Peter first got back to his apartment.

Say hello, the e-mail screamed.

She downloaded the picture attached to the file.

And she saw the creature. So strange, alien, vicious-looking—she pulled back from the screen.

"Oh, God," she said. She knew she had to print this, fax it, e-mail it too. Whatever tests Peter had done, however he had handled the code, they could do it too. She could show them what was hidden in the code.

Time to call Peter, she thought.

She punched in his number. Mark appeared at the door, his face concerned, the joviality drained away by Elaina's panicked intensity.

Peter's phone rang, and kept ringing. Nine, ten times, until a recorded voice came on and offered the chance to leave a message.

"Hit star," the voice said.

Elaina did.

"Peter, I got it out, and I sent the picture. Whatever GenTech was doing, whoever they were doing it with, whoever they were doing it for . . . it's out there now. And the amazing thing is . . . I'm still alive. So . . . where are you, Peter? Out celebrating your fantastic bit of code work? Call me, okay. Call me just as—"

"Message complete," the recorded voice said. "If you would like to leave another message, please redial the number."

Elaina put down the handset.

Sure, Peter had to be out. She pushed aside the bit of worry she felt.

No need for another message. They were both alive, and GenTech would be stopped.

She turned and saw Mark at the doorway.

"All done?"

"Yes. For now. Sooner or later, I'll have to tell people in person, talk to them." She smiled. "But, for now, I'm done."

Wherever GenTech got the code from, whatever part of the world it came from, for now they were stopped.

For now . . .

"Then how about a nice glass of Pouilly Fuisse? I must say you look like you need it."

She laughed. Actually . . . laughed.

"Sure. That sounds . . . wonderful."

It was time for a glass of wine.

There'd be time for sleep—lots of sleep—later.

Nick didn't hesitate walking in the door. Every minute he waited was another minute something could happen to Maddy.

He felt ridiculous wearing what looked like a NASA

flight uniform and head cameras. He heard Harris, so calm and collected, in his ear.

Then Nick walked into the building.

The entranceway didn't seem much different from a foyer of some modern museum, with pillars, doors, and—

"Look up, Nick," Harris prompted.

And he did. To see what looked like intersecting glasslike slivers, massive, a giant Calder mobile suspended above him.

"What the hell is that? And am I crazy, but do you see how far—"

He saw one of the glasslike planes shiver, then as he watched, a triangular chunk snapped off and started falling toward him.

He ran to the wall.

"Nick, you better get out. It wasn't like this for—"

But then a complete plane snapped free and plummeted toward the floor. Nick went flush against one wall as the glass plane shattered on the floor. A hundred small pieces exploded into the air.

"It's all falling," Nick said. "The fucking roof, the—"

And—

He remembered Sophie's words.

What you imagine becomes real.

He had been thinking about . . . Henny Penny, and the story of the sky falling. And here it was falling.

"Get out, Nick. Now."

He turned around, and there was an opening that wasn't there before, some kind of dirt burrow. Was it a tunnel, he wondered, or just a cave?

He ran to it, as more massive pieces smashed behind him.

He went in, surrounded by darkness. The noise of the pieces shattering was deafening, and he saw that they were beginning to pile up outside the burrow, pile up and—as he watched, he could see them begin to bubble. Bubbling, melting.

They were melting, bubbling, turning to shimmering sea.

"Sophie, Sophie . . . are you there?"

A pause. Had he lost communication already? And how strange was it to be depending on a young girl to somehow help him.

"Soph—"

"I'm here. They didn't want me to watch the TV screens."

"Let her watch," Nick said. "She's seen all this before."

In the background Nick heard Cosgrove agree.

"Sophie . . . I'm not imagining those things . . . can you see them? . . . melting. Turning to liquid. You said—"

"No. You're not. But someone is."

"What do you mean? Someone is?"

"Someone is. Somewhere."

"Somewhere? You mean in here? Or at the camp?"

"It could be . . . anywhere."

Nick had nothing to say.

Anywhere. And he watched as now a small sea of molten glass—if it was glass—began to form. The molten sea started inching toward the entrance to his burrow.

"Shit." He caught himself. "Sorry, Sophie. I don't know what to—"

He spun around.

The burrow was a cave. He felt the earth, not much different than the loamy soil he used to play with in his backyard while his father planted, digging, while he . . . as his father said . . . "dug a hole to China."

It was pitch-dark ahead.

Back to the glass. Now the pieces as they landed fell into the molten sea and sent a steaming splatter flying up to the walls, even shooting into the burrow.

Back to the depths of the burrow.

He had no choice.

"Can you still hear me?"

No response.

"Can you still—hear—me?"

"Yes, Nick . . ." Harris this time. "Don't know . . . what to say, what to tell you."

Harris's voice was filled with hopelessness.

But Nick knew one thing. He had no choice. He had to go deeper.

He started crawling.

thirty-two

Maddy reached out during the last tumble in this room and grabbed the edge of the floor about to turn into the ceiling.

She looked behind—though she had told herself the old adage from mountain climbing . . . never look down.

Or, in this case, never look back.

But she had to—to know if she had a chance.

She saw the room still imploding, and from the way the new floor curved up, it was only meters away from her, away from one last gulp.

"No," she said. And she pulled as hard as she could to propel herself out of the room, out into the space, the purple rose-colored space that—for all she knew, could be suspended miles above any land or sea.

It could be a final suicidal act.

Her arms were strong enough, and she found herself flying out of the room, arms in front of her. She saw the sky, a near-mythic sunset kind of sky, the purple and lavender swirling around such sweet puffy yellow clouds.

She looked down.

She wasn't so high.

In fact—it was like tumbling off her bed. She fell forward onto some leafy plants, swamplike reeds and bushes, before landing in some muddy muck.

She turned around and watched the room she came from vanish in one tiny wink.

The gravity-mad room no longer existed.

She lifted up her hands. The mud . . . wasn't mud, but more like a clay. She tried to tell the color. Was it greenish, like the algae on the side of a fish tank or the green on a rock sitting in the shade by a sleepy brook?

Or was it really black and merely picking up color from the sky or from the plants? She rubbed the ground muck on her outfit . . . and it stuck to her leg.

Like a mucky burr, it stayed on her leg.

She quickly checked her fingers. But outside of a little discoloration, they looked okay.

Then the plants.

At first glance, they looked like ordinary marshy shrubs and plants. But she looked a few seconds longer—and Maddy knew that she had never seen any one of them before. The leaves had odd shapes, symmetrical swirls and twists. And those leaves moved independently of any wind—because there was no wind. They weaved and dipped and—

They're alive, Maddy thought.

Not just like plants, they're alive, capable of responding.

And when a nearby bush seemed to be weaving toward her, dipping, diving, she decided to stand up, rise above the plants to see what this place really looked like.

She stood up.

And when she did, she moaned.

• • •

Nick scrambled through the burrow.

He could almost hear his father's gravelly, cigarette-ravaged voice . . . "Digging to China, son?" Then laughing . . . "Keep digging."

His fingers clawed at the loamy dirt while he heard the sound of something coming behind him.

A molten river of glass, rushing toward him.

The burrow tilted down, and Nick went sliding forward.

"Can you hear me?" he yelled. "Can you see anything?"

There was no answer.

Just as he knew there wouldn't be.

All radio signals, everything, all gone. Because who knew where he was.

Then he thought . . .

Sophie . . . you there?

He guessed it was too much to hope. That the girl really had a connection—unwanted—with this place, this wonderland of horror.

But then—

He heard a breeze. He felt warm air. He looked ahead, and saw a pinpoint of light.

Something fell on his shoulder, burning through the uniform.

He looked to his left and saw another ball of molten glass—if it was glass—land beside him.

He didn't have much time.

He scrambled toward the light.

Sophie curled up and kept her eyes closed.

She tried to see where they were, to make the nightmare something she could see.

I can help them, she thought. *If only I can see them.*

The feeling of . . . connection . . . came in short waves, like a gentle sea lapping at her feet when she used to dig in the sand, just at the point where the ocean waves stopped.

Please, she thought.

So many times she hated seeing things there.

But now, she needed to, wanted to—

And then—

She saw everything.

Maddy looked around.

She saw things moving . . . at first they looked like misshapen rocks weaving back and forth, but then one turned, and she saw something that had to be a head.

A single eye from the thing looked in her direction, then returned to what it was doing . . . pulling at something stringy it had found . . . something stringy, wet.

Then, from behind her, she heard a loud guttural scream, a struggled, twisted sound unlike anything she had heard before.

An alert, a warning . . . someone is here.

She sucked in the air—amazed that there was air here.

The sound again, and Maddy felt more alone than she ever had before.

She sensed movement all around her, but could see nothing.

Something brushed her foot, and she watched a grayish-colored thing slide over her foot. It had two back legs and finlike feet. And no mouth—

That is, until Maddy felt its underside start to dig into her foot. The thing's grasp, sharp and immediate, provoked a quick reflex.

She screamed and kicked the thing into the air.

I'll be dead in minutes here, she thought.

Here. Alone here. Where . . . the hell . . . is here?

All alone—when she heard a voice.

"Help . . ."

Paul's voice.

Her brother's voice. Calling to her. Nearby.

And she wasn't alone anymore.

•   •   •

Nick flew out of the burrow and rolled down to the ground so mucky, and with a smell that made his stomach heave.

I'm over my head, he thought.

Not cut out to play the hero.

I won't find Maddy, won't get out, and—

An insect the size of a hummingbird, looking more like a flying shrimp, landed on his arm. Nick watched as its pincerlike snout began to pull back.

The thing wants to dig into me.

He whacked it away, with its massive stinger just about to break his skin.

The noises from the surrounding . . . jungle—the only word he could use to describe it—filled his ear.

Sounds of another world.

He thought: *I can't move.*

I don't know where to go, what to do—

He felt the breeze again, the same warm breath of air, sweet, untainted air.

He inhaled.

And then he heard Sophie. The voice not even a whisper, a child's voice in the night telling you about her nightmare, the terrible scary nightmare, that just woke her up.

She's here, Nick. She's close. Keep . . . keep walking.

Then the breeze was gone.

For no good reason, Nick pulled out his gun.

Last time he had a gun out, he couldn't use it.

Here . . . it would be different.

But would it make a difference? He heard the sound of something stepping behind him.

He turned.

Maddy moved in the direction of Paul's voice.

He's alive, she thought. Her brother was here, and somehow, incredibly, he was alive.

"Maddy? Over here."

She turned, and walked through a swamp with knee-deep puddles. She felt things in the water moving around her leg.

Hurry, she thought. *Don't give them a chance to land. Whatever they are . . .*

She slipped into a deeper hole, and stumbled into the water.

And for the first time she could feel it, slimy, slippery, but also it had a silky feel.

She shot up as fast as she could, and sent a splash of water flying up to her lips . . . so close to her tongue, so close to *tasting* it.

That wouldn't be a good thing.

"Maddy? I'm here."

The voice now seemed to come from the other direction, but it sounded closer.

I'll find Paul and somehow we'll get out of here.

Because there had to be a way out of here.

Keep going . . . don't look at those things.

If they see you—they'll come for you.

Nick heard Sophie, that strangled child's night whisper. *It's like she's been here,* he thought. *And in some way, she has been.*

It was bad enough to come here in a dream.

To be here—for real—was—

Something landed on his back.

He reached around and felt something with a spiky fur start to hurriedly cut into the uniform, touching his skin. Then—he felt porcupine-like spikes start to go deeper. His back felt a sudden burn, and he fell to his knees.

He reached around and—in an awkward grab—pulled at the thing and with a massive tug ripped it off.

Still . . . on his knees.

He knew—he had to get up. Not good to be too low to this fucking ground.

You have to hurry . . . you have to go fast, 'cause—

Sophie?

The voice had stopped.

Did someone break her concentration?

Or was he cut off?

"Maddy!"

No answer, only the strange strangled noises that now— he was sure—were closer, circling, coming toward him.

"Sophie, you okay?"

It was the woman in the wheelchair. She had wheeled over.

Sophie needed to keep thinking, to keep . . . talking to the man inside the house. He had the picture. She had to stay with him.

The woman wheeled a bit closer.

"I need to be alone," Sophie said.

The woman nodded.

"I'm not sure"—a bit closer—"that you *should* be alone. Maybe we should get you some food. It's too scary here."

Sophie looked at the woman's legs.

So close together, since they were supposed to be crippled—

Supposed to be . . . Sophie thought.

The woman saw her looking. And her smile faded.

She leaned close to Sophie.

"They want you, Sophie. You're here. And they can come out and get you—unless . . . you run . . . now . . ."

Sophie was cornered by the woman. She looked around for the colonel, but he was up front, looking at the dead screens.

"And you know what they'll do to you? Do you want to hear what they did to your father? Sure you do—"

Sophie shook her head. No, she didn't want to see that.

"Here's what they did. Just—watch—"

No, Sophie couldn't see that. They needed her help inside.

But then the images were there. She was back in the house, with her father, alone, when her father heard a noise at the door . . .

"Paul!"

Then—his voice was there, just to Maddy's right.

She pushed past a meters-high purplish plant, but the plant seemed to push back, slashing at her, cutting through the material.

She emerged into a small pool—and saw Paul, sitting in the water.

He smiled. That same small cocky smile she both loved and—at times—could hate.

"Paul, you're alive. I didn't know—"

"You bet I'm alive—though if things here had their way—but hey, give me a hand. Got stuck in the muck. We'll get out of here together."

She smelled something then. A strange odor filled her nostrils, burning them, leaving a foul taste on her tongue.

She looked down at her brother.

Funny, he'd never ask for help. Always so much the bigger brother, independent, strong . . .

"Here—give me a tug and we'll find"—a grin—"a door out of this place."

She hesitated. She didn't know why she hesitated. But she stopped and looked around. The smell was stronger, suffocating, and—

The atmosphere. It was changing, slowly turning from something unbreathable.

She looked down to the pool that Paul sat in. The dark oily water didn't let any light through. No way to see *below* the water.

Something . . . is wrong here.

She looked around, seeing shapes moving in the distance, coming closer.

Back to Paul.

"Get up, Paul. We have to leave. We have to—"

He shook his head. "I'm stuck here. Come on, Maddy, give me a tug—"

His arms outstretched.

She should just help him, grab his arms, pull him out and—

She looked at the water. A small oily bubble popped to the surface—then exploded. She couldn't see below his waist line, couldn't see there.

She backed up a step.

"Get up, Paul." A quick look around. "Get up now and we can—"

And her brother tilted his head, looking at her, the face filled . . . with a realization.

"Okay," he said slowly. "If that's what you want."

And then he pulled back his arms as if balancing himself on a high wire, and his body started to rise out of the murky liquid. Rise up until she saw that . . . he had no legs below his waist.

No, he had something else, something that had all the crazed definition of the slimy meat of an oyster, the puffy swirls of grayish flesh. Something extended from the bottom and—her brother—

(Not her brother, it wasn't her brother, he was gone, he was gone, he was—)

—jumped at her, splashing only inches away, and those arms encircled her.

She thought of the gun.

She couldn't. Not her brother.

The other creatures, the insane assortment of shapes and colors, narrow heads, gaping open mouths—were close, watching, screaming—

Watching.

• • •

"You better leave her alone."

The woman turned away from Sophie.

Cosgrove was there. He must have seen her come over. Sophie looked at Cosgrove and made her eyes go wide, sending a warning. Cosgrove looked confused.

"I think the girl should go away. There's nothing happening here."

Sophie sat up, her voice shrill, loud. "She's one of them. She's helping them—"

And now the woman stood up and threw herself on Cosgrove.

I know what they did, Sophie thought. *She can walk again—for helping them. They can make things happen like that.*

The woman's hands went to claw at Cosgrove's throat.

And Sophie yelled. Such a small sound at first, then louder, until finally the soldiers at the computer monitors heard the noise, and pulled her off, babbling, yelling, cursing—

She was just one person helping them—but there were so many more.

But now everyone will know, thought Sophie.

Cosgrove came over to her. "You okay?"

She nodded. "I have to close my eyes. They're alone in there."

"Yes. I'll make sure no one bothers you."

And Sophie closed her eyes.

Maddy held the gun against her brother's head. She was crying. It was an impossible act, impossible . . .

I can't do it, she thought. *Please—don't make me do it.*

But when that head opened its mouth—she pulled the trigger.

It exploded—but she didn't see the expected blood and

bone flying. It was like a giant puffy spore erupting, sending grayish-white fibers into the air.

The smell made her empty stomach retch, vomiting nothing.

And those arms holding her—amazingly—pulled tighter, as she felt whatever was below . . . move against her legs.

I'm lost, Nick thought.

Trapped in—what is this—a world? A house that becomes a world or—

He remembered what Sophie had told him.

What you imagine becomes real.

I never imagined this, he thought.

Who had?

And then—Sophie's hushed voice was in his head.

She's close. She's in trouble. You have to hurry.

Left, right, which way? Nick thought. Then aloud, "Which way?"

I—I . . . go left. Hurry!

Nick raced through the surreal swamp.

"Maddy?"

He didn't expect an answer. Could Sophie really *see* here?

He didn't expect an answer but then he heard a moan, just ahead. He jumped over something small with a gaping teeth-lined hole at the top of its head.

Landing in a shallow pool, where he saw Maddy.

thirty-three

Maddy felt the arms tighten around her, holding her, pinning her. For a moment, she didn't see what those arms were doing. It felt as though they wanted to consume her.

But then she looked around—and saw the others moving close, hurrying now. Long-necked creatures that looked as though they had slid out of narrow yet mammoth mouse holes, then immediately swelled up, inflating.

Another creature whose teeth—if the shining, metallic things snapping at the air were actually teeth—made a constant chattering as they *snap, snap, snap*ped at nothing—for now.

She looked over her shoulder, wondering what horror she'd see there.

And she saw Nick.

Nick froze.

There were so many of those things moving toward Maddy. He wanted to run away, to close his eyes from this nightmare.

There was nothing he could do. She turned around and looked right at him.

That face—

So different from the day they had gone to that ancient site, the Norman mound in Kent where she took photographs and her smile had all the power of the sun.

Now, the terror, the grimace, the fear were so incredibly painful to see.

Maddy saw Nick. And for a moment, she thought of the day they had spent . . .

On that mound, raised high on the ancient earth, its treasures, its secrets, its . . . bodies . . . hidden beneath.

And then—

She was on a mound.

Nick watched the ground around Maddy *rise,* a silent upthrust of land as if the rock and mud were nothing but some endlessly expandable taffy.

She was high above the creatures.

Maddy turned away to see the creatures below beginning to climb the mound to her, then back to Nick, also scrambling up the mound.

He remembered . . . *I was thinking about that day, the mound*—had Maddy flashed on it too?

Sophie rocked in the corner. She sensed Cosgrove standing close by, protecting her, as she thought, and concentrated. Of course, she could see it all. As much as she wished she could turn it off, open her eyes, and run outside, she knew she couldn't. They needed her.

And more . . .

This was all so important.

She saw the small hill *rise* in the horrible landscape. It just rose from the ground . . .

The woman did that, as they moved to her.

And Sophie knew then that—though this was a trap—there was a way out.

If only they could do it.

Listen. She imagined the two of them. *Listen . . . it's a trap. A trap, and everyone inside it makes it stronger, feeds into it, makes the trap . . . stronger.*

But . . . but—

Did he hear? Did he know already?

But you can stop it. You can undo it . . . if—if—

If they hear me.

Nick was clambering up the hill when he felt tangling vines suddenly wrap themselves around his legs, trapping him. They weren't vines at all, but a jumbled creature curled up on the side of the hill, waiting.

He looked at Maddy.

I tried, he thought. *I tried. I didn't blink this time . . .*

He reached down for the gun by his side. But already both arms were also pinned, as the vinelike things tugged at his arms, pulling, hard, harder—

Ready to rip them off.

"Maddy!"

He screamed, but he felt the words fading, failing as if there were too little atmosphere to carry them. Then again: "Maddy!"

Now she looked trapped in her own agony, another part of the thing wrapped around her, pinning her too.

Maddy looked at Nick. He wasn't far away, but his voice was hollow, empty, barely a whisper.

She looked at his lips, repeating the same words over and over, but unable to make them out.

Then—

Like tuning in some distant radio station and—in a brief moment—the signal becomes clear.

"What . . . you . . . imagine . . . becomes . . . real."

She saw Nick entangled, then saw his face twisted in pain.

No. That can't happen. She didn't want *that* to happen.

His words, so absurd, as if imagining had anything to do with reality.

Still—she looked at him and made herself see him . . . free.

Free.

And then he was.

The vines vanished. She had heard.

Nick scrambled up the hill. Had this place wanted Maddy all along? Did it want everyone who went in here—or did it pick them? Using them to build this hell world, all the other worlds in here, an army of demented worlds?

He got to the hill with the other creatures only yards away from Maddy.

"Thanks," he said. He looked around the hill. "Now make them . . . gone."

"I don't know if I can—"

"Make them go, Maddy, and fast. They wanted you here. Now they got you. Picture them—gone."

Sophie saw all those things that she had seen in nightmares—so close to the two of them.

Please, she thought. *Let them get away. Please . . .*

Maddy looked around. She looked down at the mound. She looked at Nick. She felt so alone—

When there were three people there.

An old woman, and someone middle-aged, and a young girl, all looking at her.

Maddy looked at them.

More tricks, more danger, who are they, who could they be—

She looked at the girl, maybe fifteen. The frizzy brown hair, the green eyes, and the funny way she half smiled, as if . . . too embarrassed to let her dimples shine.

She wasn't alone. She knew that girl.

The young girl, perhaps dreaming this, the other two, tossing in their sleep, *remembering* this.

Now—here to help—

Then Nick reached out and took a hand—

The three women joined hands, and the young girl took Maddy's hand.

"Come on, beautiful," Nick whispered . . . "make this place . . . beautiful."

And in a moment, they were back there, in the Kentish hillside, and Maddy was free.

The rest of the sick world still surrounded them, but they floated on this small English green hillock, safe—and now alone.

She hugged him close, and nothing had ever felt so good.

"My brother . . . he's—" she said.

"I know. I saw. We have to go. I'll try to get us out. Can you"—Nick gestured at the world around them—"try to make this go away."

Maddy nodded. "I can try."

"Let's go."

Sophie rocked faster. They were so close. What if they didn't get out?

She could see them, close together on the mound, holding each other. *They won't know how to leave these worlds.*

She thought—

It's a straight trail.

Just keep running straight. Don't let anything stop you. Just keep running.

And then—
And please . . . please . . . please . . . don't forget.

Straight.

Straight was deeper into this hell. But Nick knew he had to trust Sophie. She knew this place's tricks, its twisted geometry.

"Come on," he said.

He pulled Maddy off the mound, running straight ahead.

"Is this right?"

"Trust me—I'm getting a little help."

Together, they splashed into the murky pond, dodged the slashing bushes, and hopped over smaller creatures that leaped into the air to snap at them.

"Maddy," Nick said, panting. "Can you imagine it all gone? You can shut it down. Make it all go away."

Something reared up in front of them, completely blocking the way, eyes as big as saucers, and a craggy, giant head with so many openings.

Nick squeezed her hand tighter.

"Gone, Maddy . . . *gone* . . ."

Then it was.

Maddy looked around, that first flush of power.

"More. Go on," Nick said.

Maddy looked around the world, and she thought of that moment in a nightmare—when you become aware that it is a dream, that nothing really bad can happen to you, not here.

They could both die in here.

But only if Maddy let it happen.

"This place is so . . . ugly—I hate it," she said.

Then, like a gentle wave breaking on the shore, she watched all the overgrown trees and ancient plants vanish. The creatures screamed and howled, a moment of bedlam as they too vanished in this newly imagined world.

Which became a stainless-steel hallway. Clean, clear, antiseptic.

And at the other end, a door.

A way out.

Nick pulled her tight.

"Let's go," she said. Then, turning to him and giving him a smile . . . she was happy with her dimpled smile these days. "Before I get any bad ideas . . ."

She took a step.

Nick grabbed her hand and stopped her.

What's this? she thought. Another trick. Nick about to turn into . . . something else.

Instead he reached into his pocket and pulled something out.

Nick pulled out the photograph.

He handed it to Maddy.

Then he pulled her tight, kissed her on the lips, and— moving his lips to the side of her face—he whispered to her . . . what he wanted her to do . . . what he wanted her to try.

Then . . . the words . . .

"Your brother, Maddy . . . your brother . . ."

"Jesus, the door is opening!" Harris yelled. "Get the gate open. Someone's coming out!"

Sophie's eyes shot open.

She sprang to her feet. And on monitors, she could see the door to the place opening.

Sophie didn't wait for the others. She turned around, and ran to the door leading out . . .

Out to the open air, where the guards were opening the gates, and everyone was running, hurrying to the gates.

Sophie ran as fast she could, flying, pumping her arms.

She hit the gates just as they opened, and kept on going,

knowing that now she too was on the screen, racing for the doors.

They were coming out, was all she thought. Coming out.

And that wasn't all.

That couldn't be all.

Twenty feet from the open door, she stopped.

The woman—Maddy came out first. And someone with her, not Nick . . .

Her brother.

Sophie looked at Maddy's legs, the material of the uniform ripped off, cut into pieces, the skin bloody.

Still, the woman—whose eyes looked puffy from tears, who was in fact still crying, heaving, her arm around her brother—smiled at Sophie.

Then Nick came out.

He was alone.

He walked over to Sophie. He put a hand on her shoulder.

He didn't say anything. It was as if he just wanted to touch her for a moment, check her before—

Someone else came out of the door.

Sophie looked up, her mind racing, her heart still thumping from her dash, and her eyes already stinging with the idea . . . the hope—

As her dad walked out into the afternoon sun, blinking, smiling.

And Sophie burst into tears as she threw herself at him, wrapped herself around him and held him tight, tighter and closer than anything she had ever held before.

This was all she could expect, more than she could have ever dreamed.

She couldn't expect any more . . . she shouldn't expect.

Then someone else stood beside them. Someone she hadn't seen in years and years. Almost a stranger. A woman. So . . . unexpected.

Sophie almost couldn't say it, couldn't say the word, almost a baby again . . .

"M . . . M . . . Mom."

Maddy looked up at what appeared to be the whole base waiting for them, holding up her brother.

All with so many questions—especially Paul.

Did they have any answers? Did they know what had just happened?

"I . . . I don't know if I can handle . . . that."

"We'll tell them we'll talk tomorrow. Now you need to have your wounds looked at."

Maddy ran a fingertip across a small gash on Nick's face.

"You too."

Then she looked at the crumpled photograph in her other hand, and they both looked at Sophie . . . and her parents. Standing there, unbelievably . . . standing there in the sunlight.

Back to the photograph showing the happy little five-year-old girl on the beach, pail in hand, one hand held by a mom who was only days away from disappearing into the Atlantic Ocean on a jumbo jet and a father who would be destroyed in his own lab.

Nick pulled her tight.

"Like what you did?"

She turned to him. "It scares me. Is it just me? And Sophie. Or could anyone go in there—and—"

"I don't know. And I'll tell you one thing, it won't be you . . . or me . . . who ever goes in again to find out."

She nodded, reassured.

She remembered how she had thought of Nick as damaged goods.

Not looking too damaged now.

Sophie and her parents started walking to the gate out,

uncontrollably holding each other, clutching each other so closely.

"Come on, enough miracles for today," she said. "I need to talk to Paul . . . and have a cup of tea."

And Nick smiled as they walked out the gate and—she was sure—away from this place forever.

epilogue

Nick's cell phone rang in the noisy bar of Mezzo in London. He looked at Maddy, indicating that, yes, he would take the call and be fast.

"Sophie!" he said, smiling.

He saw Maddy's eyes widen.

"Great. So glad to hear it. Yes, sure we will. I'm here for a few weeks—and I don't think Maddy is going anywhere."

Maddy leaned close to the phone, and spoke loudly. "Ask her if she'd like a trip to Kenya during her next school break."

Nick laughed. "Yes, you heard right. Africa. Uh-huh. She says buy her ticket now. Her parents say that she can go anywhere in the world with you."

Nick felt—a rush then. The kind of sentimental adrenaline that hits your system with such a feeling of sweet sadness, beauty, wonder . . . a mixed sensation of love and loss.

"Give me the phone," Maddy said.

Nick handed her the cell.

"Sophie, I'm serious. A week shooting pictures in the Kenyan game reserve. All the ostrich you can eat. Great. See you soon."

She handed the phone back to Nick.

"And Sophie . . . keep sending those e-mails." Nick had found that he loved finding an e-mail every day—every day—from Sophie, about her life, her thoughts about what happened. He knew that, even if he and Maddy would not ever get anywhere near Einbank again, Sophie's story about the place wasn't over.

"Bye Soph . . ."

"Bye Sophie," Maddy said.

Then Nick clicked off the phone.

Maddy finished her cosmopolitan.

"Another?" Nick asked. "Why not."

It had been weeks since what Nick called their "trip." Days were spent in debriefing, talking to Paul, then to her and Nick, where they detailed everything they had seen, heard, and thought inside.

Most of the scientists and the U.K. military, joined by a team from the United States, were unbelieving. But the evidence—was irrefutable.

Cosgrove, now joined by Sophie's dad, tried to put together some kind of explanation of the whole thing.

The lunacy of quantum physics was . . . exactly what the physicists said. The universe that can be imagined, can be real. The number of universes is . . . infinite, as infinite as thought. And the key to what is real—what we perceive as real—is very much what we believe we see.

The implications . . . were staggering.

"What are you thinking about?"

Maddy held her pinkish cosmopolitan. Before answering, she took a sip.

"Cosgrove, his explanation."

"Oh. Yeah, me too. I mean, it's all so . . . Alice."

"Alice?"

"Alice in Wonderland."

Maddy smiled, another sip. "Too right. Old Lewis Carroll was way ahead of his time."

"Or considering how really screwed up the space-time continuum can get, maybe *behind*. Maybe the Alice books were . . . a conservative view of reality."

Maddy laughed and shook her head. "So it's all rabbits down holes and crazy tea parties?"

Now Nick smiled. "If something can be two places at the same time, guess anything is possible."

A man in a sleek black jacket came beside them.

"Excuse me, Ms. Hodge, your table is ready."

She turned to him. "Thanks."

Then to Nick, "Dinnertime."

Their eyes locked. Nick held the look for a moment.

"You . . . hungry?"

Maddy took a moment to respond. "Not particularly."

Nick's smile broadened.

"Then let's get the hell out of here and head—"

Maddy finished the sentence.

"To my place."

"Exactly . . ."

Colonel Harris walked beside the inner gate.

What . . . now? he thought. *We know so much more, but what do we really know? Do we know what the place was trying to do?*

Is the place alive, trying to get a foothold in this world? Raising an army of supporters who know—with luck— we're in chaos?

So much more to find out.

For now they would continue to contain it, watch events around the world, and hope that they would never again have to send someone inside.

• • •

The road from Yellowknife in the Yukon could hardly be called a road.

More of a flat gravel pit that, when driven over at even a moderate speed, sent a spray of rocks flying up to chew the gas tank into ribbons.

Only specially outfitted vehicles like Jackson Thomson's Expedition, with an understanding of half-inch metal, could travel the road at any speed at all.

Thomson was hoping to get in some early fishing up at the base of the mountains that ran just west of Yellowknife. The first snow had yet to fall—but it would any day now.

Today, though already a chilly thirty-one degrees, might be the last decent fishing day till next May.

The car-destroying road climbed into the low-lying hills, then briefly down again, before curving around a stunningly clear and flat lake that—despite a summer of being fished—still was heavy with bass.

And if Thomson got bored, a small river alive with trout was a short walk away.

He stopped the Expedition.

That's . . . funny.

Across the lake, through a narrow foot trail, he saw something . . . shining.

Strange, like a big mirror reflecting. He backed up the car, and caught the reflection again.

You could easily miss it, but the angle of the sun was right on whatever it was hitting.

Something was over there, all right.

And Thomson thought . . . maybe before he started fishing, he'd walk over there, through the pass, to see what had caught his eye so early in the morning.